Goodbye, cowbo

"The ranch has served families and guests for over ninety years. Here at the Lazy River, we aim to be stewards of the land..."

Amanda closed the distance between them and laid her hand on his arm. "Is that your brother's script, your grandparents' or your own?"

"A bit of each."

Too aware of his physical presence, she jammed her hands into her jacket pockets so she wouldn't give in to the impulse to touch him again.

"How about we mosey around the pond as Amanda and Seth, and not as the marketing executive and ranch manager? Totally off script," she suggested.

Wanting to be in his presence went beyond work.

"Sure, but I'm a little disappointed. Crosby wrote some corny jokes into his script, perfect for getting a few laughs."

"You make people laugh just fine on your own."

"I hope I make you laugh."

The truth was, he did exactly that. But she needed to protect her heart.

Dear Reader,

Thank you for making a return visit to Violet Ridge, Colorado, the hometown of the four Virtue siblings. Each sibling has a connection to their grandparents, and the multigenerational bond is one of my favorite parts of this series. I also love the Rocky Mountains and nature. The Lazy River Dude Ranch sounds like my ideal vacation destination.

For manager Seth Virtue, the dude ranch is more than a business; it's his home—and he wants to ensure the ranch thrives, for his family and future guests. However, times are tough. His grandparents hire marketing executive Amanda Fleming to increase guest capacity so they can make the necessary repairs. Amanda has plenty of ideas about the best way to lure customers back to save the ranch, while clashing with Seth, who wants to go in a different direction.

I hope this book is like a vacation at a dude ranch for you. I love hearing from readers. You can send me a note at tanya.agler@tanyaagler.com or follow me on Facebook at Tanya Agler Author or sign up for my newsletter at my website.

Happy reading!

Tanya Agler

SAVING THE RANCHER

TANYA AGLER

HEARTWARMING

Harlequin®
HEARTWARMING™

Recycling programs for this product may not exist in your area.

ISBN-13: 978-1-335-05147-9

Saving the Rancher

Copyright © 2025 by Tanya Agler

Harlequin Enterprises ULC
22 Adelaide St. West, 41st Floor
Toronto, Ontario M5H 4E3, Canada
www.Harlequin.com

Printed in U.S.A.

Tanya Agler remembers the first set of Harlequin books her grandmother gifted her, and she's been in love with romance novels ever since. An award-winning author, Tanya makes her home in Georgia with her wonderful husband, their four children and a lovable basset, who really rules the roost. When she's not writing, Tanya loves classic movies and a good cup of tea. Visit her at tanyaagler.com or email her at tanyaagler@gmail.com.

Books by Tanya Agler

Harlequin Heartwarming

The Single Dad's Holiday Match
The Soldier's Unexpected Family
The Sheriff's Second Chance
A Ranger for the Twins

Smoky Mountain First Responders

The Firefighter's Christmas Promise
The Paramedic's Forever Family

Rodeo Stars of Violet Ridge

Caught by the Cowgirl
Snowbound with the Rodeo Star
Her Temporary Cowboy
The Triplets' Holiday Miracle

Visit the Author Profile page
at Harlequin.com for more titles.

To my grandfather Ted Balewski, whom
I affectionately called Dziadzi. A military
veteran and lifelong fisherman, he would take
me on long drives and top it off with a trip to our
favorite pizza restaurant. This book is dedicated to
you with lots of love.

CHAPTER ONE

Saturday

SETH VIRTUE GREETED the family of three heading toward the check-in desk and reached for an old-fashioned room key from a tier of hooks. "Welcome to the Lazy River Dude Ranch. You've picked a great week to stay with us. Spring is at its finest around here during the end of May. You'll be checking out next Sunday, eight days from now."

The man wound his arm around the woman's shoulder. "I'm Brian Carr, and this is my wife, Colleen. We were married a week ago." Then he tilted his head toward the young girl on his other side. "This is my eight-year-old daughter, Mabel."

Colleen smiled and leaned into her husband's touch. "I'm glad you could accommodate us at the last minute. You'll love it here, Mabel. Brian and I first met here when we were in high school, twenty-three years ago."

That was the last summer Seth's parents were alive.

Mabel bounced with excitement. "I wanted to go on the honeymoon, but you said no. Then my mommy called my daddy and he said I could come." The little girl grinned.

Colleen winced. And Seth sensed an awkward situation that needed a little levity. "And we're happy to have all of you. There are some important rules, though, you need to follow for me. No feeding the ducks cotton candy and watch out for our goat Winnie, who nibbles on anything leather." He winked and launched into his corny routine about the lodge's policies, eliciting giggles from Mabel. "Most of all, though, we want you to stay safe, so listen to the adults around you." Then Seth handed Brian the key to the Periwinkle Cabin, which had become available after the previous guests had abruptly canceled their reservation.

"There's a thirty-dollar fee if you lose this, so be careful," Seth said while accepting Brian's credit card.

Brian ruffled his daughter's short red hair. "Sorry, Mabel. No key for you."

Mabel's cute face puckered into a frown. "I'm very responsible. All my teachers say so."

"Glad to hear that. Being careful and quiet is especially important around the horses." Seth processed Brian's credit card and returned it to him. "The other guests have already checked in and their luggage has been delivered to their cabins. If you're interested in the ranch tour, it starts in thirty minutes in the dining hall. Some of the guests are already enjoying the refreshments there, and others are enjoying our library, which is down that hall. Please feel free to explore the main floor of the lodge and then mix and mingle when you're ready."

Seth pointed toward the room where urns of coffee and cider waited along with a variety of snacks, including Ingrid's finest oatmeal cookies and blackberry bars. At least Ingrid, their long-time baker, hadn't quit like two of the housekeeping staff and their desk clerk did last week.

Seth watched the Carr family, the last of the guests he was expecting to arrive, walk toward the group in the dining room. With a minimal staff, the week's amenities had been reduced to the basics, which would at least make sure the ranch lived up to its reputation and still provide cherished memories. He hoped. He finished updating the group's itinerary and printed enough copies for everyone. Then he headed to the great hall.

"By now, I hope you all have had a chance to get acquainted. You're part of our family for this week, and as such, you're stuck with me, unfortunately." Seth waited for the polite chuckles to fade away before he picked up the box of cowboy hats adorned with the Lazy River brand and distributed one to each guest. "You are now officially cowboys and cowgirls."

Mabel tugged at the rim of her hat, a smaller version of the others. "Look at me, Daddy! I'm a cowgirl."

Brian whipped out his phone. "Stand next to Colleen over by the horseshoes and pictures of the Rockies. I'll take a photo for our new home in Birmingham."

Mabel posed on one side. "Can't you get one of me without Colleen?"

Seth stepped in and extended his hand toward Brian. "In addition to being your trail guide and wrangler, I'm a great photographer."

"Appreciate it." Brian stepped between his wife and daughter for the picture.

Seth snapped a couple of shots and returned Brian's phone. Assuring them that their bags and luggage would be delivered to them after the tour, he escorted everyone to the library and gift shop before leading the guests outside, encouraging them to take a long whiff of the fresh Colorado mountain air. He did the same and smiled when the deep breaths bolstered his spirits as always. Introducing guests to the lodge was one of his favorite parts about managing the facility. For the past ninety years, the Virtue family of the Lazy River Dude Ranch had hosted business retreats and vacationing families, and seen its fair share of weddings, including his sister's recent affair. Daisy had met her new husband, Ben, when the military veteran came home to Violet Ridge and directed the town's annual holiday play. Seventeen months later, that particular production was now part of the town's folklore.

Seth gathered the motley crew of guests and navigated them toward the seven guest cabins, giving brief speeches about each. He especially appreciated the chuckles at his bad puns.

A compact car whizzed by them and stopped on the gravel driveway. A blonde emerged from the back seat while the driver sprang forth and opened the trunk. Two floral rolling suitcases landed at the blonde's feet while she handed the driver some money. With a nod, the driver hurried back into the car and performed a U-turn before zooming off.

Of average height, the newcomer had a certain presence about her, like she'd set things right no matter the circumstance. Her green plaid flannel shirt fit into the setting, as did her curvaceous blue jeans and brand-new cowboy boots.

"Can someone direct me to where I check in?" Her smile was as broad as the Rocky Mountain range that loomed behind them. "This is the Lazy River Dude Ranch, right?"

Seth was at a loss for words, which was saying something. He quickly composed himself. Any other year they'd have been full without a vacancy for months. Now, even with two cabins sitting empty, he'd have to turn her away since one had faulty plumbing, and the other was missing shingles on its roof. He'd see to those repairs as soon as the guests were settled.

Still, Seth disliked turning anyone away, especially since everyone here was family. For over twenty years, Grandpa Martin and Grandma Bridget had engrained that message into him and his three siblings. It was more than a motto, though. It was his way of life.

Seth tipped his hat at her and tried to find a way of accommodating this new paying guest. "Howdy. Welcome to the Lazy River. You picked a great time to visit since you get an extra night as it's our first week open for the season." Last week was a five-day dry run with the employees. "If you're by yourself, we have three suites in the main lodge that would be a good fit."

Murmurs started circulating behind him.

His best wrangler, Buck, passed by, and Seth hailed him over so he could take a moment to get to the bottom of this woman's situation. Within seconds, Buck was continuing the tour by escorting the other guests to the stable. With that problem solved, Seth turned his attention to the woman, who was texting. He waited until she was finished before acknowledging her again.

"You're fortunate you came this week, seeing as you don't have a reservation. The Porcupine Suite on the second floor has the nicest view, so that seems the best route." Seth smiled, trying to be as gracious as possible.

"But I do have a reservation." She sounded as sure about that as the sun setting over the Rocky Mountains tonight.

He removed his hat and scratched his shaggy brown hair. With everyone pulling double duty around here, he hadn't had time for a haircut in a couple of months. "With all due respect, ma'am, you must be mistaken. Is your reservation at the Rocky Valley Guest Ranch?" That last line almost caught in his throat, but he managed to spit it out anyway. The new luxury facility on the other side of town had put a huge dent in their reservations.

"Could you direct me to Martin or Bridget Virtue?" The blonde squared her shoulders and gripped the extralarge suitcase's rolling handle. "They're expecting me."

The hairs on the back of his neck prickled at the mention of his grandmother, who had mostly recovered from a recent stroke. Since then, Seth had made it his mission to protect her as much as possible.

"That's funny." He folded his arms and traced a line in the dirt with his scuffed cowboy boots. "My grandparents didn't mention you to me."

"Oh, you're Bridget's grandson. Seth, right?" The woman relaxed, her blue eyes sure about her knowledge. "I was expecting you to be younger."

And he wasn't expecting her at all. "I'm the oldest of the four siblings." At thirty-two he was six years older than his youngest brother, Crosby.

"You're more than welcome to make yourself comfortable in our dining room while I contact them. Please enjoy coffee or tea and Ingrid's cookies."

Even if she had made a mistake about having a reservation here, Seth started feeling bad for the woman. In late May, the Lazy River was a sight to behold with sunrises prettier than a foal and the wildflowers as plentiful as the grass on the plains.

"I'm exactly where I'm supposed to be this week and next." She stopped talking when another car passed them and then reversed, halting alongside them.

The passenger door opened, and a cane tip emerged, followed by his grandma Bridget, who looked stronger than ever after eighteen months of physical therapy. Tall and wiry, she had raised her son but also his four children after the tragic accident that claimed Peter and Rosemary. Her faded brown cowboy hat with a dark brown ribbon brim hid her short silver hair.

Now that she and Grandpa Martin had returned from their weekly breakfast with his sister, Daisy, her husband, Ben, and the triplets, Seth intended to get to the truth about the situation.

"Seth, is something wrong?" Grandma Bridget reached him and then noticed he wasn't alone. A wide smile replaced the look of concern on her tanned, lined face. "Amanda, it's so good to meet you in person. Let me hug you."

The blonde embraced his grandmother and then

stood next to her giant luggage. "Thank you for the warm *welcome*." He noticed the slight glare in his direction before she returned her attention to his grandmother. "I still haven't checked in."

"We'll get you settled while Martin parks the car. We didn't intend to stay so long at Daisy's, but it's hard to say goodbye to those adorable triplets." Grandma Bridget's brown eyes glowed with a vitality Seth hadn't seen since the stroke.

He was grateful for that and for her recovery.

And he wouldn't let anyone take advantage of her giving spirit. "Grandma," he whispered low enough for her ears only, "Amanda isn't on the list of paid guests."

"Piffle, Amanda's here at our request." Grandma Bridget moved one hand off the intricate bison carved on the handle of her cane and reached out for Amanda's, giving it a squeeze. "We'll show her a grand time and, in return, she'll wow us with a marketing campaign that will breathe new life into this old ranch."

What marketing campaign? Seth reeled seethed and tried to make sense of what was happening while Grandma motioned for Amanda to follow her. Amanda placed her smaller suitcase on the larger one and began wheeling it along the path.

As manager, he should have been consulted about this. Besides, what good would a marketing campaign be without a full staff and a slate of activities? Seth had advocated giving the re-

maining staff a raise or offering better amenities
like a sauna and nicer towels. Anything so they
could compete with the high-end Rocky Valley
Guest Ranch. With a little bit of money, he could
convert the third suite into a salon-and-spa experience. Anything to stanch the flow of customers
canceling their reservations in favor of the luxury
retreat on the other side of town. So far this month
alone, four families had canceled their June reservations. Grandpa Martin insisted this was temporary and they'd work through these lean times
together. Seth wasn't quite so sure. Upgrades were
the only way to attract new customers.

And now the money he'd earmarked for improvements was destined for this marketing expert, who was freeloading a vacation from them.
Seth fumed at how Amanda had obviously found
his grandparents easy targets for her sales pitch,
wheedling a free week at a dude ranch from them.
This scam was more than enough reason to find
the earliest opportunity to catch his grandparents
alone and reason with them.

This was a family ranch. As far as he was concerned, Amanda wasn't family and had no business here.

SETH VIRTUE WAS unhappy about her presence at
the Lazy River Dude Ranch. Then again, Bridget
Virtue had given Amanda Fleming the distinct impression that Seth was a teenager, so this was a day

for correcting faulty assumptions. Not that Seth's age mattered as far as she was concerned, especially as people often thought she was younger than her own age of twenty-nine. However, she liked starting a campaign with everyone's cooperation.

Getting to know the clients and their expectations was in her wheelhouse. She accumulated the material Parkhouse Promotions would need for the client's marketing campaign, everything from an updated website to researching demographics for their ideal consumer, while Pamela performed her magic presenting the finished proposal.

Although Amanda had arrived in an official capacity, this trip, a so-called working vacation, also marked her first time off since Pamela hired her three years ago. It couldn't come at a better moment. She needed these two weeks, maybe more, to relax and regroup. Hopefully, when she returned to Phoenix, she might have received good news that the current owners accepted her offer on what would be her perfect house. After a childhood where her family relocated when her father was fired from one job and flitted to the next, she was looking forward to her first real home. No more cramped one-bedroom apartments or nomadic lifestyle for her. She'd live five minutes from her best friend and might even rescue a dog from the local shelter.

She pushed those personal thoughts aside and

tried to focus on the task at hand. Keeping pace with Seth was a challenge in itself, his strides were so long. That was no big surprise though as he had a good six inches on her.

"There are seven cabins, all with names of Colorado flowers. Couples and individuals often stay in one of the three suites on the second floor of the lodge. My grandparents and I live have our own suites on the third story." He pointed at each as he hurried past. "Here at the Lazy River, we incorporate local history and nature for our guests to get a true taste of Violet Ridge."

"I'll enjoy the tour more if I can breathe." She wasn't winded, but she'd prefer to stroll through the property rather than sprint. She intended on savoring every minute at the ranch. That started by taking in the majestic mountains and spring wildflowers.

Seth stopped and faced her. His piercing brown eyes seemed perceptive, and he was making a strong impression on her with his tall frame and beard. Too bad it was a negative impression.

"Ms. Fleming…"

"*Amanda* has a nicer ring, don't you think?" She smiled, but he kept his lips pursed in a line.

"Can't you handle this matter online?" Seth obviously had an issue with her presence, but why? Parkhouse Promotions was a bustling marketing agency.

Besides, if any of these adorable cabins were

unoccupied, the ranch definitely needed her services.

"In this case, my presence is necessary. I want to get a feel for the ranch's personality, and I assure you I've worked on an account for another dude ranch. Parkhouse Promotions has a slate of satisfied clients, and I can provide references upon request." This was the same background information she'd given to Bridget and Martin. Why hadn't their grandson been included on the meetings? "Our consultation fee is reasonable and non-refundable."

"I wouldn't unpack my bags just yet. I intend on reviewing the contract before discussing your stay with my grandparents. It seems like we should have hired someone from town rather than an outsider."

She had to hand it to Seth. He wasn't holding back, but that was yet another reason for her to stay. Tact and finesse were important communication skills, and the ranch needed someone diplomatic and professional to tackle the marketing and public relations.

Besides, even if Seth talked to his grandparents, the consultation contract was ironclad, and she was staying. As far as regarding her as an outsider? That didn't concern Amanda. She was used to being the new kid at school.

He kept up his brisk pace, and she adjusted her strides.

"As I mentioned, I handled the campaign for Tumbleweeds Dude Ranch, located outside of Phoenix. Their reservation rate increased by fifty percent last year. Take a look at their website. There's a contact link if you want to email the owner for a reference."

"I'll do that." Seth didn't look her way but headed toward the other guests, who were exiting the stable and walking toward a large log cabin.

"Where are we going?" Amanda asked.

"The rec center. I'll be resuming the tour and relieving Buck so he can return to the stable. One of our mares, Rosa, is expecting a foal soon." Seth's voice softened when he talked about horses. She saw her first glimmer of a different Seth, a more positive and content cowboy.

Standing back, she let her gaze flit over him. He was everyone's image of a Colorado cowboy: attractive with an air of independence. If she could capture his essence in her campaign, the ranch would be turning guests away.

"We'll finish our conversation later." Preferably with Bridget and Martin nearby.

Amanda followed Seth and mingled with the other guests. She introduced herself to a couple in their early fifties. The woman smiled and pumped Amanda's hand.

"I'm Tiffany Zimmerman, and this is my husband, Derrick. You might have heard of us. We're from Kentucky and won the lottery." She pumped

Amanda's hand more vigorously and motioned to her husband.

Derrick nodded. "Last week we visited Napa Valley in California and stayed at a winery. We're gonna visit all the states before we go home."

"Sure do miss Princess and Earl." Tiffany pulled out her phone bedecked with rhinestones. "They're our cats."

Tiffany showed Amanda at least fifty pictures of the two felines. That reminded her of something important. She'd have to approach each person and ask them to sign a publicity release so she could have freedom in photographing the different activities and accommodations. That shouldn't pose a problem. People usually loved having their picture taken although she sensed Seth was an exception.

Seth thanked Buck and sent him back to the stable. She could already envision a campaign centering around Seth. Tall and solid, he exuded a confidence that would be perfect for the publicity push. The scuffed-up boots, muddy jeans and worn cowboy hat would go over well with families wanting to spend some time in the great outdoors. His tanned face covered with a brown beard possessed some wrinkles, just the right amount to make him rugged.

The group's laughter shook her from her reverie. The four women who stood together in a tight circle were laughing the hardest.

How had she missed Seth telling a joke?

He motioned toward the rear of the recreation hall, where they headed next. "This is where you sign up for different activities. Some are self-guided. In that case, you check out the equipment and return it when you're finished. You're required to take a life vest for each kayaker when you borrow our paddles."

Seth was definitely selling her on the activities. A sunrise kayak outing seemed like the perfect way to greet the morning, followed by the delicious breakfast buffet.

Then Seth ushered everyone to the other side of the hall to a foosball table, Ping-Pong table and shelves full of board games. A rainy day paradise—the owners had thought of everyone.

A pair of teenagers cheered and ran over to the foosball table.

"Hey, Mom!" An older teen with long red hair grasped one set of knobs while his younger brother did the same on the opposite side. "Eli and I found our place for the week. This is sweet."

Whitney Berggren, their mother, rolled her eyes upward and looked at Seth. "Please tell me they'll get some fresh air."

"They should. Our horses are the finest around." Seth reached for the white ball and pocketed it, ending the impromptu game. He stayed silent until the teens stopped roughhousing. "Tomorrow I will be demonstrating lasso skills and teaching a beginner's class. If you two attend, you'll be fine cow-hands in no time."

The younger brother poked his sibling. "Isaac, we can't learn how to lasso back home."

Isaac made a hand motion as if lassoing. "Yeah, we can practice on Mom's favorite lamp."

Seth must have seen the look of terror on the mother's face and reassured her. "We haven't lost a lamp or a teenager yet."

One of the women, all the same age, raised her hand. "I'm Melissa, and we're the four *M*'s. Where's the Lazy River?"

Seth seemed nonplussed at the question. "It's on the southern trail. We offer fly-fishing on Mondays and Wednesdays, weather permitting."

"No, I mean the lazy river by the swimming pool and hot tub. The one with the mai tais and apple martinis." All four women turned their gazes toward Seth.

"Um…" He took off his cowboy hat and scratched his head. "We don't have a hot tub."

"That's not what it said online." The woman came over and showed him her phone, thrusting it in his face. "This is our annual college reunion, and it's my turn to choose the destination. We're going to kick back and swim around the lazy river every day."

Seth accepted the phone and handed it back to her. "That's a different hotel. We're the Lazy River Dude Ranch. Horses, cowboys and hiking."

Melissa gulped. "Cowboys?" Then she grinned. "We can work with that, right?"

The tallest with ebony skin hugged Melissa and looked at the others. "I've never ridden a horse before." All of them murmured similar sentiments. "This will be different but fun. The four *M*'s together again."

A young girl approached Seth and planted herself in front of him. She pulled on his jacket. "The horses are really big. Is it scary to ride them?"

"That's a good question, Mabel." Seth stroked his beard as if he was giving the girl's question careful consideration. "Everything is relative, even size. What's important here is that we find you the right size pony to ride. Then it won't worry you, right?"

"I'm not sure if I like honeymoons or not." Mabel scrunched her face and stared at him.

Seth stroked his beard and then nodded. "I've never been on one myself, so I can't give advice there, but I know horses. Once you get to know her, Strawberry isn't scary. She's a sweet mare. Everyone around here loves her."

"Then I'll love Strawberry, too." Mabel pointed toward the closed-off part of the hall. "What's over there?"

"Well, Mabel, I should hire you to give the tours. You're way ahead of me." He led the group over to the sheltered alcove. "Mabel, if you like pretty bracelets, you'll want to sign up for my sister Daisy's jewelry class, especially designed for anyone eighteen and younger."

"I'm eight, and I love pretty bracelets!" Mabel grinned and gave an emphatic nod.

"Great. That finishes our tour. I'll meet everyone in the dining room for supper in an hour. See you then," Seth said.

The families dispersed. Eli and Isaac sent a lingering look to the foosball table and then followed their parents.

Seth started for the exit when Amanda caught up to him. "We can finish our conversation now."

Seth faced her. "I haven't had a chance to review your contract yet. I have work to do."

The charming cowboy was gone, replaced with this stiffer man who seemed convinced she'd be returning home sooner than later, which was hardly the case. She'd earn every dollar of her paycheck this week.

"It's my job to get a feel for the ranch. Its mission, its values, its brand." More than ever, Amanda regretted that Seth, who obviously wore several different hats around the ranch, hadn't participated in the online calls with Bridget and Martin. "These two weeks will be a working vacation for me. While I'll have fun, I'll be observing you and taking photos of the different activities."

"Watching me?" His deep voice showed his disdain for that idea. "That won't be necessary."

On the contrary, she found it imperative that

she shatter his formal facade and see the real cowboy underneath. Bridget and Martin had made it clear that Seth was the future of the ranch. He had a way about him with the guests that made him perfect to become the ranch spokesperson and communicate that special something that made it stand out from its competitors.

"Let me be the judge of that." Amanda found herself talking to his back as he was already at the door.

Good grief, did Seth ever stand still and listen?

She followed him, and he must have finally realized how determined she was. A look of exasperation crossed his face, and he motioned toward the stable. "There's an office in there where we can talk."

They entered the stable, and Amanda longed to reach out and touch the velvety muzzle of the horse who greeted her with a soft whinny. The paint horse's butterscotch color reminded her of many rides on Roxie back in Texas. That was about the time her father convinced the owners of an oil rig that he'd previously managed an offshore site and could do the same for their operation. His position lasted eight glorious months before it came to light how he'd exaggerated his previous experience. He was fired, and they moved to California, the sixth move in four years.

Seth reached the end of the corridor and opened a door. Ribbons of every color lined the opposite wall, interspersed with horseshoes and the occasional picture of a smiling woman leading a horse. Amanda sat in one of two chairs flanking a desk while Seth settled on the other side. He removed his hat and placed it atop the closed laptop. He didn't seem in any hurry to talk so she started.

"These two weeks will go by much more smoothly with your cooperation. Your grandparents have already given me carte blanche—"

"What?" That caught his attention. "I thought you'd take some photos and be on your way."

"Photo ops and the new website are only one part of what my marketing team provides." Technically, it was Pamela's team, but that wasn't important for Seth to know right now. "Give me a chance. When your grandmother offered me room and board at the ranch in addition to the consultation fee, I pitched this project to my boss. She agreed on the condition I use my vacation time for this."

Her plea seemed to make an impression on Seth. "Grandma Bridget made the offer? You didn't impose on her?"

Seth proved, once again, that he got straight to the point.

"Of course I didn't. For several days I'll be researching and assembling data behind the scenes, focusing on the ranch's strengths with targeted demographics. Then my boss, Pamela, will arrive toward the end of my two-week stay and deliver the final presentation. At that point, we'll review our long-term contract to monitor social media, update your website and arrange for publicity in magazines and news outlets. I'll do that in Phoenix."

In the privacy of her first home, a place she could call her own. If the current owners accepted her offer, that was.

Seth mulled over what she said, his fingers steepled next to his beard. "I'll do anything to protect Grandma Bridget." He paused, a tender expression coming over him. "She had a stroke a little over a year and a half ago. At the time, they didn't think she'd talk again, but she's a strong woman who defies the odds."

She sounded just like Amanda's kind of person, much like her grandmother Lou had been during her lifetime. Amanda would love to have someone as supportive and caring as Seth in her life. She stood and nodded. "Then I'll arrange a time to interview you tomorrow since I plan on making you the main attraction."

She sailed away, leaving Seth behind with his mouth wide open.

CHAPTER TWO

Sunday

THE WISPS OF orange and pink peeking over the Rocky Mountains meant the start of another beautiful spring day. Good thing the skies promised sunshine and low humidity since guests preferred outdoor activities although those teenage brothers liked the rec center. Today's lasso lesson should give them reason to venture beyond their comfort zone. That was part of the experience here at the Lazy River.

Seth wiped his forehead with his bandanna, sweat forming while he guided the horses from their pasture to the eastern paddock. He and Buck moved bales of hay to the feeders before they filled the water troughs. The sight of his mustang, Mocha, buoyed Seth's spirits after a restless night. He'd kept his retired Australian shepherds Hap and Trixie up half the night with his tossing and turning. No matter how hard he tried to put Amanda Fleming out of his mind, the more firmly she became entrenched. Whatever Amanda thought she could bring to the ranch was surely something Seth could do himself. Then again, building a website had remained on his to-do list for over a year, and he'd never gotten around to it. Why spend time on a computer when he could lead guests on a trail ride?

Seth used his sleeve to wipe sweat from his brow. Somehow, he'd have to design that website. Either that, or hire someone closer to Violet Ridge, someone who wouldn't invade Seth's privacy. Besides, it seemed to him someone local would know the ranch a sight better than a visitor who negotiated a free vacation from his trusting grandparents. If Seth persuaded Amanda to return to Phoenix, that would save the ranch unnecessary expense. He'd get on that at breakfast.

The matter settled, at least in his mind, Seth sneaked Mocha pieces of carrot before brushing the mustang's coat and picking his hooves. Seth dislodged a nasty pebble from a tight spot while soothing his horse. "That must have been painful."

If only it would be that easy to remove Amanda from the lodge.

After he groomed Mocha, Seth headed to the stable before breakfast. He licked his lips at the thought of Ingrid's homemade blueberry compote.

But when he caught sight of the tack room in disarray, he frowned. Down two grooms, he couldn't rush his responsibilities even at the prospect of catching his grandfather bright and early. The saddle pads looked most neglected. He began remedying that, glad for extra busywork. Anything to keep his mind off the blonde who seemed convinced she could bring guests back to the Lazy River.

Seth finished brushing the saddle pads and returned them to their designated place. Once more they were supple and ready for use, as were the saddles and reins. Good thing, too, with the upcoming lasso lessons followed by the first trail ride, a short trek to prepare the guests for longer excursions. He took pride in the mountain trails unique to Lazy River. The vast expanse of land had everything: mountain climbing, fly fishing and vistas that showed the area's full glory. Return customers always highlighted these horse rides as a reason they'd come back in a heartbeat.

That, plus Ingrid's cooking and his grandmother's hospitality.

As long as Killian Wilshire, the CEO of Wilshire Development Corporation and head of the Rocky Valley Guest Ranch who was intent on poaching Seth's staff, didn't lure Ingrid away, the Lazy River would eke by somehow. Seth left the tack room and caught sight of his elusive grandfather, heading out of Rosa's stall. He should have known his grandfather would personally check on the mare, who was expecting her first foal any day now. Grandpa Martin was renowned in these parts for loving his wife and family, for caring for every animal on his ranch and for his stubbornness.

Unfortunately, the apple didn't fall far from the tree. His siblings had accused him of being rather obstinate on occasion, and Seth was determined to win this battle.

"Grandpa Martin!" Seth wasn't going to let his grandfather escape this time.

The older man continued to exit the stable until Seth repeated his command with more volume and urgency now that he was far enough from Rosa as not to startle the mare. Grandpa Martin stopped, turned and tipped back his Stetson. The sunrise glow highlighted the change in the elder man's hair color. When had his mustache also started displaying more streaks of white and gray than blond? Upon closer observation, Seth also noticed his grandfather's wrinkles were craggier and more numerous. Had this happened overnight? Or had he been so focused on Grandma Bridget during the past months years that he hadn't seen how time had finally crept up to the man who always seemed ageless?

His grandfather jammed his hands into the pockets of his flannel-lined denim jacket that was older than Seth. "Whatever you're going to say, make it quick. I don't intend on missing Ingrid's buckwheat pancakes."

Martin's mustang, Thunderbolt, approached the fence and whinnied until Martin extracted half an apple out of his jacket pocket. Thunderbolt accepted the treat, and Seth stayed back. Horses came first. His grandfather rubbed the mustang's muzzle with the wariness rolling off him like ripples on Lazy River.

"Seems like you already know what I'm going to say," Seth said.

Grandpa Martin gave Thunderbolt one final pat before the horse trotted toward the open pasture. "Give Amanda a chance. Can't hurt anything."

"I read the contract Grandma Bridget forwarded to me late last night. The consultation fee alone will put a huge dent in our bottom line." Seth hurried with his plea since Grandpa Martin looked ready to devour a stack of pancakes. "Wilshire has already poached several of our best employees. Putting Amanda's fee into a bonus for the remaining staff and select improvements will pay off. Might even lure back a couple of our cowhands with extra incentive. I just need your authorization to ask Amanda to leave."

Grandpa Martin stared at Seth as if he was finally seeing him as an equal instead of a boy of ten. Was this a day for everyone to see the person standing before them instead of only seeing their past selves? So much time had elapsed since his grandparents broke the news to his siblings about his parents' car colliding with a deer. Peter and Rosemary were killed instantly while Seth's brother Jase, who'd been asleep in the back seat, was spared.

However, Seth was no longer the scared and sad little boy who'd grown up in a hurry because his brothers and sister needed him to be strong.

Being the oldest came with its own set of privileges and burdens.

Before his grandfather could respond, the Carr family waved from the path between their cabin and the lodge. Seth and Martin dipped their hats and shouted the same greeting in unison. That broke the tension. Grandpa Martin tilted his head toward the stable. "Come on. We need a little privacy to talk."

Seth followed in his grandfather's boot steps until they stood on opposite sides of Rosa's stall. "Why didn't you tell me you hired a marketing firm?"

Grandpa Martin rested his arms on top of the stall, staring at Rosa. "Because of Bridge."

His grandfather continued gazing at the horse, the man maintained a calmness Seth sought for himself. "Grandma? But why? I'm the manager, and I should be consulted about big decisions like this."

Grandpa Martin didn't meet Seth's gaze. "Then you're not going to like the next part. When the medical bills started arriving, I discovered we had let the supplemental insurance lapse. I took out a mortgage to pay for her care and treatment."

Seth leaned against the post for support. Grandma Bridget had stayed in the hospital for a month, then headed to a rehab facility, followed by months of physical therapy, still ongoing. The bills must have been substantial if Grandpa Martin went to the bank for help.

Guilt flooded Seth at his grandfather feeling he had to take on this responsibility by himself. Both of his grandparents were irreplaceable.

If anything, he should have asked about the bills before now. "Why didn't you say something sooner? We could have found a solution together as a family."

The vein on the side of Grandpa Martin's neck bulged. Maybe it was talking about finances with Seth. More likely, it was facing how he could have lost his beloved wife. The stroke had devastated all of them. Seth could handle it if Grandpa Martin was protecting his wife. But if he was trying to protect Seth? He clenched his fists by his side. His grandfather should trust Seth by now.

Perhaps Grandpa Martin really saw that same little boy from the day after the accident rather than the man standing before him now.

"Didn't want Bridge to know. Still don't. You know your grandmother." Grandpa Martin's voice barely rose above a whisper, holding the same note of fear Seth had heard while Grandma Bridget was in the hospital.

Grandpa Martin had survived the loss of his only child, but life without his beloved Bridge? That would devastate him.

And Seth knew his grandmother well. If Grandma Bridget believed for one minute her medical costs were hindering her family's welfare, she'd hesitate before telling them of any future issues. "So, you've kept the bills a secret?"

Grandpa Martin's eyebrows sank until they almost formed a V. "There was never a good time to tell her about the mortgage."

That was debatable, but Seth kept that to himself.

Rosa ventured over to them, her low whinny echoing in the wide expanse of the stable. His grandfather reached into his pocket and pulled out the other half of the apple he'd given to Thunderbolt. Rosa accepted it and whinnied again, this time in thanks for the treat.

His grandfather seemed to take comfort from rubbing Rosa's muzzle as the weight of everything bore down on him.

Then it hit Seth. His grandfather had just presented the best solution to the problem that was Amanda.

"More reason than ever to send Ms. Fleming and no doubt her pricey contract back to Phoenix and deal with the marketing ourselves. I'll get Daisy and Crosby to help. We'll knock out a new website and work on social media together."

At this pronouncement, Grandpa Martin grabbed Seth's arm and shook his head. "I don't want your siblings to know. Even Jase."

"Why not?"

"Daisy just got married and has her hands full with the triplets." Grandpa Martin smiled at the mention of his great-grandchildren. "And Crosby has to finish his doctorate. Besides, his job occupies his attention in a way the ranch never has."

That was a polite way of saying Crosby was the epitome of an absent-minded professor when it came to his doctoral dissertation. However, his siblings deserved to be in on a secret of this magnitude. Even Jase, who had his own demons to confront about Violet Ridge. Whenever his brother, the Denver police detective, was ready to come home, Seth would greet him with open arms. At least Seth hoped there was still a dude ranch to come home to.

"You're underestimating them," Seth said.

"I want them to be happy. Same as you." Martin squeezed Seth's arm.

"But we need to tell Grandma Bridget and my siblings about the mortgage. The sooner, the better."

A shadow crossed over his grandfather's face. "If I do, Bridge might not go to physical therapy or the doctor when she needs to."

Seth's heart went out to his grandpa. How he'd worried about this alone caused a deep ache in Seth's bones. His grandfather wouldn't have to do that anymore. "I thought the same thing. But she deserves to know. You've trusted her with so much over the years. Trust her with this." Close to sixty years of love was a bond Seth envied. "And I'll explain to Amanda her services are no longer needed. She'll be gone by the end of the day."

Martin frowned. "I need the right moment to tell Bridge." His face softened when he referred to his wife by the nickname unique to him and him alone. "If Amanda leaves, Bridge will know something's wrong. Amanda has to stay."

Keeping both a secret and Amanda on the ranch? Seth looked at Rosa as if the mare would come to his rescue. Instead, Rosa contentedly chewed on hay, ignoring Seth's dilemma.

Seth let out a huff of air. "Tell me the loan details on the way to breakfast."

"You won't say anything to Bridge?" Grandpa Martin raised his eyebrows in an expression that almost bordered on hope.

"I'll let you face Grandma's wrath on your own. She's going to be mighty riled at you." Come to think of it, only Grandpa Martin would be able to beg for forgiveness about keeping this from her. "But I need to know everything. You can't hold anything back."

Grandpa Martin jammed his hands into his pockets, his face showing each of his seventy-eight years. "I had the best intentions, you know."

"Yeah, I love her, too." Seth placed his arm around his grandfather's shoulders. "Grandma Bridget is a strong woman."

"Has to be, married to an old coot like me." Grandpa Martin's laugh was hollow.

Seth steered him toward the stable's exit. On the trail to the main lodge, the first person to cross their paths would have to be Amanda Fleming.

Even Seth had to admit she was a ray of sunshine this morning with her yellow plaid flannel shirt paired with denim jeans that emphasized her long legs. Seth blinked. Amanda was a guest and a subcontractor. He had no reason to notice her legs or any of her other features.

"Good morning! It's a gorgeous day." Amanda's smile was as genuine as her greeting.

"You've slept away half the morning." Seth's statement sounded like a warning growl from one of the ranch's working dogs, and he immediately regretted it. Just because Amanda was the first person they met after his grandfather informed him of that enormous secret didn't mean he could vent his frustration on her.

To her credit, Amanda waved away his bad manners. "That's what you think. I watched the sun rise over the duck pond with a blanket and a cup of coffee. It's amazing what wonders coffee does for my mood. You might want to take note of that, Seth, and see if coffee sweetens your disposition."

"You deserved that, Seth." Grandpa Martin chuckled and faced Amanda. "My grandson is all bark and no bite."

Seth stared at his grandfather. Whose side was he on, anyway? After all, who had just promised to keep a huge secret from Grandma Bridget? Even if that did mean giving up any remaining opposition to the marketing contract.

For now, though, that zap of attraction on his part scared him. While he'd like to get to know her better, that wasn't his priority. That contract was one-sided to say the least, and he was sure her firm had the upper hand. Keeping his curiosity to himself was reason enough to maintain his distance.

Seth opened the lodge's door for Amanda and Grandpa Martin. Seth's retired senior Australian shepherd, Hap, bounded over, having seemingly forgiven him for his restless night. After Seth lavished affection on him, Hap investigated Amanda, who scratched his ears and then gave him a belly rub.

To Seth's relief, one of the three twenty-something guys who were staying in the Lupine Cabin motioned to him. Seth excused himself and headed over to the man whose name eluded him.

"What can I do for you, Todd?" Seth hoped he'd guessed right.

"I'm Trevor. Todd is shorter." Trevor indicated for Seth to come closer. "Where's today's clue for the scavenger hunt?"

Seth wracked his mind and came up short. "What are you talking about?"

"It's why Todd, Kevin and I are here. You know…" Trevor must have seen the blank look on Seth's face because he rolled his eyes. "The treasure. A million dollars in gold hidden somewhere in the Rockies."

Seth rubbed his forehead. This was a first in the ranch's history books. "We're not a part of that."

"Dude," Trevor said and furrowed his brows. "Everything pointed here. The Lazy River. Your last name. Seven cabins."

Seth shook his head. "Really. I don't know anything about that."

Trevor wrinkled his nose. "Whoa. Then what are we supposed to do here?"

Seth blinked and wondered if Trevor had heard anything Seth had said on the intro tour. "We emailed everyone today's itinerary. You can learn how to lasso or take a trail ride or—"

"No clues? No million dollars?"

Seth gave Trevor points for persistence. "The real treasure here is the ranch. It's up to you how involved you get with the activities." Seth's stomach grumbled and he excused himself for a much-anticipated breakfast.

With minutes to spare until Ingrid closed the breakfast buffet, Seth plucked a plate off the stack and loaded it high with pancakes and plump sausages. He spotted Amanda talking to his grandmother at his favorite table overlooking the pond where ducks and geese glided across the smooth, glassy surface.

Seth considered his options. Be rude and sit by himself or join the ladies' conversation. It was a no-brainer. Besides, he never passed up time with his grandma Bridget. A bundle of energy, she'd taught her four grandchildren how to fish, throw a lasso over a running steer and use a sewing machine. The stroke hadn't diminished her presence. For those close to her, however, there were noticeable signs that no amount of physical therapy could change. The slight downward tug on the left side of her face. The use of a cane in the evening when she was tired. Still, she was the glue that held the Virtue family together. Seth could never blame his grandfather for mortgaging the ranch to pay her medical bills.

Seth cleared his mind. Otherwise he'd reveal everything to Grandma Bridget when his grandfather needed to be the one to tell her. A few seconds minute later, he approached the table where Amanda was examining his grandmother's favorite shawl.

Amanda admired its softness. "Thank you for letting me see it for a minute." She handed it back to his grandma. "I'd love to know how to knit, but I've never been able to learn how to cast on."

Grandma Bridget positioned the shawl back on her shoulders. "This is a cherished present from a childhood friend." His grandmother stared at

Amanda. "I have to confess something I should have told you sooner. Your grandma Lou visited this ranch many times when she was younger. We became really close before she stopped coming here."

Amanda gasped. "You're Bridie?"

Grandma Bridget nodded. "We kept in touch for decades, but the Christmas cards stopped coming about fifteen years ago."

Amanda took a sip of her water. "That was about the time she passed away. I never made the connection before now."

"Your name sounded familiar. Then the first time we had a videoconference, I knew you were her granddaughter." Grandma Bridget swiped at the corner of her eye. "I hope you don't think badly of me for not telling you earlier."

Amanda shook her head. "On the contrary. I hope you'll tell me many stories about her while I'm here."

"And if I can teach my grandsons how to knit, I can teach anyone, including you."

Amanda arched her eyebrow in his direction, and Seth shrugged. "I can also darn socks and make a soufflé."

"Chocolate?" Amanda asked.

"Is there any other kind?" Seth scoffed.

"I'd like to try one before I leave." She smiled at him, and the world tilted on its axis.

Seth girded himself. It wasn't like a woman had

never smiled at him before. He just hadn't seen anyone light up the way Amanda did.

Every week he welcomed visitors, and every week he said goodbye. She was no different from every other guest.

"Thanks." His voice came out funny, and he cleared his throat, pointing toward the beverage station. "Amanda, join me."

He supposed he should have phrased it as a question rather than a statement, but Grandma Bridget hadn't taught him the skill of subtlety.

They waited until his grandmother was settled in her seat before walking to the coffee urn. He poured a large mug to the brim, the robust aroma of fresh beans giving his system a welcome jolt of energy. "Care for a cup?"

"Decaf for me." Amanda reached for the pot with the orange handle and helped herself. Amanda added cream and sugar to her decaf and held the cup to her face, her look of bliss as appealing as a newborn colt.

"I had my daily dose of caffeine at sunrise. Too much of even the best things in life can leave me with a bad taste."

After yesterday and this morning, he had a feeling she'd categorize him with the bad things.

For his grandparents' sake, he had to find some way of correcting that terrible first impression. "I'm sorry we got off on the wrong foot. Despite my behavior yesterday, my grandparents instilled good manners in me." He spared a glance toward his grandmother, choosing to ignore the interesting way she was staring at them, a knowing spark lurking behind her eyes.

"Glad to hear it." Amanda turned her attention in the same direction. "We've left your grandmother alone for too long," she said.

She made a beeline back to the table. Seth hesitated before following in Amanda's footsteps. How was he going to keep the new mortgage a secret from his grandmother?

And if he acted strangely, would Amanda believe the worst of him?

It would take more than words to show Amanda he wasn't a bad guy, just a cowboy looking out for his grandmother.

He joined the two women, trying to worm his way onto one's good side while hoping to remain in the other's good graces.

IN THE MEADOW within eyesight of the stable and paddock, Amanda settled her professional camera on the tripod and adjusted the aperture. The low ISO setting ensured quality photographs for the updated website, which she should have up and running by the time she left. Together, the still photos and video footage would provide topics for newsletters and other material for months in advance. Fingers crossed she'd be working on those in her new home. Her real estate agent's text, a mere ten minutes ago, was most encouraging since her offer was now under consideration.

Too bad she hadn't found this part of Colorado before she moved to Arizona. The commanding Rockies beckoned to something deep within her, most likely a connection to her late beloved grandmother, but it was just the vacation talking. Once she returned to Phoenix, she'd be relieved to sleep in her own bed again.

For now, though, she welcomed that beginning-of-vacation vibe where everything was shiny and fresh. Somehow, she'd have to convince Pamela that days away from the job without mixing work with pleasure was needed more often than once every three years. No matter how often she raised the subject, though, Pamela's response was always the same. Until Parkhouse Promotions became *the* top marketing firm in Arizona, or at least a consistent contender, she needed Amanda hard at work.

At least the Lazy River Dude Ranch was exceeding expectations, both in terms of scenery and culinary delights. Her opinion of Seth Virtue, however, was still in doubt.

From here, she could see the cowboy, tall and lean in the glow of the morning sun, adjust the sawhorses for the lasso lessons. Even if she had a thousand photo résumés before her of male models pretending to be cowboys, none of them would fit the bill like Seth. Everything about him screamed authentic from his posture to his "aw shucks" method of telling stories.

Part of her wanted to give Seth the benefit of the doubt. As much as she wanted to move on from her first impression, she was wary about doing so. Clients often said something kind to her face to get them out of a public relations disaster, but then didn't back up their words with commendable actions. In this case, Seth had believed Amanda a fraud, willing to scam his grandparents into a free vacation. It would take more than an apology to prove he'd accepted the truth and changed his mind about her.

Speaking of the cowboy, she kept her sights on him through the viewer. He plucked Mabel from the gathered guests, and the little girl responded with glee. Around other customers, Seth was patient and witty. Maybe he was really a nice guy who just wanted the best for his grandparents, shielding them from outsiders or strangers.

That should make her job easier. It was clear he loved the Lazy River Dude Ranch, and having a client who believed in the service's mission and values was beyond ideal. She stepped away from the camera and blinked. She couldn't let herself get carried away by an idealized version of Seth. She needed to remain a consummate professional, starting with snapping these photographs and following up by seeking out signed releases from the guests and staff.

She focused her attention on her camera, taking photographs of Seth teaching Mabel how to hold the rope. Unless she missed the mark, Seth's photogenic appeal would go a long way in making her proposed campaign a success.

"Amanda?" Seth's voice broke through her reverie. She looked up from the camera and saw him holding a length of nylon rope toward her. "Want to learn how to lasso?"

She'd learned years ago during her father's oil rig job fiasco. In those eight months, riding had become her favorite way to while away the hours. She loved western Texas with its open vistas and desert landscapes.

She moved the tripod for a better perspective. "It's best I capture this experience for the website." Amanda gave a flicker of a smile, placing her hands on the camera, hoping he wouldn't take her no personally. "Soon, I'll obtain the releases from your guests and staff so I can use these photos. Thanks anyway."

"Amanda." Seth kept holding out the length of rope. "We need to establish some ground rules about this."

The olive branch he'd extended at the beverage station snapped in two. Bristling inside, she should have known better. She'd actually believed he'd had a change of heart about a bad first impression. Instead, he'd just been trying to persuade her to accept his rules even though his grandparents had given her carte blanche.

"Thank you, Mr. Virtue, but I'm finished here for the time being." She uncoupled the camera from the tripod and stowed it with the rest of her gear.

If Seth wanted to establish ground rules, he should start by embracing her presence on the ranch. Enough was enough. It was time to reach out to Bridget to intervene. Still, she bristled at what this meant. Her parents had always shown favoritism to her sister, Sami. She'd never been good enough for them, and now she wasn't good enough for Seth Virtue.

Somehow she'd find a way to avoid his presence for the remainder of her stay at the ranch. Let the handsome cowboy work his magic on the other guests, the ones who paid for the privilege.

CHAPTER THREE

WITHIN MINUTES, Amanda found herself heading toward the ranch so she could track down Bridget and talk to her. Laughter from the paddock caused her to linger. She turned and saw Seth giving a high five to Isaac, who sported a grin a mile wide, no doubt due to the lasso tied around the prop sawhorse.

That could have been her, proving herself to Seth that she was more than what she seemed on the surface. Had she been too hasty in her eagerness to get away from him?

She ignored that thought and entered the lodge, her eyes adjusting to the softer lighting as opposed to the brighter sunshine. Tails wagging, the retired Australian shepherd dogs, Hap and Trixie, greeted Amanda. Dogs never showed a different side of themselves to people. Unconditional love was their nature inside and out. Amanda set her gear to the side and petted both of the sweet Australian shepherds.

After stowing her gear in the Porcupine Suite

on the second floor of the lodge, Amanda found Bridget in the library where the older woman was teaching Whitney, Eli and Isaac's mother, how to knit, not an activity Amanda would have associated with a week at a dude ranch. Still, this was a vacation, and sometimes people needed a quiet escape from the hustle and bustle of the everyday world.

That begged several questions. Where did the Lazy River Dude Ranch fit into people's lives? A return to a simpler time? A week with cowboys in the mountains? Amanda was sure if she figured out the answer to her question, she'd pinpoint the heart of the presentation. Then that would be the springboard to a long, illustrious relationship between Parkhouse Promotions and the Virtue family.

"Amanda! Join Whitney and me. I promised to teach you how to cast on, remember?" Bridget's warmth was a definite selling point to the ranch, an antidote to her grandson's cooler nature. "I'll have you knitting in five minutes."

The ambience of the library lured her inside. Hap and Trixie entered and warmed themselves near the fireplace. True to her word, Bridget, with an assist from Whitney, taught her to cast on. A sense of accomplishment flowed through Amanda.

She was working on the second row when the door opened. Three men in their late twenties entered and searched the room.

"This could be where the next clue is hidden.

They probably didn't tell Seth about the scavenger hunt." The tallest guy stopped talking while the other two nodded.

"Gentlemen, the true treasure before you is in the extensive collection of books and the joy I find in knitting. The Lazy River is not part of any scavenger hunt." Bridget was firm but gentle in her admonition as she laid her handiwork on the table. "I'd be more than happy to teach the three of you how to knit."

They looked at each other and shrugged. "I still have the blanket my nana made me. I wouldn't trade it for all the gold in Colorado." One pulled up a chair and sat next to Bridget. "I'm Kevin."

Todd and Trevor introduced themselves, and Bridget gave them each a ball of yarn and knitting needles. A companionable silence came over the group while they made progress on their individual projects. Almost an hour had elapsed when Bridget flexed her fingers and called for a break.

Amanda took the opportunity to explain the photo release, which the three guys signed before leaving. Then Whitney accepted the stylus for her signature.

"This place is performing miracles," she said. "Back home, I've tried everything to get Eli and Isaac outside for some fresh air. Nothing has worked. One day at this ranch, and they're running all over, from one spot to the next."

The happy mother excused herself for her family's scheduled horse ride. She passed Seth on her way out of the library. The tall cowboy tipped his hat in her direction before entering the room.

He kissed his grandmother on her cheek. "Why are you inside? Vitamin D is the best therapy of all. I want you to stay healthy and vibrant, Grandma."

"Thanks for your concern. But, as you well know, it's time for my daily knitting lesson." Bridget pressed her hand against Seth's face before he resumed his standing position. "Why are you inside instead of finishing your lasso performance?"

"I was looking for Amanda." Seth pasted on a winning smile, one that could surely secure cabin reservations in a heartbeat, and faced her. "And here you are."

That smile was already making her pulse race, and Amanda couldn't risk being swayed by someone's appearance.

The release could wait until later. She wasn't going anywhere. Amanda gathered her tablet and supplies, taking care to leave nothing behind. "Sorry I can't stay longer, but work awaits." She stared at Seth. "But you're probably relieved I'm not around to take advantage of Bridget and Martin."

"What are you talking about? What's happening between you two?" Bridget frowned and picked up her knitting needles, the clicking and clacking as soft as the slow hum of the gas fireplace.

The ball of lavender yarn fell to the cherry hardwood floor, and Seth placed it back on the table.

"Nothing," he said, his voice perplexed. "I thought we mended fences at breakfast."

Huh? What about those ground rules? How had he conveniently forgotten them? The cowboy's unpredictability threw her off-kilter. Why did he have to look exactly like a cowboy with a rumpled flannel shirt, dirty jeans and faded boots? Worse still, that added to his appeal rather than detracted from it.

Still, his family ran the ranch, so she had to follow their orders.

"I'll try to stick to your ground rules and keep you out of the promo material." If she captured his signature on the release form now, she could avoid him for the rest of her stay. Once more, she pulled her tablet out of her bag. "But I snapped photographs of you teaching Eli and Isaac how to throw a lasso so I need your signature for the release."

Bridget's needles stopped clicking. She stared at Amanda, then Seth. "Is there a problem I need to know about?"

No! Ever since her previous unfortunate employment experience left her without a reference, Amanda prided herself at keeping her nose to the grindstone and her manner professional. However, the Lazy River was a family-run enterprise. If Bridget sensed any disharmony between Amanda and Seth, Bridget would side with her grandson, same as Amanda's former boss sided with his son over her.

It went deeper than that, though. Amanda genuinely liked the older woman, who cared about everyone on the ranch, employees and guests alike. Having Bridget look at her like she stole Ingrid's apple pie didn't sit well with Amanda. She sought some foothold to regain her composure.

"Seth reminded me there are ground rules for this week. I'm trying my best to accommodate him. Just so you know, my goal is to formulate a plan that will increase your visibility and result in full occupancy." Amanda felt better discussing business. This was familiar and safe. "That starts with a website highlighting the best about the past and the present. Bridget, can I schedule a time with you to go over the history of the ranch?"

Before Bridget had a chance to answer, the library door opened. Tiffany and Derrick stepped into the room, laughing until they spotted the trio at the table. "Can you believe Princess and Earl put a hole in the cat sitter's sneaker?" Tiffany's hand flew to her mouth. "Did we interrupt a business meeting? I'd like to borrow a book."

Derrick frowned. "Honey, we can do anything. Go for a horse ride, feed the goat, explore the trails. Anything you couldn't do when you were working three jobs."

"I didn't have time to read then," Tiffany explained.

"The library is always open for everyone at any time. Martin and I have read most of these books." Bridget reassured the woman with a smile as her knitting needles resumed their progress. Trixie came over and lay down at Bridget's feet. "We have mysteries, romance novels, science fiction."

The empty nesters each chose a book and left the library as the Carr family entered. Mabel bounced over to Seth, her grin spreading joy throughout the room.

She brought out a small vial and launched into her day's activities. "There are real gold flakes in here! I can't wait to show my friends and tell them about my honeymoon."

Seth chuckled and examined the vial with a smile before returning it to her. "You're a genuine miner, a real forty-niner."

Mabel frowned. "I'm not forty-nine. I'm eight."

Seth explained and then listened to the rest of Mabel's adventures while Colleen and Brian selected books. The trio departed with Mabel dragging Brian out of the room, urging him to go faster as she was ever so hungry. Colleen trailed behind, her demeanor rather stiff and formal. Amanda felt for Colleen, who was obviously trying to gain Mabel's affection.

Bridget laid her knitting needles on the table. "It's busier in here than the Rocky Mountain National Park. Seth and I will meet you in your cabin so we can enjoy a smidgen of privacy. I'll arrange for Crosby to come out to the ranch this week. He's the town historian. Which cabin are you staying in, Amanda?"

"I'm upstairs in the Porcupine Suite," Amanda said.

"Seth Peter Virtue! You didn't." Trixie startled at the vehemence in Bridget's tone before laying her head on her paws once more. "Two cabins are currently vacant, correct?"

"The Bluebell and the Marigold, but I saved those in case someone booked them at the last minute. I fixed the shingles on the Bluebell this morning," Seth said. "But the plumbing still needs work in Marigold, and Rich is out sick. Grandpa and I are handling everything in his absence."

Bridget reached for her big knitting bag and stowed her needles and yarn. "Rich is our head maintenance tech, and he's been under the weather. Amanda, you'll love the Bluebell. All seven cabins are beautiful, but that one is especially lovely. The bedroom has a breathtaking view of the Rockies. You'll be back every summer."

A sweet sentiment, and Amanda saved the phrase for a possible theme for her presentation. However, she wouldn't book another week here, not with Seth believing she was taking advantage of the situation. Besides, once she clipped the key to her new home on her key chain, she'd savor days off with friends or exploring her corner of Arizona, home to many natural wonders.

Most of all, she didn't want Seth thinking she was asking for special privileges.

"I'm content where I am," Amanda said.

Bridget clicked her tongue. "The Bluebell is vacant and stunning, and I won't hear any objections. Seth, help her move her belongings, and we'll meet there after dinner." Bridget limped out of the room, Trixie following on her heels.

Amanda faced Seth, his expression unreadable.

"Surely the lodge has another room for conducting business?" There was no need for her to change her lodgings, let alone for Seth to help her.

"Grandma Bridget doesn't take no for an answer. Come on."

A bit like her grandson. Amanda preferred that Seth stay clear of her personal space seeing how he was already invading her thoughts. "I'll pack by myself and meet you in the lobby in twenty minutes."

Seth agreed to the compromise, and it didn't even take her ten minutes to gather everything together. With time to spare, she checked her phone and found a text from her sister, Sami, asking if she had time to talk. Amanda groaned and sat on the edge of the bed. Had their mother finally relayed the message Amanda would no longer fund Sami's headshots and acting lessons?

There was no need to jump to conclusions. Still, she'd have to postpone a sisterly chat until she was back in Phoenix. She texted Sami she was busy with work. Three dots immediately came up on Amanda's screen.

What about tomorrow night? Can u talk?

Amanda sighed as Sami must, indeed, have taken a page from Wendy Fleming's playbook. She replied in the affirmative, wanting to take a page from Seth's instead as he seemed to know when to be direct and when to turn to a story as a roundabout way of addressing a situation.

Still, she had to be firm in her resolution. It was time the Fleming family stopped using Amanda as an ATM.

Twenty minutes had flown by, and she hurried to the lobby. After dealing with her sister, she'd prefer to settle into the Bluebell by herself.

"Give me the key. I'll find the cabin on my own," Amanda offered.

"I'll help." Seth pointed toward her rolling suitcase. "May I take that for you? My grandmother would drill me about common courtesy if I didn't treat a valued guest with respect."

"I can take care of my luggage myself." Amanda kept her hand on the suitcase handle. "But that's the issue, isn't it? I'm not a guest—I'm a subcontractor."

"We've gotten off on the wrong foot. My grandmother is a good judge of character. She approves of you, and so do I." Seth nodded at a family heading toward the dining room before turning back to Amanda. "As far as I'm concerned, you're a guest."

"You're the one who insists on establishing ground rules." Why couldn't he just give her the key and be done with it? She'd managed just fine over the past few years traveling by herself.

She'd find another cowboy on the ranch to feature in her campaign. There were plenty of them although none had a bearing like Seth or brown eyes that burned with the same intensity.

Seth scratched his beard and looked perplexed. "What are you talking about?"

Amanda rolled her suitcase toward the exit, and Seth obliged by opening the door for her. She continued down the path. The silence grew between them until it was practically a crescendo.

She halted and he did the same. "When you were teaching Mabel and the Berggren brothers how to lasso, you said we need to establish ground rules. As hard as it is for me to accept that, you've gotten your message across. Your grandparents hired my firm for a job, but you don't want to be featured in the promo material. Don't worry. I won't use your name or likeness."

Amanda walked a few steps before she realized Seth wasn't keeping up with her any longer. She glanced back, only to find those brown eyes contained a touch of disappointment rather than their usual spark of cowboy crustiness.

"This is your cabin." Seth pointed toward a gorgeous log cabin at the end of the path.

On the front porch, baskets of petunias, pansies and geraniums hung from hooks. Two rocking chairs with plump cushions provided respite for the guests. This was exactly the look she wanted for her new home. She couldn't wait for the current owners to accept her offer; she'd actually have a front porch!

Seth traversed the trail and unlocked the front door with Amanda on his heels.

The inside was spectacular even if it was a little faded and worn. Directly across from the door, a stone fireplace showcased a wooden mantel with climbing plants on the end and a framed painting of a buffalo. Plush indigo blankets and blue pillows with embroidered bluebells occupied space on an older leather couch. Seth led Amanda on a tour of the rest of the cabin. Her mouth dropped at the size of the bathroom although the fixtures looked like something out of her late grandma Lou's house. She parked her suitcase in the master bedroom with an inviting king-size bed and a floor-to-ceiling glass window. Bridget was right. The view was spectacular.

Then Amanda met Seth in the galley kitchen.

"Dinner will be served in thirty minutes at the main lodge." Seth laid the key on the counter, his voice more formal than it had been at the beverage station this morning. "At the present time, we're not offering room service due to lack of staff, but I'll let you know when we resume that amenity so you can add it to the website."

Amanda missed the more jovial Seth that made him such a hit with Mabel, Eli and Isaac, but perhaps it was for the best they added a touch of formality to their business relationship.

Partnership, not relationship.

She ran her hand over the laminate countertop. "Thank you." She searched for the words to describe how much she appreciated this space. Although words were part of her livelihood, she couldn't find the appropriate ones to convey her emotion.

"See you around." Seth started for the door and faced her with his hand on the knob. "For some reason, I say the wrong thing around you. Earlier while I was conducting the lasso program, I should have said I wanted you to take part in the activities as a guest."

She failed to find the right words, and he was saying the wrong ones.

Was the undercurrent between them responsible for that? She blinked away any notion there was chemistry between them.

Then his message infiltrated her brain. "But you mentioned ground rules?"

"Yeah, so you can enjoy yourself." Seth rubbed his beard. "Everyone who comes to the Lazy River, whether on vacation or as staff, becomes part of our family, some for a week, some longer. Do what you need to do but then enjoy yourself."

Here she was in marketing, a profession that revolved around bringing out the best in a service. She prided herself on seeking out every angle and studying it until she knew all aspects of the product, good and bad.

Something about Seth was drawing out the worst in her. Amanda needed to take a page from her own playbook and spin this in a more positive manner. She'd find a way for Seth to bring out the best in her.

"Thank you for your honesty." She held out her hand in a gesture of peace. "Let's mend that fence, once and for all. I can't think of a better place for a truce. This cabin is peaceful, and I already love it."

He hesitated and then slipped his hand in hers. Tiny shocks traversed through her. They were anything but peaceful. In fact, it was alarming. The last time she'd mixed business with pleasure with a coworker, she'd been burned and on the unemployment line without a reference.

"Ranchers do like their fences in proper repair." Seth released her from his grip, the wariness in his brown eyes giving way to something close to mirth.

If the cowboy had a sense of humor, it was a good thing she lived in Phoenix.

"Keeps away the predators, huh?"

To his credit, he laughed and headed back to the front door. "I like to think of a fence as a protective barrier. Then everyone can sleep well."

He dipped his hat in her direction and took his leave. Amanda brushed aside the turbulence in her stomach that screamed danger, a far cry from feeling protected and secure.

She set aside her qualms and removed her boots, placing them near the front door. A more thorough tour made her fall even more in love with the surroundings. Everything about the space called to her. She lingered in the kitchen, her fingers tracing the label of a small jar of chokecherry jelly. Then she did the same for a package of ground coffee with beans grown in Colorado.

This place was a dream come true, and a genuine respite away from work and her family. Returning to the bedroom, she bounced on the bed and wiggled her toes, sinking into the mound of pillows. Then she rested her head against the plump blue headboard. This was the most relaxed she'd felt in years, perhaps ever.

Now that she and Seth had they'd cleared away the misunderstanding between them, she found herself lingering over times he made Mabel laugh. Changing her opinion about the winsome cowboy was enough for a truce, but that was as far as it could go between them. There was no use fanning the flames of a fire to the point where they were out of control. She'd been burned once before, and she'd take care she wouldn't suffer that kind of downfall again.

CHAPTER FOUR

Monday

THE COLD, misty drizzle proved Colorado weather would always keep ranchers on their toes. Seth chipped away ice from water troughs and ventured over to Wilma and Betty, the two oldest mares on the ranch. For twenty years, they performed above and beyond in their service to Martin and Bridget. They earned their retirement, and more. Wilma seemed bothered by the elements, and Seth fetched a horse blanket for her. After making sure both horses were content and grazing, he washed up in the stable before hurrying to the main lodge for breakfast.

Seth shook off the excess water from his Carhartt jacket. Then he made a beeline for the dining room. Only the sound of his grandfather calling out his name halted his progress toward a stack of Ingrid's waffles.

Grandpa Martin stopped him in the lobby. "Your fly-fishing lessons are canceled for the day."

That wasn't a surprise. Most guests didn't want to spend hours in a freezing river in the rain. There were still plenty of activities in the rec center for them.

And Seth had enough chores to keep him busy for the rest of the week, let alone a morning. "I'll fix the leaky faucet in Marigold." While Grandpa Martin was a captive audience, he pressed his case about the necessary changes. "Once Amanda spreads the word about the Lazy River and capacity is back to normal, what about adding some new features to the ranch? Even now, there are some simple updates that won't cost much. I could paint the cabins with paint stock from our storeroom. That won't cost a penny."

Grandpa Martin shook his head. "Customers will find us again. We just need to be patient."

Seth blew out an exasperated breath and glanced around the lobby. Thankfully Grandma Bridget was nowhere in sight. "The mortgage payments will take a big chunk out of our operating budget. Did you tell Grandma about the loan yet?"

"She fell asleep as soon as she was done visiting Amanda." Grandpa Martin pursed his lips, his mustache almost bristling with concern for his wife of almost sixty years. "Didn't have the heart to wake her up."

Guests started flowing into the lobby from the dining hall. One of the college reunion guests interrupted Seth's conversation with his grandfather to ask for an umbrella. Grandpa Martin directed the guest to the front desk. Then they were alone once more.

"I'll get my toolbox and head over to Marigold," Seth said.

At least he'd be keeping his distance from Grandma Bridget today. That would reduce the chance of him spilling the beans.

"Seth!" Before he could take another step, his grandmother called his name.

That was too close. Once Grandma Bridget found out about the mortgage, Seth might have to board a plane for anywhere until she cooled off. Not that he'd blame her if she was upset with him for keeping this from her.

She headed his way, hobbling on the cane she depended on at night and during inclement weather. "Martin, I just posted a note at the rec center. Your archery lesson is canceled."

Perfect. That would give Grandpa Martin a chance to get everything into the open, and Seth knew just the place. They could talk while he fixed the faucet.

"Grandma Bridget." The more Seth reflected on how everything came together, the more he liked it. "Grandpa Martin was asking me where you were. He has something to tell you."

He sent a pointed look in his grandfather's direction. At that moment, Amanda came into view carrying his grandmother's knitting bag on her shoulder. Her bright pink flannel shirt and jeans fit right into the rustic lodge lobby almost as if she belonged here. Other guests over the years had worn similar outfits, and he never considered any of them as belonging at the ranch.

She's only here for a short while, Seth. Just like Felicity. He thought his ex-girlfriend wanted the same things as him, loved the ranch as much as he did, but he'd been wrong.

"I could say the same about you, Seth." Grandma Bridget asserted herself in front of Seth, hands firmly on the cane handle. "I have plans for you."

Amanda neared with mirth on her pretty face, enough to give Seth pause. What had the two of them cooked up over breakfast?

"I already have a full slate for this morning." It wasn't just the plumbing in Marigold. There was a host of other issues that needed attention with a reduced staff. "Amanda, my sister, Daisy, is giving a silversmith demonstration this morning. Everyone who attends leaves with a special bracelet. A perfect photo opportunity for you."

"Actually, I'm meeting with a different Virtue sibling today." Amanda adjusted the knitting bag onto the other shoulder. "Your brother Crosby."

Grandma Bridget nodded. "Seth, show Amanda around Violet Ridge and then take her to the Miner's Cottage. Crosby is going to fill her in on the ranch's history."

Even if Seth wanted to show Amanda his hometown and, glancing at her, he realized that was exactly what he wanted to do, the ranch was too short-staffed to spare him for an entire morning. "What about Grandpa Martin? He can drive Amanda into town."

His grandfather flexed his fingers and then rubbed his hip. "Arthritis is acting up something fierce this morning." Seth raised his eyebrow at the flimsy excuse. His grandfather averted his gaze and continued, "So you can stop at the saddlery and pick up my order."

With his grandparents united in their mindset, Seth knew it was fruitless to argue with them.

He shrugged and glanced at Amanda. "Can you meet me at my truck in forty-five minutes? It's parked in the employee lot behind the maintenance shed." He patted his stomach. "I haven't eaten breakfast yet."

"Ingrid outdid herself today. I've never tasted waffles that delicious." Amanda licked her lips. "My oatmeal won't taste half as good when I return to Phoenix."

The perfect reminder her visit was temporary. Same as Felicity, who had no ties to bind her to the Lazy River or Violet Ridge.

Seth noticed his grandparents sneaking away.

"Grandma! Grandpa! Not so fast."

They faced him with guilty expressions. He knew what Grandpa Martin was hiding. It was the thought Grandma Bridget also possessed a secret that was most concerning. Now more than ever, he had to find some way to talk to them in private. Better yet, he just thought of the perfect solution for his grandfather to find time to tell his wife about the loan. "Since I'm going to Violet Ridge, Grandma can help you fix that leaky faucet. I'll walk you there before I eat breakfast."

"Nonsense. I've been repairing faucets long before you were born." Grandpa Martin dismissed Seth while flexing his arm muscles. "I'll fix it before you finish your first waffle."

"And I'm manning the reservation desk." Using her cane, Grandma Bridget walked over and checked the computer. "Martin, get going. Two families just reserved the Marigold. It seems as though we're going to host a destination wedding."

Seth's jaw dropped. "That's not our niche. So many last-minute details." His mind reeled.

"For their dogs. They're arriving this afternoon."

Seth had never thought he'd attend a dog wedding, but then anything was possible this week. Still, down one maid, Seth definitely couldn't drive Amanda to Violet Ridge. Although he was usually content to stay on the ranch, which had everything he needed, a sliver of sadness shot through him. "There's too much to do. Crosby will have to drive here to talk to Amanda."

"Everything's under control, Seth. Daisy will give it a go-over after her demonstration. We need that saddlery order today." Grandma Bridget smiled and shooed Seth to the dining area. "And pick up special dog treats for a basket for the newlyweds."

He rolled his eyes before sending a backward glance and thumbs-up in their direction. Of course, he worried about his grandparents. They had practically raised him. And this ranch was more than just his livelihood.

Was there any way to pay back the mortgage early? Since he was heading to Violet Ridge, he might as well see if he could schedule an appointment with the new manager. With a long history as a reliable customer, perhaps he could finagle a better interest rate and more favorable terms than his grandfather negotiated.

After a side trip to his office, where he made that appointment, Seth entered the dining room. Mabel Carr launched herself at him, and it was all he could do to answer her flood of questions. *Yes, he loved his job. No, he didn't want to work anywhere else. Yes, Colorado weather was always this unpredictable. No, he never got bored on rainy days.*

Mabel chatted with him while her newlywed father held hands with his wife at a nearby table. Finally, Brian and Colleen collected Mabel and set off for the rec center. Then, with a full stomach, Seth made his way to his truck, glad Mabel had provided a happy distraction from the upcoming bank meeting. In a few hours, he'd have a better idea about where the ranch stood in terms of affording more upgrades since guests expected free Wi-Fi and perks like loyalty programs and excursions into Violet Ridge in dependable vehicles.

And dog baskets for pet weddings. He let out a deep breath.

"Good morning, Seth." Amanda hailed him from beside the passenger door, the misty drizzle not seeming to impact her in the least. A tote bag on her shoulder, she held up a travel mug. "Hope you don't mind my bringing along some liquid warmth. I shouldn't have a second cup of coffee, but your lodge does make a delicious brew."

"Hold on." Seth read an incoming text from his brother. "I just heard from Crosby. He forgot about an important meeting, but he'll meet you for lunch at Brewer Brothers to review the ranch and town history with you."

"No problem. I haven't spent any time in Violet Ridge, and who better than you to give me the grand tour?" Amanda flipped the lid enough for a wisp of steam to dissipate in the chilly air. "Learning the ins and outs of the area will give me more material for my presentation. I came upon a great idea at breakfast. I'm creating a special booklet we can send to new customers with discounts to restaurants and activities in Violet Ridge as a thank-you."

"Sounds like that will provide value, but I can't guide you around town. I have an important appointment plus I have to buy dog treats." He stopped short of revealing his destination to Amanda; the pet wedding was a perfect distraction. If she found out about the ranch's precarious financial situation, she might pull out of the deal. While that had been his goal yesterday, this morning he found he welcomed her presence. "I'll be busy until lunchtime."

"Great. That will give me a chance to talk to business owners. Maybe fit in a little souvenir shopping. I'll handle the married doggy congratulations basket for you. That sounds like an excellent morning to me." She sipped her drink, and contentment radiated off of her. "Isn't it a beautiful day?"

"That's one way of looking at it." He clicked the key fob. "Most guests don't appreciate the chilly rain."

"I love cold, rainy mornings." Her smile was as sunny as the day was overcast. "Phoenix has over three hundred days of sunshine with an average of only seven inches of rain per year."

Taking care of the slippery gravel, he spotted her while she climbed into the truck's interior. Then he closed the door before heading around to the driver's side. Over the years he'd lost count of how many times he traveled to Violet Ridge by himself, valuing the thirty fifteen minutes of peace to regroup from the minor incidents that plagued the dude ranch. Like the time all the ATVs ran out of gasoline, stranding several guests and a guide in the woods. Or the family of noisy raccoons that temporarily took up residence behind the main lodge.

Those were the rare cases, however. Meanwhile, he often fed off the guests' energy.

Seth settled into the driver's seat and turned on the ignition. The chords of an Elvis Presley song blared from the truck's speakers. Heat rose to his face at her discovering his personal secret. He always cranked up the volume on return trips home. He fiddled with the knob and turned off the music. "Feel free to adjust the heat, too."

"May I?" She flipped the music back on and danced in her seat, using her hips and her hands. "I love the King's songs. They remind me of my grandmother."

That was how he'd first become an Elvis fan, as well. "Then an apology is overdue from my end."

"I'm not going anywhere."

She moved toward him, her lips slightly parted as if in expectation of a serious discussion, but this was only a thirty-minute drive. Serious conversations in Seth's book required at least thirty-one minutes.

"I'm sorry your grandmother Lou is nowhere near as fantastic as Grandma Bridget," he teased.

"I should have seen that coming." Her chuckle was a warm caress on this chilly morning. "Your grandmother is the heart of the ranch. My grandmother was pretty wonderful, though."

"Was?" Her use of the past tense didn't escape him.

"She passed away when I was fourteen." The wistfulness in her voice was enough indication they must have been close. "Grandma Lou was my shield."

Seth pulled up to the entrance gate. Amanda offered to do the honors of opening and closing it, leaving him to ponder what she said. How was a grandmother a shield? Then he understood. In a way, his grandparents had sheltered the four Virtue siblings the best they could from the harshness of losing their parents so young. They'd done a phenomenal job.

Amanda entered the truck, drops of water on her rain jacket. "Brr." She shivered. "The temperature is dropping."

"Spring in Colorado is full of surprises." Seth adjusted the heat and veered east on the road that would lead them into town. "Tell me more about your grandmother."

The opening chords of the next Elvis song filled the cab, and Amanda adjusted the volume until it was louder. "This one was my grandmother's favorite." She swayed in rhythm to the music. "Whenever Elvis came on the radio, Grandma Lou would stop everything and dance with me."

"Music might have been what brought our grandmothers together and then their friendship took off." Seth tapped the steering wheel in time to the rhythm.

Amanda stilled in her seat. "Seems like we're finally getting along. I like our truce."

So did he. It was nice having company on the ride into Violet Ridge. He'd forgotten this stretch of road could get lonely when it was just himself along for the ride.

"All cards on the table, then." Out of the corner of his eye, he saw her face him, a serious expression overtaking her. Somehow, he'd like to learn all of her expressions before she went back to Phoenix, but a week didn't seem long enough to do that. "Younger Elvis or older Elvis?"

She scoffed. "As if that's a real question. Younger Elvis by a mile. That energy, that persona."

He blew out his own sound of indignation. "Hardly. In his later years, his voice mellowed and grew richer. There was a maturity about him that came out in his music."

As they headed toward town, they continued the debate. To his surprise, she relented a tad, and he did the same.

Something about Amanda put him at ease, perhaps because she must have to adapt to handling different kinds of personalities in her career. He found himself a little regretful that the conversation would end as they arrived in Violet Ridge.

Seth pointed out different parts of the town. "That's the Over and Dunne Feed and Seed. It's expanded quite a bit and now includes a consignment store for cowboy hats and boots."

Amanda twisted her body and kept watch long after they passed the store. "I'll definitely visit there before I leave. Does the ranch have a shuttle that brings guests into town?"

"No. Most guests want to stay on the ranch since there are so many activities."

"If you could get me a complete list of the amenities, I can add them to the new website. I'll also capitalize on the pet wedding. That's a sweet angle." Amanda gasped when he cruised along Violet Ridge's Main Street. While the drizzle was limiting the usual foot traffic prominent in the growing shopping district, the mist couldn't hide the area's charm. "What a cute town."

"Speaking of cute, you have a coffee mustache."

Her swift intake of breath preceded her hand flying to the passenger sun visor. She pushed it down and opened the flap for the vanity mirror. "You were going to let me talk to people with a coffee mustache?"

"I would have told you." He opened the console between them and handed her a napkin with a wink. "Eventually."

"That's what they all say." Her harrumph struck a deep chord he'd thought was permanently dormant, same as her coffee mustache had. "Wait a second. You think foamy mustaches are cute?"

"I reserve *cute* for lambs and kittens." Although

he could see himself easily adding blondes with a dimple and a quick smile to the list. Seth neared Crosby's workplace and turned the conversation back to a safe topic that would keep their truce and boundaries intact. "The Miner's Cottage is the oldest building in Violet Ridge, dating back to the 1880s."

"Ah, Seth the tour guide has reported for duty. I get your message." She patted the tote bag near her feet. "Will the drizzle end by this afternoon so I can take some pictures? I brought my camera and gear."

"Most likely, although Colorado weather has a mind of its own."

"A little like the residents I've met." Her tone conveyed she too was making an effort to keep the conversation light and easy. "Your secret's safe with me."

"Secret?" Could Amanda have overheard his conversation with Grandpa Martin? He shivered.

"About lambs and kittens." Her revelation slowed his racing heart, his sense of relief immediate. "A rancher like yourself probably treasures an aura of toughness and authority. If word got out that you're a softie, who knows what people might think?"

What would she think if she found out he was finding her more attractive by the minute? If she didn't reciprocate his feelings, she could go to his grandmother and tell her of his unprofessionalism.

Whenever Grandma Bridget was disappointed in him, Seth always felt like the world was a little less palatable.

He found a parking spot halfway between the Miner's Cottage and the saddlery where his grandfather had placed his order.

"I'm tough enough to handle people's opinions of me." Except his blood ran cold at the thought of his grandmother thinking less of him once she found out he abetted his grandfather.

Too late. He'd made his bed and now he had to lie in it.

He turned off the ignition and caught the way her blond hair swooped over her face in a veil of shimmering silk, honey strands intermixing with gold. She pushed it back behind her ear.

He tried to ignore his attraction. Nothing could come of it. He reached for the umbrella stowed in the driver's door compartment and handed it to her. "You'll need this."

"Every time you're exasperating, a minute later, you do something that's utterly delightful." She reached for it and halted her hand above the console. "Won't you need it?"

"Nah. Tough guy, remember?" He winked and transferred the black umbrella into her capable hands, already missing the sweet vibe from the trip.

A brief twinge of guilt for leaving her on her own passed. He delivered directions to the restaurant as well as a description of Crosby before taking his leave. After adjusting his rain jacket collar, he glanced behind him. She sent him a smile of thanks, most likely for the use of the umbrella. Satisfied, he walked a block to the bank.

Another surprise awaited him when Seth was introduced to the new bank manager. Instant recognition flooded him at the sight of the president of their high school graduating class, Mateo Rodriguez, who'd left for college fifteen years ago and must have just returned to Violet Ridge. Mateo greeted Seth and steered him toward his corner office. Long triple-paned windows afforded a breathtaking view of the Rockies. Seth hung his rain jacket on a hook and settled in a comfortable leather chair.

"First week on the job, and I've already seen ten classmates." Mateo smiled and sat in the executive office chair behind a massive mahogany desk. His navy suit was impeccable as opposed to Seth's wrinkled plaid shirt. "What brings you into the bank today?"

Seth fiddled with his cowboy hat before setting it on the ground beside his boots. "My grandfather took out a mortgage on the dude ranch. I'd like more details about refinancing and possibly procuring another loan for improvements."

Mateo stroked the keys on his computer and studied the screen with intent. "I see your grandfather has filled out a power of attorney and designated you in it so I can speak freely to you."

TANYA AGLER   81

Then he frowned. "Martin and Bridget are joint owners of the Lazy River Dude Ranch, but he's the only signatory on the loan."

"He mortgaged the property for her medical bills." Seth glanced at the empty chair next to him. Rather than his grandfather or one of his siblings, however, he'd have given anything for Amanda's presence. Dismissing that thought, he continued, "And he didn't tell her yet."

Mateo gave a low whistle. "Way to make my first week easier." The echo faded as Mateo scrutinized the documents. "I have bad news for you. Since you don't own the ranch, you don't have enough collateral."

"What if my grandfather cosigns?" Seth searched for any possibilities that could bring the ranch into this decade and compete with the Rocky Valley Guest Ranch.

Mateo flicked a few more keys, his eyebrows furrowing deeper. "I'm not seeing enough here for the first loan to have been authorized."

This time Seth had the answer. "Grandpa Martin and the former manager knew each other well."

"Too well," Mateo kept a guarded expression on his face. "I wouldn't have authorized this loan without more paperwork, but what's done is done."

There was no point in wasting any more of Mateo's time so Seth reached for his Stetson. "Thanks for seeing me and not giving me a line."

Mateo extended his hand and clasped Seth's

in a hearty shake. "Business always stays in the office. A group of us are getting together soon. You're welcome to join us."

"Text me the details. You've got my number and I'll let you know." Seth dipped his head. "Sorry to waste your time."

"On the contrary. I have to dig further into the loans the former manager authorized and follow up on them." Mateo opened the door, indicating Seth should go ahead of him.

With today's order from the saddlery firmly in hand, Seth considered his next steps on the way back to his truck. Another loan wouldn't be forthcoming without Grandma Bridget knowing about the first one, and Mateo indicated the ranch might not be the recipient of any future loans.

More than ever, it seemed as though Amanda held much of his future in her hands. Seth loaded the back, slamming the tailgate a little too hard. He might claim he was tough enough to handle what others thought of him, but he was anything but that when it came to being the bearer of a secret of enormous magnitude.

AMANDA WAS IN LOVE. Downtown Violet Ridge had entranced and enraptured her like no other place she'd ever visited. Lanterns glowed a welcome beacon upon antique lampposts and cut through the misty drizzle. The pastel storefronts touted shops she'd love to explore with fun names like

Saucy Sal's Specialty Sauces and Setting Sun's Beads and More. Every time she entered a store, a friendly salesperson extended a warm greeting along with an invitation to peruse the merchandise at her leisure. After exploring the aisles of each establishment, she introduced herself and exchanged business cards with the staff. So far, she batted a thousand in her requests to photograph the stores' interiors for the upcoming Lazy River Dude Ranch website.

She stood outside of Brewer Brothers restaurant and let reality seep into her inner core.

Vacation vibes. That was why she was so enamored of the town, the ranch and the enigmatic cowboy she'd recently met. Then again, she could also be projecting her marketing ideas onto her personal life. This campaign already felt more personal than any of her other assignments, and the dog wedding was definitely more fun than her recent projects.

She just needed to make sure she carried these positive feelings back to Phoenix with her.

Until she returned to her home state, she'd enjoy this new energy feelings as long as possible while giving her best to the Virtue family. Entering Brewer Brothers, she paused while her eyes adjusted to the dim interior. Once they had, she liked the restaurant's casual ambience with metal brew kettles taking up space in a cordoned-off area. Nearly half of the wooden tables were already occupied. She glanced around, searching for Seth, but he was nowhere in sight. The only table with a sole customer was covered with books and papers, and the man didn't resemble Seth with his blond hair and black horn-rimmed glasses. Instead of Seth's rumpled flannel shirts, the customer wore a huge sweater that had definitely seen better days.

Besides, he was too occupied with his work to be expecting someone, so Amanda waited on a nearby bench.

No sooner did she pull out her phone to text Seth than he appeared. He glanced around the restaurant, paused on the man eating along, and a chuckle suddenly lightened Seth's serious bent. "Some things never change," he said. "And Crosby is at the top of the list."

Seth escorted Amanda to the table covered with books and other paraphernalia.

"You must be Amanda," the man said. "Have a seat." The man didn't look up while jotting notes on his laptop. "Hi, Seth."

"Ha. Gee, thanks, Crosby." Seth pointed to a crowded booth. "I thought you were going to ask us to sit at a different table so we wouldn't disturb you."

This close, the family resemblance was more pronounced with the brothers sharing similar builds and cheekbones.

Crosby pushed his glasses up the bridge of his nose. "Nonsense. The books won't mind, and neither will I. Please join me." He closed his laptop and cracked a smile in Amanda's direction. "Someone has to mess with him every once in a while. Gotta keep him honest."

"I think Seth does a pretty good job at being himself."

Amanda felt the heat rise to her cheeks so she hastened to sit across from Crosby while he stacked the books and laughed at her quip. "Touché. You fit in well around here."

Too bad it was just a temporary fit.

"Amanda's a visitor. She's not sticking around," Seth said.

She almost gasped aloud. Just when she thought she might be growing on him, he said something abrupt about her leaving. Was he looking forward to getting rid of her that much?

She pushed her concern aside as the bubbly female server brought menus and glasses of water.

Amanda asked her for recommendations, and the young brunette mentioned several locally made craft beers as well as their homemade root beer. Amanda chose the root beer with her order and then brought out her interview questions for Crosby. She hoped the brother was more forthcoming with details about the dude ranch.

To her surprise, Seth's brother was as effusive as Seth was efficient. "My great-grandparents purchased the land over ninety years ago. In the 1930s, they charged forty dollars for a week's stay, including lodging, activities and food." Crosby pulled up pictures on his phone and showed them to Amanda. "I'll forward some of these to you."

Amanda stopped jotting notes long enough to give Crosby her contact information. Her vision for the updated website solidified in her mind along with a new logo. Tonight, she'd take full advantage of her beautiful cabin and work on the presentation.

The server brought the bison queso appetizer. Amanda dunked a tortilla chip into the queso, and the tangy flavor delighted her just as the town had captivated her. Crosby followed her lead while Seth tapped his watch.

"This is one of my favorite appetizers, and I have the two of you to help me finish every bite," Amanda declared while passing the queso to Seth. "The ranch will survive for one meal without you."

Seth scooped a bite of queso onto a chip. Some of the tension released from his shoulders. "I'm only doing this to be chivalrous."

Seth delivered a half smile while he lifted the chip to his lips. Good thing he held back as the full deal was starting to elicit flutters in her stomach.

Crosby's mouth dropped before he blinked. His surprise faded while he crunched another chip. "Amanda, you have to consider moving here. You're the only one who's ever brought out this lighter side of him."

Seth glared at his brother, who simply brushed

him off, launching into more details about the ranch's past. The server appeared with their entrees, and Amanda's mouth watered at the sight of her bison burger and fries. "Crosby, do you have time to come to the ranch this week?" She squirted some ketchup on her plate. "I'd like to interview you for a video for the website."

The historian would appeal to some, but Amanda was still convinced that Seth, the consummate cowboy, would captivate the audience and sway their final decision to book a cabin at the Lazy River.

Crosby agreed and reached for the barbecue sauce. "Maybe you can give me some pointers for my history vlog. I'm stuck at a hundred followers."

This was comfortable territory for Amanda, and she delivered some pointers until Seth's eyes glazed over. Then she veered the conversation to more neutral ground.

Too soon the lunch ended. She and Seth said their goodbyes to Crosby, who remained behind with his books. They walked back to Seth's truck and Amanda handed his umbrella back to him. The gray, misty drizzle had departed, leaving a gorgeous afternoon in its wake. Wispy white cotton clouds dotted the blue sky while the afternoon sunlight drenched the pastel storefronts in a golden glow. This was spring at its finest.

While Seth powered up the truck, Amanda rummaged through her tote bag for the daily activity sheet.

"What do you suggest this afternoon? I'm leaning toward the mountain bike excursion." Exploring the miles of trails was a necessity before she left.

"That's been canceled for today." Seth waited at the intersection until it was his turn. "The rain started after midnight and drenched the ground."

"I imagine your sister's silversmithing presentation was well attended. Sorry I missed that." Amanda folded the paper and placed it back in the tote bag. "You, Daisy and Crosby seem close. Why aren't your siblings more involved with the day-to-day ranch management?"

"They all chose different paths." Seth halted at the town's red light, and Amanda savored the opportunity for a last, lingering glance at the shops.

"I also have another brother." Seth tapped his hands on the steering wheel. "Jase is a detective in Denver."

"A rancher, a silversmith, a detective and a historian. Your parents must have encouraged you all to follow your hearts." Unlike hers who encouraged her sister to become an A-list actress while ignoring Amanda. That was, unless they were asking her for money.

Seth's hands stilled. The light changed to green, and he breezed through the intersection. "My parents died in a car accident when I was ten."

Amanda's heart dropped to her toes. "I'm sorry

for your loss." Her sympathies went out to the four siblings.

"It was a long time ago." Seth kept his gaze focused on the road. "My grandparents raised the four of us."

Based on what she already knew about Seth, she deduced he'd done his fair share of helping with his siblings. "Let me guess. You're the oldest."

His nod confirmed her theory. "Then Daisy, then Jase. Crosby's the youngest."

"And you're the only one who lives at the Lazy River?" Amanda sought clarification as much for herself as for the campaign.

Seth shrugged and paid attention to his surroundings. "Daisy lives in town with her new husband, who's the mayor of Violet Ridge. He's in the process of adopting her triplets from her first marriage. It only makes sense for her to live away from the ranch." He pointed out the window. "See the elk."

Another unforgettable moment on her trip. They were starting to stack up fast, and yet she'd have some special times ahead of her in Phoenix once she closed on her new house. And last night, when she finally talked to Pamela, her boss had insisted she was one client away from being elevated to partner along with a pay raise.

Amanda kept her gaze on the elk until it was out of sight. "I enjoyed meeting Crosby. I can tell he looks up to you."

"Hardly. He was really young when Mom and Dad died in the accident. When he was five, I answered why to more questions about science and history than I ever thought possible. He always has his nose stuck in a book, and he's so intelligent." Seth reached for the console as if to turn on the music again but stopped himself. "What about you? Do you have any siblings?"

"One sister." Now Amanda itched to let the plaintive sounds of Elvis fill the truck's interior once more. Instead, she sought to change the subject. "Speaking of family, I have some ideas to run by you about the campaign. Have a minute?"

"Captive audience." Seth chuckled.

Heat crept up her neck as it was rather obvious he was stuck with her for the time being. "I've been talking to the families who are staying at the ranch, and they gave me the idea for your brand overhaul. I want to refine the treasure that is the Lazy River Dude Ranch and focus on your strengths."

"My thoughts exactly." Seth grinned, that huge smile lighting up his entire face. "That's what I've been trying to convince my grandparents of. We can't compete with the Rocky Valley Guest Ranch unless something changes."

"What do you mean by that? They're not your competition." Confusion about his continued focus on that hotel weighed on her, and she frowned.

"They're an upscale spa and resort with a Western theme."

"The Wilshire Development Corporation picked this town, and it's draining our resources," Seth said.

He stopped at the ranch entrance, and Amanda used the opportunity of gate patrol to compose herself. In no time, they resumed their ride. She picked up where she left off.

"The Rocky Valley Guest Ranch caters to a different clientele." Amanda secured the seat belt for good measure.

"We need to keep up with the times." Seth's grip around the steering wheel tightened, his knuckles turning pale under his rugged tan. "Guests expect top-rate accommodations during their stay. Things like Wi-Fi, high-quality towels and linens, a rewards program."

"So incorporate the latter. You deliver so much here, and you need to emphasize the positive." Amanda was running out of time to sway Seth since the ranch complex was now in view.

"It hasn't changed since my parents died. It's time I do something about that." He parked the truck and opened his door. "If you'll excuse me, I have to put up this order."

As Seth headed to the stable, Amanda considered catching up to him and finishing their conversation. Instead, she mulled over what he'd said. He might be onto something. What he considered a negative might be a positive. The dude ranch did seem as though it was stuck in the last century, but that could be the key to a campaign that centered around simplicity and family.

She reached for her tablet and considered what she had already learned from the guests. The lottery winners were enjoying Ingrid's cooking and something quite different than their normal lives. Whitney Berggren had found a place where her boys would go outside and leave the electronics behind. Colleen had mentioned this was a place where she and Mabel could bond as stepmother and stepdaughter. Even Amanda had lost herself in the calmness of her cabin, a respite from the hectic pace of the past three years. Yet the ranch had so much more potential. She just needed to think outside the box. The dog wedding was just what she needed for a unique spin. And perhaps she could take a page from the three guys and incorporate some modern takes on the idea of family. The possibilities were endless. Whichever way they went, a fun but reassuring experience like this was exactly what so many people seeking a dream vacation wanted. That dynamic would become the cornerstone of her presentation.

Now, if she could only convince Seth she was right.

CHAPTER FIVE

SETH RANG A bell and gathered the guests for his favorite part of the day. With dusk approaching, the horses galloped unencumbered from the stable paddocks to the meadow they called home. Joy emanated off the mustangs as they traversed the trail, the bells on their harnesses jingling all the way. Part of him envied that type of freedom. None of them harbored secrets or faced challenges from nosey marketing professionals.

Then again he reminded himself he got to be a part of this every day. He was fortunate to be so involved with something he loved, something bigger than himself. This "Jingling Hour" was a tradition at the Lazy River Dude Ranch since before he was born. Somehow he needed to clear the air of secrets between him and his grandmother. That would solve one problem, but he was still at a loss about what to do about Amanda.

He sneaked a peek at their on-the-job guest, who was talking to Colleen Carr and the four M's, the college roommates gathered here for their annual reunion. Amanda's hair was tied back in a pretty ponytail with a bright yellow scarf wrapped around it, one that matched her sunny plaid flannel shirt. Unlike him, her jeans were immaculate, and she looked as though she was pulled together.

For a while, he'd been meaning to drive to town and buy some flannel shirts, maybe stop at Harold's Barbershop while he was there. Every time he had a spare hour, though, something at the ranch beckoned. He stroked his beard, a way to hide a scar from getting kicked by a horse when he was fifteen. Even it needed a good trim.

Seemed as though he had something in common with the ranch. They both needed some maintenance work.

Soon the horses were settled, and he invited the gathered guests to head to the dining hall for a steak dinner with all the trimmings. Isaac and Eli picked up the pace, and Seth remembered how his stomach had been a bottomless pit at that age.

At the fork where one path led to the lodge and the other to the stable, Seth waved goodbye to the guests with an admonition to save him a piece of Ingrid's apple crumble pie. Crossing the threshold into the stable, he found Buck and received an update on Rosa's condition. Buck guesstimated the mare would deliver her foal any day now.

Once Buck departed for dinner, Seth swapped out his light jacket for his sturdier Carhartt coat with extra pockets. His Australian shepherd, Hap, came running toward him. "Can't stay away from the action, can you, boy?" No doubt his other dog, Trixie, was keeping his grandmother company.

He reached for a shovel and started mucking out the stalls. Peace seeped into him, and he placed the shovel aside for a minute. This was what he needed, a reminder of what was good with the ranch and why he loved his job.

"Can I help?" Amanda's voice broke through the silence, but he didn't mind.

He faced her, the brightness of her outfit a sign of hope, something he let slip away as the dinginess of the paint and loss of staff weighed on him. A brief image of someone like her, exactly like her, flickered through his mind until it crystallized. It wasn't just anyone at his side. It was Amanda.

What was he thinking? They had sparred non stop since she arrived. He dismissed the picture and grabbed the shovel.

"Guests aren't allowed to help in the stable. Insurance and safety rules."

"Good thing I'm a subcontractor and not a guest." She gave Hap a pat on his head before she extended her hand toward the shovel and smiled. Her sunny nature pierced deep to his core.

He relented. She was offering help, and he'd be foolish to decline. He gave her his shovel and retrieved another. Then they settled into a comfortable rhythm while Hap bedded down in one of the stalls for a snooze. After a few minutes, he broke the silence. "Thank you for your help. I'm usually more adaptable, but the Lazy River Dude Ranch is at a crossroads. Still, that's no reason to take it out on you."

"I thought we were past the apology stage." Amanda filled the wheelbarrow while he placed his coat on a nearby hook. "This afternoon we exchanged differing opinions. I suggested one way, which happens to be the right way, but you're the manager who will be here day after day while I'm directing your marketing plan from Phoenix."

Then they'd continue to communicate with one another. He hadn't considered that they'd have to keep in touch. That attraction he was trying to keep at bay flickered alive once more. Perhaps this was the beginning of something intense. Already he sensed something between them more real than anything he'd felt for Felicity.

Yet that didn't change the fact Amanda would be in Arizona while he'd be in Colorado. Keeping everything light between them until she departed might be the best strategy to tamp the sparks flaring on his end. "Your way is the right way, huh?"

He turned toward her, the stable LEDs illuminating her with a glow he'd have preferred not to notice, considering how recently they'd met.

She shoveled fresh hay into a stall, grinning all the while. "Of course it is. You have so much to learn about me."

Already he sensed he'd like to learn more about her, but he hesitated. If his grandfather, though, could keep a secret from the woman he spent the past fifty-eight years loving, what chance did Seth have of creating something enduring?

Rosa whinnied a greeting in Amanda's direction. "Why is this horse not with the others in the meadow?"

With some effort, Rosa climbed out of her resting position nestled in the hay and approached Amanda.

"Meet Rosa, my grandmother's beloved Appaloosa." He reached into one of his pockets for an apple slice and handed it to Amanda. "She's expecting her first foal in the next few days, and we're monitoring her closely."

Rosa accepted the treat, and Amanda chuckled. Then she rubbed the spotted muzzle of the bay mare. "You're such a sweetheart. You're going to be a good mother." Rosa seemed to accept Amanda, and Seth counted a horse's judgment as superior to most people's. Then Amanda faced him. "What's next? Filling the water troughs? Sweeping the aisles? Cleaning tack?"

Amanda made each chore sound like a stroll in the spring meadow where the wildflowers were in full bloom. Then again she brought a positive bent to anything she did. One look at her clean jeans and immaculate shirt gave him pause.

"It's okay. You've done more than you should.

Go ahead and eat dinner before you ruin your clothes. It can get messy around here." He wiped away sweat from his brow with the sleeve of his blue plaid flannel. "Smelly, too."

She laughed and kept a firm grip on the shovel handle. "I've worked on a ranch before. I like how a stable smells, and there's free laundry service with the cabins, remember?"

Out of excuses, Seth assigned her to the other side of the stable. Hap took off for parts unknown, likely the main lodge. After a while, he found himself tapping his foot and paused. What was that sound? He listened and chuckled. Amanda was singing an Elvis tune while she worked.

Of course she was.

When they finished in the middle of the stable, she handed him the shovel. "Thanks. I can take it from here," he said.

"I'm a pro at cleaning tack." She flexed her arm muscle and let out a contented sigh. "I miss all of this."

Despite his brain sending alert signals to his heart, Seth couldn't disappoint her.

"I'll show you the tack room." Seth led her to where they stored the bridles and other leather goods.

An extra set of hands would make the tasks go faster, and he might claim a piece of Ingrid's delicious apple crumble pie for himself. At least if he kept telling himself that he only saw her as an additional employee, maybe he'd start to believe it. Truth was, he liked spending time with Amanda. Too much.

They settled into a companionable rhythm with her humming a different Elvis melody as she scrubbed the bits with a mixture of hot water, salt and vinegar. Then she gasped, causing him to glance in her direction.

"I sing and hum whenever I clean my house." Two bright patches of pink dotted her cheeks. "I forgot you were here."

Just when he'd imagined an underlying spark between them, she put him in his place, and plenty.

"Thanks." His droll tone was drier than the rolled-up hay in the barn loft.

Those pink spots darkened to a deep blush. She traded one bit for another. "That's a compliment. I've always found that when you're comfortable around someone, your true nature comes to the forefront."

Seth wiped the saddle with glycerin soap. "No worries. You have a nice voice." Now it was his turn for heat to rise up to his face, his cheeks burning. "What did you mean earlier when you said you miss all of this? Did you grow up on a ranch?"

Amanda found a toothbrush and concentrated on the dirt caked into the bit. "No, but I worked at one when I was a teenager. Loved it."

Why did he want to curl up in the library with a

fire, the two dogs and Amanda? He'd like nothing more than to sit back and ask her more questions about her life and listen to all her answers. What was it about this blonde stranger that was taking his world by storm? He hadn't talked to anyone this much, even his siblings, since Felicity.

"How could you have ever left ranch life once you got a taste of it?" He finished dusting a saddle and moved onto the next. "I don't want to live anywhere else."

"My family moved away from Houston when I was only fifteen. I couldn't stay behind." She shrugged. "But I loved my time at the Bricker Ranch."

Seth whistled at the name of one of the largest ranches in Texas. That explained why she knew her way around a stable. "That's some good ranch land."

"The best." Amanda grimaced as she used a little elbow grease and attacked the caked-on dirt. "I worked in the stable. Most of my classmates worked retail, but I wanted something different, something outdoors."

Until recently, the dude ranch had a roster of employees who'd worked here ten, twenty, even twenty-five years. His grandparents hadn't been able to offer the same salary and bonuses as the Wilshire Development Corporation. So they had jumped ship to the Rocky Valley Guest Ranch. Seth missed many of them almost as much as he missed his brother Jase, who lived and worked in Denver.

"Why did you have to move?" he asked.

"My father lost yet another job, and my parents decided to move to California. My sister, Sami, had been racking up beauty queen victories, and my mom hoped that would translate into an acting career. Mom believes Sami will be the next major movie star." She scrubbed away the dirt until the silver gleamed. "Yes, finally! Victory."

"Your family moved around a lot?" He prodded for more information. Something was lurking beneath the surface.

"Too often for my taste."

"That must be why I can't hear a trace of Texas in your speech." He hadn't detected any Southern accent at all.

She chose another bit. "I've lived in ten different states, but no more moves for me. I've made an offer on the most darling house in Phoenix." Amanda whipped out her phone. "Want to see a picture?"

Seth murmured praise while she scrolled through the photos of the beige stucco house, a lone tree situated in the front yard. The large bright rooms matched Amanda's sunny personality, and he could see how happy she was at the prospect of making her imprint there. "Congratulations."

She pocketed her phone and returned to her task. "The house is everything I've always wanted." She laid aside the toothbrush and bits. "That, and a better relationship with my sister, Sami. At lunch, you and Crosby seemed close. Your bond is evident."

"Hmm." Working on his doctorate, Crosby lived and breathed history whereas Seth never wanted to look at another textbook. Yet no one was prouder of his sibling than Seth. "We try to keep each other in line. Crosby tends to forget everything when he's researching history. We have that in common. I've fallen asleep in the stable a time or two myself."

Amanda's face tightened into a look of concentration as she scrubbed at the next bit. "I can relate. I like working late into the night until I find something unique to feature in each client's marketing campaigns. I really enjoyed my assignment for the Tumbleweeds Dude Ranch. That's what compelled me to accept your grandmother's request."

"Is that why you chose marketing over ranching?" That was a concept he had trouble understanding. How could anyone want to work in a profession other than ranching? It was the best. He loved mingling with horses every day.

And every season had something fresh and glorious. He loved spring wildflowers, and he already let it slip to Amanda how he felt about kittens and lambs.

"I love pointing out the positive of different products or services. It's refreshing. Every client is a new challenge."

"Same with ranching."

She reached for the final bit and started rubbing off the dirt. He wiped the last saddle at the same time she finished polishing the bits.

"Whew!" She rose and washed her hands at the corner sink, wiping them on an old towel. "I worked up an appetite."

"Then it's a good thing it's dinnertime." He whistled over the pile of bits. "Nice job."

"Thanks. I do wash up nicely." Her eyes sparkled, and she went to the door. "Are you coming?"

"I want to check on Rosa one more time." The mare meant the world to his grandmother.

"Don't fall asleep in here. Otherwise, I'll have to eat your share of the apple crumble pie." She winked and disappeared from view.

A stab of regret sliced through him at how fast this week was going by. He liked spending this past hour with Amanda, but the Lazy River Dude Ranch was just another client to her.

Still, he was impressed at her willingness to help wherever needed. A trooper, Amanda was proving her worth this week. Could he place the same trust in her as his grandparents had done, giving her carte blanche for her marketing campaign?

He fingered the silver dollar at the bottom of his pocket, the last gift from his father, one he hadn't appreciated at the time. Now it was his most treasured possession, a reminder to slow down and notice what was around him.

Including this short time with Amanda.

NIGHTFALL CAME OVER the ranch, and Amanda zipped up her fluorescent yellow windbreaker jacket. She walked along the path around the duck pond, the sunset touching something deep inside her. While she loved the sunrises with the orange glow bringing everything to life, the sunsets were equally magnificent.

One of the ducks emerged from the pond and shook the water off its feathers. She smiled at the sight and commenced her walk, only to find the duck now following her. She sped up, and a few more ducks joined in the pursuit. She stopped and faced them. "I don't have any bread or any food."

They seemed to understand what she was saying and headed back to the pond once more. Whew! She'd have to ask Seth if there was anything safe to offer them.

A stand-alone bench swing affixed to a wooden lattice structure beckoned, the perfect place to enjoy the quiet of the evening before Seth's astronomy lesson.

She settled on the swing and pumped her legs. The cricket chirps and frog croaks provided a sweet lullaby. Having gone nonstop for the past three years, she relished someone else preparing the meals and planning adventures for a week.

Even compiling the research for rebranding hardly seemed like work. Crosby deserved credit for most of that since he sent her the historical information. She quieted her mind, teeming with what would go where on the revamped website and how to incorporate little touches on social media, like the dog wedding.

Speaking of Crosby, watching him interact with Seth might have been her favorite part of today's lunch. She yearned for such a sibling relationship with Sami, yet her drive to succeed at the agency and her sister's string of beauty pageants and auditioning for roles conspired against them. Amanda merely transferred money to her sister whenever their mother texted about the latest expenditure from headshots to acting lessons.

The chains on the swing jingled, and Amanda fingered the cold metal. Sami seldom talked directly to her with their mother often acting as the conduit, claiming Sami was too busy. So why did Sami choose tonight to talk to Amanda? Then again, connections didn't happen on their own. Seth and Crosby lived in the same town and made time for each other. Perhaps the first link in an adult relationship with Sami started with Amanda reaching out and returning her call. Only then could they start building something close to what the brothers had.

Amanda pulled out her phone, only to have it ring. She held her breath that it was Sami with impeccable timing but, in reality, caller ID flashed Pamela's profile.

"Amanda." Pamela's breezy greeting unsettled Amanda's stomach. That tone always preceded a special request. "How's Colorado?"

"It's wonder—"

"That's nice." Pamela cut her off and continued, "You won't believe this. My niece Paisley arrived on my doorstep this afternoon so you're going to have to take over constructing the website for Innovative Buildings and More. Then I need you to schedule the promos for the landscape architect firm who signed with us after my fabulous presentation last month."

Amanda had personally interviewed and done the legwork with each of those clients. While it wouldn't take her long to do these tasks, Pamela was supposed to handle the details this week. "I'm on…"

"I haven't seen my niece in three months, far too long to be away from her sparkling personality. Hold on a sec." Pamela muffled the phone, and Amanda stilled the swing, halfway tempted to disconnect the call.

However, Pamela would just text her the information and then turn off her phone. That had happened before.

"Pamela! I have something important to tell you." Amanda stopped wasting her breath when it was obvious Pamela wasn't paying attention to her. She tapped her boot on the brown dirt under the swing and spoke forcefully into her cell. "*I'm on vacation.*"

"Good, that's good." Pamela's voice came back on the line, and Amanda breathed a sigh of relief as Pamela seemed to be relenting, which didn't happen often, if ever. "You don't have anything important to do and can whip up those two things in no time. I'm emailing you the information. Paisley and I have tickets to a play tonight, and you know what that means. I'm switching to Do Not Disturb. Talk soon."

Amanda stared at her phone and blinked at the email notification, signaling Pamela's instructions. Groaning, she opened the file and found three accounts, not the mere two Pamela mentioned, waiting for updates.

It was a good thing her cabin was comfy and isolated so it would be quiet while she burned the midnight oil. She started on the trail when her phone rang again. Sami! Amanda settled back on the swing, the metal echoing in the night air faintly traced with the sweet smell of nearby peonies.

No sooner had Amanda connected the call than Sami's frantic voice could be heard over the sound of persistent knocking. "Where are you? How long until you're home?"

"At least a week from Saturday. I'm working at the Lazy River Dude Ranch in Violet Ridge, Colorado."

Her sister's wail almost punctured Amanda's eardrum, and concern prickled her nerve endings.

"That long?" Sami asked.

"Sami? Are you in trouble?" Amanda stilled the swing, her body suddenly tense. "What's going on?"

"I'm at your doorstep." Sami let out another wail. "You're always home when I call you."

"You're in Phoenix? Why?" Amanda switched her phone to her other ear. "Are Mom and Dad with you?"

Had she emptied the dishwasher? When was the last time she hung fresh towels in the bathroom? Did Mrs. Gustafson still have that spare key?

"How long do you have to talk?" Sami's voice was weary, a side of her younger sister she'd never heard before.

"As long as you need." The words slipped out without hesitation as did the directions to Mrs. Gustafson's apartment. "Call me back once you're inside."

"Thank you, Amanda." A more humble, huskier timbre sent chills through her.

If need be, she'd leave for Phoenix tomorrow morning.

While she waited for Sami to call back, Amanda opened the file for the landscape architect's marketing plan. All of the graphics Amanda had designed prior to her departure had been approved, so she scheduled them on the social media sites.

She clicked the button for the last post when her phone signaled an incoming call from Sami.

"I'm inside. You have such a cute apartment. I see touches of you everywhere." Sami's relief was palpable.

Amanda relaxed, and the tension in her shoulders eased away. "I hope I'll be moving soon. I placed an offer on a house, and my real estate agent is optimistic that it'll be accepted."

Squeals of delight left Sami's lips. "Oh, Amanda! I'm so happy for you." She paused and then continued, "Any chance you're looking for a roommate?"

Amanda let out a slow, long sigh. This was why she hadn't told Sami or her parents she'd made an offer on a home. She'd had a sneaking feeling the three of them would eventually talk their way into living with her. "My apartment only has one bedroom, and the house has two bedrooms."

She didn't mind a visit; she just minded being the sole source of income for the whole family.

"If you don't mind a roommate, I'll stay on your couch until I can get my cosmetology license transferred and find a job," Sami said. "I can pitch in with the rent and help you with housework."

This night was providing one surprise after another. "You're a cosmetologist?" Amanda hopped off the swing and started walking around the duck pond, the night perfect for a casual stroll. She kept a careful eye on the ducks now on the other side of the pond. "What did Mom and Dad have to say about that? If you need to put me on speaker so they can listen, that's okay."

"No need for that." Sami almost sounded out of breath. "Mom and Dad have moved to New York on the heels of Dad's latest job. I think it's a pyramid scheme."

Amanda's legs wobbled for a second, and she almost stumbled over a tree root. She would have preferred sitting down for that news. Mom and Dad hadn't even bothered to tell her that they'd moved. "Do you want me to leave immediately? I can be home by tomorrow."

"Don't you dare! I'll be fine until you get back."

Amanda breathed a little easier at Sami's protest. "Why don't you start at the beginning?" She made a complete loop around the duck pond while her sister poured out everything that had happened over the past few months.

"Once they figured out I was serious about becoming a hairdresser and was no longer going to auditions, they called me ungrateful and left for New York."

Amanda's heart went out to her sister, and she wished she were in Phoenix to hug her. This was the first time Sami had ever experienced their parents' disdain even though Amanda had been on the receiving end more times than she could count.

"You'd love this dude ranch." Amanda breathed in the fresh mountain air, wishing her sister were here to enjoy it for herself. "Martin and Bridget

Virtue are the owners, and they're a real inspiration. Their grandson Seth is the manager, and he's the image of a cowboy. He teaches guests how to lasso and ride horses. Tomorrow, he's taking a group out on the mountain bike trail."

Amanda kept talking about Seth in glowing terms.

"Seth's a cowboy, huh?" Sami already sounded calmer and more like her bubbly self. "Tell me more."

Amanda felt her cheeks grow warmer by the second. Hadn't she learned anything by getting too involved with her boss's son, her coworker at her previous place of employment? Until she heard herself rave about Seth to Sami, she hadn't realized she was developing romantic feelings for him. She'd best stanch those now. "The dude ranch is a family-run enterprise with something for everyone."

"Are they looking for a hairdresser?" Sami perked up, and Amanda disliked bursting her bubble.

"They don't have a spa or salon. That sounds more like Rocky Valley Guest Ranch, the luxury resort on the other side of town."

"Too bad. I'd like to meet this Seth of yours." Sami laughed, and Amanda could picture her curling up on her comfy sofa, spreading the blue diamond quilt over her. "I have a little saved, enough to chip in my share of the rent while I transfer my license and get a job here."

"He's not my Seth." Of all the things to correct, Amanda zeroed in on that. "If anything, I wish you could afford to spend a night at the Rocky Valley Guest Ranch."

"Ooh, a spy." Sami was sounding more like her old self. "How exciting."

"Except these two places aren't in competition with each other. They have a different customer base." Amanda changed gears before she bored Sami with marketing details. "I'll be back in Phoenix early next week. Help yourself to anything in the refrigerator and don't worry about money. We'll get everything straightened out once I'm home."

Sami let out a sigh that blended contentment and relief. "Thanks, Amanda. See you soon."

Amanda disconnected and found she'd been on the phone with her sister for over an hour. She'd best head back to the cabin and get started on the new client's website. So much for taking part in Seth's astronomy outing.

She looked up and gasped. In Phoenix, light pollution disrupted her view of the night sky, but here, in the heart of the valley, with the crags of the mountains shadowy and distinct in the moonlight, the stars twinkled and sparkled their way into her heart. Happiness spread through her.

"Pretty special, isn't it?" Seth's voice startled her, and she calmed her racing pulse.

A large group lingered behind Seth, including

the three guys, who finally seemed resigned that the ranch was not part of the scavenger hunt, as well as the couple from Kentucky, Tiffany and Derrick.

The Carr family brought up the rear with young Mabel running over to Seth, yanking on his brown jacket. "Are all these stars yours?"

Seth's chuckle was warm, rich and as decadent as a decanter of aged Scotch. "I borrow them on occasions like this, but they don't belong to anyone."

Mabel's grin grew as wide as her face. "Thank you for sharing them." She spotted Amanda and bounced over to her. "Hi, Miss Amanda. I'm glad you're coming with us. Mr. Seth is teaching us all about cons...const...the stars."

"Constellations." Seth repeated it until Mabel could pronounce it on her own.

Amanda felt like she was missing out on a special part of this ranch, but her job awaited her. Earning her paycheck and moving into her new home was now more important than ever. This was her chance to get to know Sami as adult siblings. Together they might form a bond like Crosby and Seth's someday.

Amanda stepped backward, dipping her head at everyone. "Work is calling my name. Have a good evening."

Seth stared at her and, for a split second, she thought she saw moonbeams reflected in his eyes. Then she dismissed the notion. It didn't escape her that her romantic side, something she thought lost after Blake betrayed her, was returning. Who wouldn't get in touch with that on a night like this?

Seth moved toward her, looking every inch the cowboy in his Stetson. "I insist you come with us. You deserve a break after working above and beyond at the stable. Enjoy your vacation tonight."

He tilted his head toward the sky, letting the stars talk for him.

Sixty minutes, precious time with Seth and the other guests, couldn't make that much of a difference, right? "One hour. Then I have somewhere to be."

Seth clasped her hand and pulled her along the path. "I'd best make every minute count."

His fingers entwined in hers, and something passed between them, a spark. She caught her breath. In two weeks he'd still be here, teaching different guests how to lasso, and she'd be in Phoenix, salvaging a relationship with Sami and hopefully preparing to close on her new home.

But Seth was right. She deserved to enjoy tonight. For once, she would be happy with the stars and friends surrounding her.

Without another word, the group walked to a nearby field. A slight breeze rustled the top of the aspens, and the temperature cooled to a comfortable level. They formed a large circle, and Amanda swung her arm, their hands moving in harmony. He must have realized they were still connected about the same time as she did, and he let go with a mumbled sorry.

She wasn't sorry. There was something about Seth that intrigued her. Maybe it was his beard. Maybe it was his aura of independence. Everything about him pointed to someone who cared deeply for what was around him, from the land to his grandparents and siblings. Yet she couldn't shake the feeling that it was about the romantic nature of these surroundings, with the mountains and a real-life cowboy in her midst.

Who wouldn't be swayed by all of that?

Tiffany shivered, and Derrick gave her his coat. "Tomorrow I want you to pick out your favorite sweater and jacket in the gift shop," Derrick said.

Tiffany protested. "Your coat's all I need."

"You'll need it next week for our Miami yacht trip," Derrick countered. "You deserve the best, sweetheart, after working such long hours for so long—"

"Hold on. The cat sitter is texting. She just assembled a new cat tower for Princess and Earl and sent me pictures. Aren't our cats the cutest thing ever?" Tiffany squealed and showed everyone her phone. Then she turned to Derrick. "Did you send the tower to them?"

"They were bored if they were putting holes in things—" Derrick stopped talking when Tiffany hugged him.

Seth called for everyone's attention and launched into an explanation of the origins of astronomy.

Mabel shot her hand into the air. "Mr. Seth, I have a question."

Seth grinned. "Just Seth. This isn't a classroom although, in a way, this is nature's classroom."

"Why are there so many more stars here than at my house?" Mabel yawned and then nudged her father until he stopped holding hands with Colleen and placed his arm around her.

"There are the same number of stars. You see more of them here because this has been designated as a dark sky zone. Violet Ridge makes sure there's as little light pollution as possible at night. Our place in the valley between the San Juan Mountains and the Rockies gives us a special perspective so the stars have a place to shine." Seth stopped when Mabel yawned again.

The young girl faced her father, who lifted her until she nestled into his shoulder. "Somehow you've tuckered out Mabel," Brian said and tilted his head toward the cabins. "We'd best call it a night."

Mabel gave a faint protest before her eyelids lowered. Brian carried his daughter, and Colleen waved good night before starting down the path to their cabin. The other guests followed. A lingering glance at their departing figures sent a pang of regret through Amanda. She'd best head back to her cabin since a few hours of work awaited.

"I'll say good night, as well." Amanda started following in their footsteps.

"Hey, have a little mercy. You're an audience of one, and I'd like to finish my talk. Astronomy's a hobby of mine." Seth's voice halted her steps with a pleading note under the lightness.

How could Amanda resist a cowboy under the stars?

She returned to his side. "Instead of a practiced speech, why don't you tell me what you love about astronomy?"

Seth motioned above him with a sweeping wave of his long arms. "The sky speaks for itself. You can't get this view anywhere else."

Amanda was starting to feel the same way as him. There was something special about the Lazy River Dude Ranch with the lowing of the cattle in the distance and the faint trace of peonies in the air. If she could communicate that through branding and increased social media presence, there'd be a waiting list of guests a mile long.

"Sell me on that, and I'll sell that to others." As soon as the words left her mouth, she wanted to take them back.

Even in the darkness, she sensed she'd struck a sensitive chord. It was almost as if he'd donned his manager persona again.

Goodbye, cowboy. Hello, manager.

"The ranch has served families and visitors for

over ninety years. Here at the Lazy River, we aim to be stewards of our legacy…"

Amanda closed the distance between them and laid her hand on his arm. "That sounds like something you've practiced over and over to tell the guests. Just talk to me from the heart."

His muscles tensed before his lips quirked upward. "That obvious, huh?"

Too aware of his physical presence, she jammed her hands into her jacket pockets so she wouldn't give in to the impulse to touch him again.

"How about we mosey around the pond as Amanda and Seth and not as the marketing executive and ranch manager? Totally off-script."

Wanting to be in his presence went beyond her work. He was loyal and dependable, and his congenial presence was drawing him to her.

Seth shrugged. "Sometimes it's easier to entertain the guests as Seth the manager, rather than just be myself."

"You make people laugh just fine on your own. Take Mabel and the Berggren boys. They hang on your every word."

"I hope I make you laugh."

The truth was, he did exactly that. But she needed to protect her heart. She set forth around the pond with Seth by her side.

Once more, Amanda gazed at the wide expanse of stars surrounding them. "Is this one of the places where you can see the Milky Way?"

"Wrong time of year." Seth motioned for Amanda to follow him off the gravel path and onto the grassy knoll at the pond's edge. "Watch your step."

"What can I see in the spring?" Amanda halted beside him, the ripples of the pond softly lapping at the water's edge.

She looked out at the ducks slumbering with one eye open and one eye closed, peaceful now.

Seth pointed toward the horizon. "See that bright star?" He paused until she answered in the affirmative. "That's Regulus, part of the Leo constellation."

"Leo the lion?" Amanda asked, as fascinated by the galaxy as by the man next to her.

He nodded. "Do you know the Greek myth about him?"

"No. Nothing."

She leaned in and he continued. "Leo the lion was supposedly unable to be harmed, but Hercules conquered him with his bare hands and placed him in the stars as a way to memorialize their battle."

Amanda shivered. "Are any of the other constellation legends less gruesome?"

Seth searched the sky and then aimed his arm in a different direction. "That red star is Arcturus and belongs to a constellation that's a favorite of farmers and ranchers. The legend goes that Demeter rewarded the inventor of the plow with a special constellation."

Amanda smiled. "I like that story better. Tell me more about astronomy and why you like it."

"The view of the stars is a part of this special place as much as the pond, the animals or the range." Seth's simple explanation conveyed so much about him. "In the daytime, I love the ranch with all its activity and noise, but there's something about the night, too. The quietness and stillness speak to me. Reminds me of what's real, why I love what I do."

Another pang traveled through her, and she sought to understand it. It wasn't regret. Or sadness. It was almost as though she recognized something innate in him that she wanted to get to know better but couldn't.

Instead, she curled up and sat close beside him on the grass. She laughed at his anecdotes and then asked follow-up questions that led to another and another. Three hours slipped away faster than a shooting star.

"It's almost midnight!" she exclaimed while jumping to her feet.

That website wouldn't update itself.

Seth himself startled at her pronouncement and escorted her back to her cabin. "Next time don't let me ramble."

He stumbled into her. His face neared hers, and she held her breath. He was about to kiss her, and she found she wanted that even more than her new house. Would his kisses be tender and slow? Or breathless and long? She parted her lips, but then he righted himself, tilted his Stetson toward her and left her on the front porch. He disappeared from view before she extracted her key from her pocket. He'd been a gentleman, making it too easy to keep her promise to herself about maintaining a healthy distance between them. Any feelings she had for the enigmatic and charming cowboy were a figment of her romantic nature, and nothing more.

She slipped into the cabin, wondering what it would be like to be by Seth's side as he looked out at the stars and savored the stillness for more nights than just this one. Though she wouldn't be on this ranch for long, she intended on enjoying whatever her next adventure here might be.

CHAPTER SIX

Tuesday

FOUR O'CLOCK CAME too quickly this Tuesday morning for Seth's liking after staying up late with Amanda. He climbed out of bed and managed the transfer of the mustangs from the meadow to the paddock, taking time to watch some horses trot to the water trough while others headed for their favorite grazing patches.

Seth closed the gate and wiped the sheen of sweat from his forehead. Thankful for the exertion, he welcomed anything that kept his mind off the beautiful marketer. Time collapsed upon itself whenever he was with her. Hours slipped away as though mere minutes. It had taken all of his willpower not to kiss her last night with her hair tousled from the night breeze and her cheeks pink from their brisk walk to her cabin.

And yet she made it no secret she was returning to Phoenix, and he made it a policy never to get involved with guests or employees, especially after the Felicity fiasco.

The moment they met, he felt a connection with Felicity unlike any other. For three months, they'd done everything together. Night after night, they talked until the wee hours of the morning as he confided his hopes and dreams to her. She'd listened and agreed she wanted the same for herself. When he proposed, she hesitated before saying yes. But not even twenty-four hours had passed before she went back on her promise, without so much as an apology, and returned home, taking his heart with her and leaving the ring behind.

Now, given time had passed, he wasn't sure if he missed Felicity or simply that kind of connection again.

He walked toward the main lodge, eager to wash off the grime and dive into a stack of pancakes. Something caught his eye as he passed the Shooting Stars Cabin. Worn weatherstripping had loosened to the point where it was flapping against the log siding. He jotted a note to talk to the head maintenance technician, Rich, who was finally back on the rotation schedule after a brief illness.

He went to his suite on the third floor and washed away the morning dirt, watching the water drain in the sink. If only his problems could wash away that easily. Grandpa Martin's secret. The mortgage. His growing attraction to Amanda.

Was he using Amanda as a refuge from his problems?

He had no answer for that, no positive spin as

Amanda would phrase it. He wiped his hands and hurried to breakfast. In the dining hall, he spent a pleasant hour answering Eli and Isaac's questions while keeping watch for Amanda without a single glimpse of her.

As soon as he could politely break away, Seth escaped to the manager's office and closed the door behind him. Groaning at his inbox full of urgent matters, he went through them one by one. With Rosa set to give birth any hour now, concentration was at a premium. He wasn't Crosby with a college education and an ability to get lost in books. This part of managing the ranch came the hardest to Seth, but he'd learned a few tricks over the years.

He reconciled the invoices and was about to start going through the mail when someone knocked.

"Come in," Seth said.

His maintenance technician, Rich, and head gardener, Vickie, appeared and crossed the threshold, serious expressions on their faces. Seth turned away from his computer at the same time Rich handed him an envelope.

"This is for you." Rich's deep voice filled the room, and Seth's stomach clenched in knots.

Then Vickie did likewise.

Seth frowned while accepting the sealed envelopes. "What's this?" Although he already had a sneaking suspicion of what was contained therein.

Rich removed his Stetson and shuffled his feet.

"Killian Wilshire added more money to his sign-on bonus. My son's getting married this summer, and that pay is too good to pass up. The rest of my crew, Nancy and Al, are staying here. They're good workers."

Rich had served as head maintenance technician for fifteen years. How would this place get by without him? Just a few days proved how much he was needed here. Seth thought of Rich as more than an employee; he was part of his extended family. His stomach clenched at yet another resignation. He tapped both envelopes on his desk. "You too, Vickie?"

She nodded, her silver hair bobbing with the movement. "It'll be strange taking orders from someone I trained, but for twenty extra dollars an hour, I can handle it." She glanced around the office and swiped at her eye with the back of her hand. "This is harder than I thought it would be."

For all of them. Knowing the dude ranch was now down two more of its hardest workers eliminated any possibility of change. It took every bit of his energy to manage the place, let alone on a bare-bones staff.

He thanked them for their service and ushered them out of the office but not before consulting the employee schedule wall chart. Grandpa Martin was at the archery range. Seth grabbed his jacket and headed that way.

Sure enough, he found Grandpa Martin at the

target field, doing his daily check. Safety and security were his grandfather's hallmarks. Headphones in place, Grandpa Martin was clearing the field of debris from the last rainfall and singing at the top of his lungs. Bruce Springsteen didn't have to worry about his grandfather taking over his job.

"Grandpa!" Seth strode toward the older man, having no time to waste since his schedule was jam-packed. He repeated himself, but his grandfather started to dance, a sure sign he didn't see Seth.

Despite a full docket, Seth stood by and watched with amusement as his grandfather could still move with style. His grandfather turned around and spied Seth. Grimacing, he removed the headphones. "You heard and saw all that?"

"Heard what?" Seth's laughter gave him away. Then he remembered what he had to say and grew serious. "Rich and Vickie just quit."

Grandpa Martin appeared nonplussed, and Seth struggled to understand his lack of concern. He'd built this dude ranch into a premier vacation destination, taking what Seth's great-grandparents had managed and expanded the offerings. How could he be so calm when this ranch's future hung in the balance?

"Don't look so glum. We'll get by." Martin neared and patted Seth on the back, only making Seth feel worse. That only tightened his chest to a breaking point. He was the one who was supposed to make life easier for his grandfather, not the other way around.

"We need to address the changes that we have yet to make." Every time Seth finally cornered his grandfather, something else took precedence. Too soon Rosa would need Martin when it was time to deliver her foal. "And are you sure you can handle these archery lessons?"

"Yes, and I'm starting in thirteen minutes." Grandpa Martin's jaw clenched. "How many times do I have to tell you? Archery is the best medicine for me. It helps me keep up my arm strength, which has come in handy the past few years." *After Grandma Bridget's stroke and its aftermath.* He didn't say the words aloud, but Seth knew they were thinking the same thing.

Seth held up his hands as if surrendering. "We can still cancel. There are enough scheduled activities today."

Grandpa Martin huffed. "Archery promotes flexibility, something everyone needs. Besides, I'm hale and hearty. After all, I fixed the plumbing in Marigold, and the family arrived last night during your astronomy lesson. How'd that go? Good attendance?"

"I put Mabel to sleep." Seth kept his voice as droll as possible. Better to be dry than let the concern drip out of him. "Eventually, it was just Amanda and me."

"I like Amanda. You keep harping that we

need to hire more employees." Grandpa Martin picked up a branch and set it in the debris cart. "We should hire her."

"I doubt we could afford someone of her caliber." Seth followed his grandfather's example and reached for the last stick. "Besides, she's buying a house in Phoenix."

Was that sympathy or hope lurking on his grandfather's face? "Sounds like the two of you have exchanged more than the current weather forecast."

Perhaps, but it wouldn't do any good. Dwelling on Amanda and everything they had in common would only result in a sore heart next week when she left. A true connection needed proximity for sticking power. Best to nip that in the bud before he experienced another heartbreak.

In Colorado, if you didn't learn from a bad experience the first time, you might not survive a second encounter.

For the good of his mood, Seth changed the subject. "What are we going to do about the employment vacancies?" His phone pinged, and he read the incoming text.

Seemed as though the new guests in Marigold had some demands for the pet wedding. Their officiant had canceled at the last minute, and they needed a speedy replacement. Then there were tiny tiaras and other wedding details he needed to help them with. Seth sighed and stuffed his phone back into his pocket. He'd do his best to smooth those ruffled feathers, but everything in that text confirmed what he already knew. They had to up their game to compete with the Rocky Valley Guest Ranch.

While he'd been reading the text, his grandfather had unlocked the shed where the archery equipment was stored.

Grandpa Martin turned around and bumped into Seth. "Get those bows for me."

Seth did as directed. "I could talk to Ben and see if he knows anyone looking for permanent work."

Grandpa finished loading the cart and headed outside. He locked the bolt and faced Seth. "You're right. It's time for change…"

"Hold that thought." Seth held up his hand as his grandmother approached, her face the picture of a fierce Colorado thunderstorm.

"Martin Peter Virtue!" Lines furrowed deep in her forehead, she waved a piece of paper at them, her cane nowhere in sight. "What's the meaning of this?"

"Tell me you found a way to tell her last night." Seth hissed the statement under his breath, but he shouldn't have wasted his time. One look at Grandpa Martin told him everything.

"Do you have a spare bed in your suite?" Martin said in a voice low enough for Seth's ears alone.

"Seth, if you don't mind, I have a matter to discuss with your grandfather." Grandma Bridget's eyes blazed with a fury Seth had never seen before. "I'll see you back at the lodge."

"Why don't we get comfortable for this conversation, Bridge?" His brogue thick, Grandpa Martin attempted to extend his arm around her waist.

Darting away from her husband's reach, Grandma Bridget raised her eyebrow. "This is one time you won't be able to sweet-talk me, Martin. We're alone and out of earshot of the guests." Her gaze traveled over Seth, and she huffed. "You're still here."

He was no longer ten and able to be dismissed so easily when people wanted to discuss matters that concerned him. "What's that piece of paper?"

Grandpa Martin's shoulders slumped. "You can talk in front of Seth."

She waved it under Grandpa Martin's nose. "This is a letter from Mateo Rodriguez at the bank. He'd like to review the mortgage with you and see if he can negotiate better terms. What mortgage? We own this land free and clear."

It was as if his grandfather aged ten years in the blink of an eye, the same as he had when Seth awakened for a glass of water and hid in the kitchen while the police officer delivered the news about Seth's parents to Grandpa Martin.

Seth wanted to protect those he loved, and he was doing a poor job of it.

Seth stepped between two of the people who

mattered most to him. "Grandma, Grandpa, there must be a better place to discuss this."

The whole point of borrowing that money revolved around her health, and this type of shock wasn't good for her, let alone discussing it in the outdoors without her cane or a heavier jacket.

Grandpa Martin shrugged out of his coat and placed it over his wife's shoulders despite her protests. "Seth's right, Bridge. Let's go to our suite and have a cup of tea."

She handed him his coat and fumed. "If you don't know by now that you're not alone in this venture, Martin, then tea won't help you get on my good side again."

She spun around and limped toward the lodge.

Eli and Isaac were heading toward the archery range and nodded at her, respect in their faces. Grandma Bridget stopped and engaged them in a brief conversation until the teens were laughing. Seth wasn't surprised. A consummate pro, she treated each guest like a member of her extended family.

Seth turned toward his grandfather. "Go to her while she's talking with the Berggren brothers. She won't refuse you in front of them. I'll take over the class."

Grandpa Martin didn't need a second invitation, hurrying toward the small group. Seth finished the equipment check and readied everything for the archery lesson. Late tonight, he'd finish the paperwork he'd started before he became sidetracked with resignations and revelations.

Guests began arriving for the archery lesson, but Amanda wasn't among the attendees. Too bad as he could have used her advice about spinning today's confrontation into something positive.

Last night, he'd felt an undercurrent between them. There was so much about her that he liked, already appreciating how she managed to give everything an optimistic spin. With her expertise in marketing, perhaps she'd have some ideas for the pet wedding. After the archery lesson, he intended to find her and ask her advice about tracking down those items.

Eli and Isaac arrived at the equipment table, and Seth got his head out of the clouds and focused on archery.

AMANDA WAITED IN line at the rec center and relished the chance to enjoy the outdoors. After a morning of building a website for Innovative Buildings and More, the mountains beckoned, and she heeded their call. A calm afternoon on horseback was exactly what this cowgirl ordered.

Finally, it was her turn. Buck's horseback ride was full, but spots still remained for Seth's mountain bike excursion. Her nerve endings tingled at spending time with Seth, but was this a wise choice? The more time she spent with the attractive rancher, the more she feared he would lasso her heart.

Alas, the only other activities were indoors with Daisy demonstrating silversmith techniques and Bridget teaching knitting. Amanda's scarf was coming along, but this was a day made for the great outdoors.

Before she could regret it, she signed up for the last spot and hurried over to the staging area. Seth was pairing each participant with a fat-tire bike.

He sent a wide smile to Mabel. "I hear you had a birthday last month. Happy belated birthday." Mabel giggled as Seth presented her with a pink bandanna with the Lazy River Dude Ranch logo before turning to Colleen and Brian, asking questions about Mabel's height and weight. "Congratulations!" Then he gave Mabel a high-five. "You and your father can ride the tandem fat-tire bike together."

Then Seth called for quiet. The four women attending their college reunion did just that, as did the family who must be staying in the Marigold Cabin that Amanda hadn't met yet. At that moment, the rec room attendant brought out an extra bike and delivered it alongside the others. When Seth's gaze connected with hers, a funny quiver traveled through her.

She never felt this way around her former boyfriend, the landscape architect who had landed on a local magazine's Top Ten Bachelors of Phoenix list. This afternoon with physical exertion, sweat and other guests around would be exactly what she needed for any type of romantic feelings to dissipate into the wind.

Seth reviewed the safety procedures, blending humor with precautions. Everyone tried on helmets, and Amanda chose a bright blue one. Too big. Then she selected a red model, which didn't even fit on her head. Seth purveyed the remaining helmets and handed her the white one.

"Thanks." She tried it on and felt like Goldilocks as this one did, indeed, fit. "I hope you don't think I have a big head."

"Not at all. Everything about you seems to be perfect."

His cheeks turned bright red under his beard. Someone called out his name, asking about bike baskets, and he rushed away but not before adding, "You're just the person I need for something. Don't go anywhere, please."

Amanda stood there, happiness that he noticed something positive about her winning over the jumbled mass of confused emotions flitting through her.

The participants sipped from their Lazy River Dude Ranch water bottles before mounting their bikes. These models had oversize tires for gripping the dirt of the trail as opposed to the sleeker mountain bike she rented in Javelina Canyon back home.

Thanks to her previous experience, though, she

had no trouble adapting to the differences. She braked to a stop and grinned in Seth's direction. "How am I doing?"

"You've ridden before." He nodded his approval. "You could even be the guide. Can you do me a favor and lead the pack? I'll take the rear making sure there are no stragglers."

Honored at his request, she agreed. He ventured over to the Carr family, giving Mabel some extra encouragement. To her surprise, one of the dude ranch employees came over with a basket that held two Pomeranian dogs. Seth helped attach it to one of the newcomer's bikes.

At last, the trail ride commenced. She led the procession on the double-track trail with columbine and lupine dotting the grassy meadow on either side. Soon they passed craggy red rocks, the scenery near perfection. Wispy white clouds danced near the brown peaks on the horizon. Her troubles faded away as sheer joy took over. A golden eagle soared in the sky, its wingspan as impressive as its screech. Even the dogs in the basket looked as though they were having the time of their lives. Out here everything and anything was possible. She would form a bond with Sami. She could live up to Pamela's ideals, and she was good enough to own her own home.

Seth called the group to a halt and produced a picnic lunch, laying out an impressive spread on several red plaid blankets. Fried chicken and roll-up sandwiches occupied space next to bowls of diced fruit and a veggie platter. The families filled their plates and found shade or a soft spot in the grassy meadow to enjoy their meal and the sunny day. Seth introduced the newcomers, who excused themselves to tend to the dogs, while the college roommates were chuckling over something in the distance. With Brian and Colleen entertaining Mabel, that left Seth as the only unaccompanied person.

Something had happened to him since last night. Fine crinkles around his eyes commanded her attention, and there was a wary look about him.

Amanda loaded her plate and settled next to him. "Want to talk about it? You'll feel better."

"If only it was that simple." Seth chomped on a chicken leg and chewed, his gaze wandering off into the distance, no doubt keeping an eye out for predators.

"Why don't you tell me what's bothering you?" Amanda popped some of the delicious raspberries in her mouth. "The food is really good, too delicious to devour it without savoring it."

Seth lowered the chicken leg. "How do you do that when we haven't even known each other a whole week? I feel guilty about relaxing. There's so much to do."

"Sometimes a breath of pure mountain air can put everything in perspective. Take last night for example. Pamela called with some tasks, and I waited until after we talked under the stars to tackle them. Glad I did, too." She speared a plump blueberry and the flavor exploded in her mouth. "I was fresh and the ideas flowed out of me. Balance and all that."

"I thought you're on vacation? Except for us, that is." Seth selected a whole apple and crunched his teeth into it. Some of the juice landed on his beard along with a small piece of the peel, and she handed him a napkin.

"Pamela's niece is visiting, and I'm helping out." It wasn't anything new, and it was better than the time Pamela texted while Amanda was recovering from a dental procedure and had to work through the pain. "What happened this morning?"

Seth wiped one side of his beard, and she motioned that it was the other side. He still swiped at the wrong place, and she reached over, guiding him to the right spot. The contact with his calloused skin was electric.

She jerked away and concentrated on a plump strawberry.

He folded the napkin and used his plate as a paperweight for it. "I pride myself on keeping it light around the guests so they can enjoy themselves."

She clicked her tongue against the roof of her mouth. "There you go again. I like to think of myself as a special guest or Bridget's subcontractor. I love how she treats everyone like family." His swift intake of breath was her first hint about what was bothering him. "Is everything okay with your grandparents?"

"Physically, yes. I do everything I can to make life easier for them." Seth wore his mantel of responsibility well, that innate protector quality of him coming out around Mabel and the other guests. "Yet Grandpa Martin is…"

"Is what?" Amanda's phone rang, and she glanced at the screen. Her real estate agent would only be calling, and not texting, if this was important. "Hold that thought. This is my Realtor."

Amanda excused herself and found a private place to answer the call. Her toes started to tingle. In a few minutes, she might actually own her own home. For the first time, she might have a little corner of heaven with two bedrooms, a garden room and a laundry room all to herself.

Once she talked to her real estate agent, however, that tingle turned to dread. The homeowners had received a better offer, yet they were still giving Amanda a chance to make a counteroffer. Without a raise, which Pamela hadn't authorized since Amanda started working for her, the counteroffer's monthly payments would be a few dollars more than she could afford. All her hopes for a home of her own were falling apart. Her Realtor assured her she had forty-eight hours for her decision. Amanda ended the call and returned to the picnic.

Seth opened a tin of cookies and was passing

them out to the other cyclists. Amanda settled back into a sitting position on the hard ground. Suddenly the food didn't interest her as much, and she pushed around the mound of potato salad. Seth nudged the tin of sweets in her direction.

"To steal a line from my newest friend, Ingrid's cookies can spin your day into something better. Oatmeal Craisin or chocolate chip?"

She guffawed. "A real friend knows that's an impossible choice."

"Duly noted, friend." He plopped one of each on her plate. "Rough phone call?"

"The counteroffer bid my Realtor suggested is on the high end of my range but, in this market, I don't know when another house this perfect will come my way again." The location was close to her best friend's house and convenient to work.

Yet it was more than the location or the awesome laundry room. This was going to be her home, her haven of rest. It represented the culmination of her dream to settle in one place. Maybe she could adopt a senior dog like Hap or Trixie without worrying about landlord restrictions. There would be no moving boxes staring back at her. No real estate agent on speed dial.

"This ranch is my piece of perfect," Seth admitted before selecting one of the oatmeal Craisin cookies.

"This land is part of the ranch, too?" She marveled at the nearby red rocks. While she had never thought of rocks as majestic, these qualified with their heft and presence.

"It backs up to a national park, and we have permission to use the trails for our guests." His gaze never stopped searching the perimeter.

"It's beautiful here. I can see why you and your family love it so much. What were you about to say about your grandparents earlier?"

He demolished the cookie in two bites. "I'm not sure it's my story to tell."

Amanda hesitated. Getting too involved in a work relationship had burned her once before, leaving a scar that was still raw. One look at Seth threw caution to the wind. She'd only be here until the end of next week. Even she, with a romantic streak as long as the Lazy River, couldn't fall in love that quickly. "If you need a friend to listen, I'm here."

He sighed and reached for another cookie. "Thanks, but Grandma Bridget and Grandpa Martin have to clear this matter up by themselves. But I would like to bounce something else off you."

"Go ahead." She nibbled the oatmeal Craisin, relishing the cinnamon taste.

"The family that arrived last night requested nicer linens and towels for them and their dogs. Isn't that proof of what I've been saying all along? Upgrades like that are vital if we're going to keep ourselves current and relevant in today's market."

She finished the oatmeal cookie and started on

the chocolate chip. "Depends on what you classify as your competition." She outlined how the target demographics for luxury hotels and dude ranches were different. "Sometimes it's enough to offer the experience of a lifetime without the extras. If someone wants luxury, let them go to Rocky Valley. Do what you do and do it well."

"I'm not sure this town has room for two dude ranches." Seth swallowed and coughed. Then he sipped some water. "Cookie got stuck in my throat."

But Amanda had seen that look before. He was trying to keep his concern to himself, and she struggled with how to get through to the elusive side of the cowboy. Highlighting the basics like the horseback riding and living like a cowboy for a week in a setting that blended charm and magnificence—that was what she wanted from her approach.

Still, she understood what he feared. Guests wanted the shiny, all-inclusive resort. Beneath the surface, it hit too close to her situation. Her parents lavished love and attention on the beautiful daughter who won beauty pageants. Amanda, the ugly duckling, had never been good enough for them.

Still, this ranch had so much to offer, and she would do her best showcasing what made this place special.

"Take a different approach." She finished the

last bite of her cookie and brushed crumbs off her shirt. "This town has enough room for a luxury hotel that happens to call itself a guest ranch and the Lazy River Dude Ranch with its unforgettable family experience."

He himself was proving to be pretty unforgettable with that protective nature guarding his grandparents. A mix of corny jokes and action, he went out of his way for each guest. Add in that cowboy charm, and he'd be part of her memories for a long time.

But she'd create new memories in Phoenix with friends and, even better, bond with Sami.

Seth pulled her out of her thoughts. "We need to head back. It's almost time for when the horses run to their meadow. After that, I have to check on my grandmother."

"Your grandparents are wonderful. Their love for each other is an inspiration." So far, that was another highlight of the trip.

His hand stilled, and he frowned. "Is that your personal or professional observation?"

Amanda had never known a scowl could reach someone's eyes, but in Seth's case, his whole face reflected scorn. "Both, I suppose. Why?"

"They've been through enough in their lives." Seth packed up the tins and loaded them into his bike basket. "I don't want their story exploited as a selling point."

"Their story is part of what sets you apart from

the Rocky Valley Guest Ranch." Amanda handed him the stones that had kept the blankets in place.

Seth shoved the stones in the basket. "I don't want them publicized for personal gain."

"Bridget gave me carte blanche for the website. The ranch's history is part of my presentation, and that includes their love story." Amanda couldn't understand what was happening. It wasn't like she was writing an exposé about the Virtue family; she'd be emphasizing the good. Then the truth dawned on her. "That's not the problem, is it? This goes back to my original question. What happened today?"

Seth snapped the basket closed and stared at her. "Two more employees resigned. If Rocky Valley snatches any more of our staff, there won't be a Lazy River Dude Ranch." He ran his hand through his thick, wavy hair before reaching for his Stetson. "And my grandmother found out I've been keeping a secret from her."

Amanda laid her hand over his. A small zing electrified her fingertips. "You'll get through it. She loves you."

"This secret changes everything, and that doesn't alter the fact this ranch should sell itself."

Getting through to Seth was harder than cycling up that last hill, but the magnificent view had been worth it. "You know how you asked me to lead the group, and I did it without question?"

"I needed an experienced biker at the front."

"I'm also an experienced marketing professional." Although you wouldn't know it with her fingers laced through his. She yanked away her hand. "You're doing your job—let me do mine."

With that, she left his side and jammed her helmet on her head. No one else had ever stirred such a tumult within her with happiness one second and consternation the next. Of all the infuriating clients, Seth Virtue was at the top of the list. Then she saw him help Mabel with her helmet, and she softened at the sweet way he approached the little girl. She knew he respected his grandparents and wanted to shield them. There was something admirable in that. Despite his obstinate stubbornness, he cared about people as much as he loved horses and this land.

She mounted her bike when shouts caught her attention.

"Juliet! Come back here!" One of Juliet's owners, a redhead in her forties, started running toward Amanda while her husband reached for the other Pomeranian, who barked at the commotion.

Amanda dismounted and darted for Juliet, who escaped her grip. Everyone except Seth joined in the chase. Juliet must have found her newfound freedom exhilarating as she weaved around guests and staff.

Suddenly, Juliet stood still and rushed to Seth, who was holding a small whistle in his hand. He scooped up the little dog, who panted against his chest.

The owners went over and thanked Seth for his quick thinking.

"You saved Juliet," the woman said, slightly out of breath. "Will you do us the honor of being the officiant for her wedding to Romeo?"

Seth handed the dog back and opened his mouth before his gaze met Amanda's. She nodded with her mind going in all directions about how she could use this in her campaign. He turned his attention toward Juliet's owner once more. "Since I'm the manager here, that gives me the authority for such an event. Sure."

Amanda got on her bike once more with yet another reason to think about the attractive cowboy.

CHAPTER SEVEN

Wednesday

AT LEAST GRANDMA BRIDGET talked Rich and Vickie into working through their two weeks' notice. That freed Seth long enough to track down his brother-in-law, Mayor Ben Irwin, this morning and ask his advice about hiring more employees. Not that Grandma Bridget was talking to Seth about anything other than work. She'd found out he learned about the secret and hadn't told her. Now he was relegated to the doghouse along with his grandfather. Seth didn't like it. He unlocked his truck, a mountain of tasks awaiting him upon his return. With no time to waste, he slid into the driver's seat.

"Seth! Seth!"

He emerged from his truck and found Amanda running toward him.

"Glad I didn't miss you. Your grandmother told me you're headed to town. Have room for me?" She bent to put her hands on her thighs and tried to catch her breath. At the same time, her smile played havoc with his emotions. "We could listen to Elvis again or maybe Patsy Cline."

The late Patsy Cline was Seth's favorite female country singer, but he'd best go alone. If she went with him, he'd have to admit he overreacted yesterday. She wasn't exploiting his grandparents, and he knew it. "I'm dropping in on Mayor Ben, my brother-in-law, about the possibility of a job fair to attract employees to the ranch. No shopping or anything else."

"Sounds perfect to me. Your sister and grandmother told me Ben has something waiting for me."

"What does Ben have that Daisy couldn't bring to the ranch tomorrow?" Seth's curiosity was piqued.

Then he realized Daisy and Grandma Bridget asked Amanda for a favor in town when they both knew he was driving to Violet Ridge. Warmth crept up his neck. It couldn't be. They weren't playing matchmaker with him and Amanda, were they?

And, if they were, did he mind?

Amanda faced him again and squinted. "Are you blushing?"

"We're wasting time. Get in the truck." He waited until she was settled in her seat before closing her door and going around the tailgate, taking a minute to pull himself together.

There was something about her that made him dig deep and want to commit to new ideas and different activities. Amanda's own willingness to see the best in everything was a good influence on him. One he'd never forget.

Including Felicity.

Once in the truck, he found her tightening her seat belt and staring at him. "You're as red as a matador's cape."

He composed himself while driving toward the front gate. "Hasn't it occurred to you Grandma Bridget and Daisy are plotting ways for us to spend time together?"

When he stopped the truck, she jumped out and opened the gate while he pulled through. After she closed the gate, she hopped back into the passenger seat and fastened her seat belt. "I think you're jumping to conclusions. They assured me this has something to do with his mayoral duties. I think it's about adding a tab regarding the town's history to its website."

"But why does Ben want to talk to you and not Crosby?" He resisted the urge to turn on the truck's stereo system and let country music fill the air. "You don't have any ties to the area, and you're returning to Phoenix soon."

"That eager to get rid of me?" Amanda's voice was teasing.

He was relieved she hadn't figured out it was the contrary. He wasn't in any hurry for her to leave.

"Yesterday you mentioned something about a counteroffer." He kept his eyes glued to the road, careful to be on the lookout for any stray wildlife. "What did you decide?"

Amanda propped her right elbow on the window ledge and watched the scenery. "Can't until I talk to my boss and she must be busy with her niece. Pamela hasn't returned my texts or calls."

He caught sight of Amanda, still staring out the window. "A home base can make all the difference, a shelter in the storm. I've lived here all my life, first in my parents' house on the other side on the ranch and then in my suite on the top floor of the lodge. I'm closer to work that way. I couldn't live anywhere else."

"Thanks for the advice." She moved close enough for him to get a whiff of her perfume. Jasmine, if he wasn't mistaken. "So you live on the same floor as your grandparents?"

They still had ten minutes until they'd be at the city hall parking lot. He hesitated, not wanting a burdensome silence to enter the cab, and yet they were entering something that bordered on friendship. Friends shared personal details. He could use a friend. Amanda was easy to talk to. There was something in that.

"Yes. For my job as well as to keep an eye on them. They're not getting any younger." And now Grandma Bridget wasn't even talking to him except about vital business.

He had made a huge mess of everything.

She must have sensed his distress for she laid her hand on his arm. "That's sweet."

"I know I'm overprotective." He disliked how husky his voice sounded. "But I love them. I'm sorry about yesterday. I overreacted."

Amanda even made delivering apologies easier.

"Thank you. That means a lot coming from you."

He turned on Patsy Cline, a huge weight lifted off him.

"Did Daisy give you a hint about what Ben has waiting for you? I hope it's not the triplets. I love them, but it would be a tight fit for all of us in this truck."

She chuckled, and he liked her laugh. "That's for sure. You're fortunate to have nieces and a nephew. Sami's a free spirit, and I don't know if she wants a family. Anyway, that's her decision, not mine."

"What about you? Do you want to be a mother someday?" Heat rose up his cheeks. "If that's too personal, forget I asked."

"I don't mind sharing that I'd like to be a mom someday." Amanda waved away his concern. "What about you? Do you want to be a parent someday?"

Ever since Felicity departed for Wyoming, he believed his dream of having children went with her. He might have Amanda to thank for helping him repair the shattered pieces of his heart back together. Felicity left him battered but not down for the count.

"I can see myself being a dad."

He pulled into the city hall parking lot and opened Amanda's door for her. They walked toward Ben's office together.

She glanced at him. "How many children do you see on your horizon?"

He shrugged. "I love my siblings, so at least two, maybe three, if possible."

"I wouldn't mind having only one child." She paused and shifted her head from side to side. "Then again, I like the number three as long as there's no favoritism."

Before he could ask her to elaborate, they entered city hall. He guided her to Ben's office, where his brother-in-law wore a harried look. Ben spotted them and extended his hand in Amanda's direction before resting in his office chair. "Bridget and Martin Virtue speak highly of you, and you've made a good impression on Daisy. Do you accept freelance projects?"

Seth decided he'd return later when Ben had some time to talk to him alone. He rose from his chair. "I'll come back after I run some errands." His schedule was tighter than ever, and he still had to pick up the order at the Over and Dunne Feed and Seed.

"Don't leave," Ben said as his assistant entered and handed the mayor a sheaf of papers.

He thanked her and turned back to Seth. "This involves you, too."

What would need his and Amanda's shared input? Seth got comfortable and immediately regretted it when Ben revealed the reason for the meeting.

"You want the ranch to host the annual Ducks for Dogs Derby?" Seth shot out of his seat once more, intending to pace the length of Ben's office, except there was no place to walk. "It's this weekend. That's impossible, especially now that I'm also the officiant for a dog wedding."

Ben's frustrated sigh echoed what Seth was feeling on the inside.

"It wasn't my first choice. And we could really use the Lazy River's help." Seth stared at Ben, who pushed his black-rimmed glasses back into position. "But I already consulted a number of other possibilities. It's a no-go from everyone. The Double I is undergoing driveway maintenance, and my sister Lizzie can't accommodate us. My stepsister Sabrina's ranch is hosting a rodeo simulation. The neighboring ranch, the Silver Horseshoe, has a passel of baby goats that keep escaping. Plus, the size of your pond makes your place the best choice, and it's within walking distance of ample parking."

"We don't have the staff to handle the event." Seth resisted the urge to return to the ranch, saddle his horse and start riding. And possibly never stop. "That's why I'm here, to find out about the next Violet Ridge job fair."

"You don't have to worry about staff." Ben sifted through papers and placed them in a binder. "The local animal shelter has all the volunteers you need. It's only the location that fell through at the last minute."

"The animal shelter?" He remembered the day they called him about a litter of puppies like it was yesterday. Hap and Trixie were those puppies, and Seth had a soft spot for the sanctuary that helped so many animals in need.

"I'll sweeten the pot." Ben tapped the edge of his desk with a pencil and flipped open an agenda. "We don't currently have an employment fair on the calendar, but I can make one happen during the last week of June."

Seth noticed Amanda, who looked confused. "What's a duck derby?" she asked.

Ben chuckled. "I only attended my first one last year. It's a fundraiser for our animal shelter where folks put down a donation of two dollars to choose one of the many rubber ducks available. They can sponsor as many ducks as they'd like to. We've got some very generous people in Violet Ridge. Anyway, the plastic ducks are released into a body of water where the current and ropes keep them corralled as they float toward the finish line, or in this case, the other side of your pond. The first three ducks to make it there earn a prize for their backers. Business owners have donated the prizes, so everything's already taken care of."

It sounded simple enough, but the logistics were anything but. Seth added, "And there's more. Food vendors, face painting and games. People come from miles around for this."

She extracted her tablet from her tote bag. "This would provide great publicity, both for future guests and employment prospects," she said.

Ben handed her the promotional binder. "That's where you come in. I need someone to help publicize the new location. Drum up buzz about the event and the town."

Amanda nodded and, and she skimmed the contents of the binder. "There are so many great photo ops for the dude ranch, and it's a charitable cause. I love animals, so I'm all in."

He knew he'd regret this, but he simply nodded. "Okay. So the Lazy River is hosting the Ducks for Dogs Derby."

They settled the details although Seth couldn't help but be concerned the brunt of the activity would fall on them. He left with promises from Ben that they would barely notice the event was there on Saturday.

Upon leaving city hall, Amanda must have spotted his added strain since she reached for his hand. "I know you're busy, but I saw the cutest little coffeehouse near here. We'll get our order to go and enjoy it on the way back to the ranch, where I'll get started on the publicity." He started objecting, but she refused to take no for an answer. "I know Ingrid makes a wonderful cup of coffee, but I could go for a matcha latte or whatever catches my eye. My treat."

The balmy spring day with a cool breeze was Colorado at its finest, the blue sky the picture of perfection. The town was crowded with tourists, another reminder of her own temporary status. He wouldn't have many more opportunities with her in person, and he wanted to get to know her better.

"The meeting was shorter than I anticipated. So, okay," Seth said.

"See." She sent him that smile that shot loud warning signals to his mind. "This will be fun. Just like the duck derby on Saturday. Whatever that is."

Amanda wove around a tourist, as did Seth, who forged ahead to the coffeehouse and opened the door for her.

"All this chivalry is going to my head." She thanked him and swept inside.

The aromatic beans tickled his nose. "Grandma Bridget raised her three grandsons to be gentlemen."

While in line, he stayed quiet while Amanda mentioned the new location for the Ducks for Dogs Derby to the customers. Amanda was amazing. Here she was on a working vacation that seemed more work-like than relaxing, taking on a project of this magnitude by diving in and getting the task done. Not only that, but she was having fun in the process. Had he been so self-involved that he stopped noticing the lighthearted aspects of his job and only dwelled on the problems?

At the counter, the owner promised to publicize the fact that the Lazy River was now hosting and jotted down their orders.

In no time, they found themselves back at his truck.

Amanda lifted the lid of her mocha coffee and inhaled, her tiny groan of contentment echoing in the cab. "You can never go wrong with mocha. I love the combination of coffee and chocolate." Seth twisted the key in the ignition, and she snapped the plastic lid in place. "But I want to know what made you so quiet all of a sudden."

He pulled out of the parking space and headed to the Over and Dunne Feed and Seed. After his order was loaded, he made his way toward the ranch. The silence drew out while he tried to fashion an explanation that wouldn't lower her estimation of him. He didn't usually care about other people's opinions of him.

Yet he valued Amanda's esteem.

Her gaze didn't waver away from him, which was something considering the awe-inspiring mountains around them.

"I'm just concerned about the ranch. I didn't consult my grandparents first about this decision.

Instead, I committed to the derby without calling them and asking for their insight and approval."

"You're missing the important point. Daisy and Bridget obviously knew about the duck derby. That's why I was sent along with you. To set up the marketing promos." She sipped her drink and gave an appreciative moan. "Ooh, this is delicious."

He considered her take, and realized she was right. Grandma Bridget and Daisy must have known about Ben needing to change the location of the derby.

"So, I was the last to know about the derby?"

"Nope. I didn't know, either." Amanda placed her cup in the holder and extracted the binder from her tote bag. She scanned the contents. "This sounds like fun. The ranch gains favorable publicity, and so does the animal shelter. Have you ever been to one before?"

"More than one. I remember when Crosby was six. He was so upset when he found out he didn't get to keep his duck."

Amanda giggled. "That sounds precious."

"Crosby still ended up having fun that day." Especially after Seth had used his allowance to buy a souvenir pirate duck that had been their bathroom mascot for years.

He hadn't used his silver dollar, though. Seth would never part with the last gift his father gave him.

Seth pulled onto the main road leading to the

ranch. Once again, Amanda opened and closed the gate while Seth added an automated one to his long list of updates.

She climbed into the cab and wiped her hands together. "I'm getting good at that." She reached for her drink and finished it off. "Everything will turn out fine with the duck derby. It'll be fun."

He scoffed at anything being that simple. "It'll be a lot of time and effort."

"Ben said his staff will handle it. Trust people and take them at their word." Amanda stuffed the binder back into her tote bag.

Too soon he found himself parking in his usual spot. He watched her leave. The trip had gone by in a flash, thanks to her. From what he gathered, she'd had a difficult upbringing yet retained an aura of positivity. He admired that about her since he sometimes felt like he was more jaded than his siblings.

He hoped she was right about the duck derby and the amount of work involved.

And yet? Even if he was right, would Amanda find some way to make the work fun? So far this week, she'd done just that.

If he let himself, those feelings of admiration could blossom into something more. For now, though, he'd focus on managing this ranch, and hoping for a successful duck derby.

STILL FULL FROM the delectable dessert buffet, Amanda decided a walk was in order before

Bridget's knitting lesson. Last night, she enjoyed Seth's astronomy program, maybe a little too much, but tonight's was canceled so Ben and his crew could start installing the equipment for this weekend's duck derby.

Amanda settled her knitting bag, brand-new, thanks to Bridget, in a corner of the library, eager for this chance to come to a final decision about the counteroffer. Her texts and calls to Pamela had gone unanswered, and Amanda's email was met with an automatic reply that Pamela was spending time with her beautiful niece. The disconcerting part of the email was Pamela providing Amanda as the emergency work contact. So far, none of their clients had reached out, but still...

Once outside, she heard someone call out her name, and she looked around the lodge entrance. Colleen waved and approached her. "I'm going for a walk. I'd love some company unless you're going back to your cabin?"

"Great minds think alike." Amanda glanced over Colleen's shoulder. "Where are Brian and Mabel?"

"They're at the rec center. Brian's teaching Mabel how to play Ping-Pong. I was heading to the library for another book, and Ingrid's cupcakes were so scrumptious I couldn't resist a second one." Colleen patted her stomach and pointed toward the stable. "I definitely need a stroll. Want to head to the meadow?"

"Sounds good to me," Amanda said.

They chatted about Colleen's job as an engineer before arriving at the fence that separated the trail from the horses. There was a freedom about roaming here in the vast expanse that Amanda envied.

The gentle sway of the breeze rustled the tops of the aspens, their silvery leaves putting on a spring display. She and Colleen fell into a comfortable silence while watching the horses in the meadow and hearing their delightful whinnies.

Amanda turned to Colleen and decided to prod a little. "Want to talk about what's bothering you?"

Colleen kept her gaze on the horses. "Do you know Brian and I met here when we were teenagers?" She zipped up her jacket and then pulled out a tin of mints. She offered them to Amanda, who accepted one with thanks. "You should have seen the ranch twenty-three years ago. There was an overnight chuckwagon ride where Brian and I snuck off and talked for hours."

Amanda perked up at the unabashed nostalgia in Colleen's voice. "What else do you remember?"

"Fishing, riding out to see the cattle, cozying up in Brian's letter jacket at the bonfire." Colleen smiled as she elaborated on other activities. "You know what? I think I changed my mind about the book. I'd like a romance rather than a thriller that will keep me awake. Let's head back to the lodge so I can swap out the books."

Amanda couldn't let Colleen escape before

knowing the rest of the story. "Those sound like great memories. What happened between you and Brian?"

Amanda opened the lodge door for Colleen, who muttered her thanks. "They were the best times." Amanda strolled to the lobby's fireplace and warmed her hands while Colleen followed suit. "Right person, wrong time and place. I moved to Seattle for my first engineering assignment, and Brian stayed in Birmingham for his family. We broke up, and he met Mabel's mother. They grew apart and divorced four years ago. I accepted a new job in Birmingham, where we reconnected."

Amanda couldn't help but wonder if there was a parallel to what was happening between her and Seth; for her there was no doubt in her mind. She would be leaving here for Phoenix, even if it meant turning her back on a potential relationship although that was probably putting the cart in front of the mustang.

Out of nowhere, Mabel ran up to Colleen, and Amanda spotted Brian not far away.

"I beat Daddy, Colleen!" Mabel hugged her and scrunched her nose. "Daddy was right when he said you'd have loved it. Next time you gotta be there with us."

Colleen tucked her hand into Mabel's. "You're right. Tell me how you beat him. We girls gotta stick together sometimes."

Over Brian's mock protests, the family left the

lobby. Brian and Colleen had fallen in love here, and yet it was just a vacation kind of love until they were ready to commit for a forever kind of love. Still, Amanda wondered. Would Colleen have made the same choice of career over love all over again? Would Amanda ever face that type of decision?

She blinked and headed to the library, choosing to mull over what Colleen shared about the ranch. Its past was the key to its future.

When Amanda entered the library, Trixie, one of the bonded pair of Australian shepherds, looked over from the hearth before resting her head on her paws once more. The library was cozy warm with a gas fire and soft lighting. Bridget patted the chair next to her while Amanda scooped up her knitting bag from its secure resting place in the corner.

"I knew you'd be hooked." Bridget laughed at her pun.

Amanda laid her knitting bag on the rug next to the chair. Maybe tonight Bridget would show her how to end the scarf that was now longer than a full-size rattlesnake.

"I never knew knitting could be soothing." Amanda extracted her yarn and knitting needles. "It's mind-blowing how something so beautiful can come from a simple ball of yarn."

"I wouldn't call yarn simple. There are so many textures and colors." Bridget's fingers never stopped moving, her nimbleness and proficiency an inspiration to Amanda.

"You're right," Amanda said.

Bridget chuckled. "Your expressions remind me of your grandma Lou. You two are so much alike."

The questions rolled off her tongue, and Bridget answered them, her needles clicking all the while. Amanda was processing everything when Seth entered.

Bridget stilled her needles and flexed her fingers. Then she rubbed her gnarled hands. "Seth."

There was a world of meaning in that solitary word. The bond between Seth and his grandmother hadn't been permanently altered with whatever transpired between them. She envied their connection. Resolved to start afresh with Sami, Amanda made a mental note to text her sister and make sure she had everything she needed at the apartment.

Trixie came over and rolled on her back until Seth obliged with a belly rub. Satisfied, Trixie resumed her spot on the hearth while Seth set his large leather bag on the table. "Grandma Bridget, I'll take over tonight so you can get some rest."

Amanda delivered a silent groan. Although she was intrigued at the thought of Seth giving her knitting lessons, this was not what she meant by adding a grand gesture to a heartfelt apology.

She glanced in Bridget's direction, the older woman's firm jawline proof she was offended at

Seth's offer. "Thank you, Seth, but this is restful for me."

Seth frowned and then pulled out his knitting needles, attached to a gorgeous chunky throw in various shades of blue. "I thought a night off would help."

Bridget rolled her eyes. "Help with what? My health? My relationship with your grandfather? Or your conscience?"

With a wobbly smile, Seth shrugged. "All of the above."

Bridget's lips formed a thin line with the side impacted by her stroke tugging downward. "For your information, my physical therapist encourages knitting. It promotes my hand-eye coordination." She glanced at Amanda. "In case Seth didn't tell you, my husband kept a secret from me, and Seth found out about it. He was complicit by not telling me personally."

Amanda felt for Seth, whose attempt at seeking forgiveness was failing on a cosmic level. Maybe she could help him yet. She crooked her finger at him. "Can I speak to you in the hall?"

Seth wrinkled his nose. "I think I better stay here."

Bridget nudged Seth with her elbow. "Go talk to Amanda." Her tone reminded Amanda of Grandma Lou's no-nonsense attitude laced with a lot of love, making her like Bridget that much more.

With grudging reluctance, Seth followed Amanda

into the hall. He shrugged. "I took your advice about a sweet gesture, and now she's more upset than ever."

Amanda folded her arms and leaned against the wall, taking care not to jostle the framed photograph of a Colorado sunset. "You didn't apologize, and the gesture needs to mean something to both of you. She values her independence." Amanda saw that same streak in Seth but chose to keep that to herself.

Seth muttered something under his breath and went back into the library. Amanda considered giving them space but ventured inside anyway.

"I'm sorry, Grandma Bridget. I should have told you the minute I found out." Seth had settled next to his grandmother on the sofa.

The knitting needles kept a steady rhythm. Minutes ticked by, and then Bridget chuckled. "As if anyone can make Martin Virtue do anything before he's ready to do it." She paused and reached for Seth's hand, causing him to put down his knitting. "Thank you for the apology. From here on, this matter is between your grandfather and me."

"No, ma'am." Seth drew in a deep breath as if this discussion went against everything he held dear. "This involves the ranch, so it includes me."

It was time for Amanda to leave. She started toward the door and was almost out of the room when Bridget cleared her throat. "Amanda, please stay. I feel like you belong here."

What if that were true? And yet she'd already committed to Phoenix. All this talk about Grandma Lou brought back that same glow of contentment she'd find whenever she stepped over the threshold into her grandmother's house. She hoped to find that same sense of belonging in her new house.

But that didn't mean she couldn't form cherished friendships while she was here.

Amanda hugged Bridget, inhaling the scent of the ranch and rose petals, a combination that worked for the lovely woman. "Thank you for making me feel so at home."

They separated, and Bridget eyed Seth's blanket. "You dropped a stitch three rows ago. We Virtues look out for each other."

Then Bridget winked at Seth, who winked right back at her. "And the ranch," Seth added.

Amanda soaked in their mutual love. For the past five days, the Virtues had allowed her access to their home and their lives.

"Tell me more about this duck derby that will happen on Saturday. Ben called today and asked Martin and I to help plunge the ducks into the pond. Celebrity Ty Darling will pluck the winners from the pond." Bridget stopped knitting and smiled. "Rosie, Lily and Aspen are so excited about it taking place here."

Amanda glanced at Seth and raised a brow, so he explained. "Ty Darling is a local rodeo star, and Rosie, Lily and Aspen are Daisy's triplets and Ben's stepchildren."

"Ben and Daisy are perfect for each other. He's been good for Violet Ridge, too." Bridget resumed her knitting. "Is something else bothering you, Seth? You look rather upset considering we're sorting out everything between us."

Seth pursed his lips while concentrating on unraveling his yarn. "Just thinking about Winnie and our real ducks and how they're going to respond to all the activity."

"Ben said he'd take care of that," Amanda reminded Seth. "And there's already been buzz from the social media posts about the change of venue. I also arranged for the television stations in this area to mention it and cover the event. Everything will come together."

A dog wedding and a duck derby. The ranch had a lot more to offer than at first glance and prospective guests needed to know about it all. Then it hit her what had been missing from her life for so long. This was the most fun, the most welcome she'd felt in ages, and certainly on any assignment.

Was it the ranch that was adding this dimension?

Or was it the cowboy who was showing a new and attractive side to him as he knit that blanket?

CHAPTER EIGHT

Thursday

SETH PASSED THE goat pen on his way to the archery range with the midday sun shining bright. Grandpa Martin unlocked the shed behind the archery range. When his grandfather asked him to conduct today's lesson so he could monitor Rosa's condition. Seth agreed without hesitation.

Something caught his eye, namely Amanda feeding Winnie the goat pieces of carrot. She looked carefree and happy in her pink flannel shirt and jeans, toting a leather backpack. He had a couple of minutes before the lesson was set to start. The closer he came to Amanda, the more his pulse raced from her mere presence.

"Has Winnie behaved herself?" Seth asked.

Amanda faced him and smiled. "She's being a perfect lady." Amanda removed her backpack and placed it on the ground before extending the bowl of carrots toward Seth. "Is feeding Winnie too tame for you?"

"Never." Seth always loved a chance to interact with the animals. It just seemed like he never had enough time for managing everything at the ranch and spending time with them, too. He liked how Amanda was making him slow down and see the positive aspects of life around here again.

He reached for a piece of carrot at the same time as Amanda. Their hands touched, and he felt a zap. The contact ended, and he fed Winnie. Soon the bowl was empty, the experience over too soon.

"I had the best morning. I conducted online interviews with local podcasters to publicize the duck derby," Amanda elaborated on her other efforts. "And then the four *M*'s and I made wedding favors for Romeo and Juliet."

He was afraid to ask, but curiosity overtook him. "Doggie wedding favors?"

"Just snacks and a bracelet," Amanda said.

Seth looked down and winced. "Uh-oh. Winnie is nibbling your backpack."

Amanda snatched it out of reach and sighed at the damage. "You warned me she likes leather."

"You can get a new one at the gift shop." Seth had gotten so caught up listening to Amanda, he'd forgotten to watch out for what was happening right under his nose. "On the house."

She scoffed and brushed his protests aside. "Now it has character." She strapped it to her back and pointed toward the meadow. "Archery, huh?"

"In about thirty minutes. I have to get everything set up first."

"Need help?"

He shook his head. "Got everything covered."

She neared him and pushed up the brim of his hat until his eyes were visible to her. "Is this another part of the cowboy credo? Always stand resolute, never offer an apology or accept a hand?"

"Interesting concept, but cowboys work together. There's always one who's better at mending fences and another who's a horse whisperer." Seth figured it was time to start listening to himself. "So, yes, thank you. I'd appreciate your assistance."

They walked to the supply shed. In no time, they had everything ready as Tiffany and Derrick made their way toward them.

"This should get your mind off home." Derrick waved when he spotted Seth and Amanda. "I've never shot a bow and arrow before. Should be a great experience for a new phase of life."

Tiffany looked uncertain. "Maybe we should spread out the trips and go home after this week. Princess and Earl have probably forgotten me."

"For years, we bought one lottery ticket a week and dreamed of what we would do if we won." Derrick placed his arms around his wife's waist and pulled her close. "Now we have that chance. You should have everything you deserve for working so hard for so long."

She kissed his cheek and slipped out of his embrace as the four *M*'s appeared with the Carr family and the Berggren brothers. Now that everyone was accounted for, Seth delivered his safety lecture and worked in turn with each group, saving Amanda for last.

"Are you right-handed or left-handed?" Seth asked her.

She approached the chalk line on the green grass and stood at a right angle to the target, her feet together at the line. Determination in her eyes, she held a bow with her left hand. "I'm right-handed."

"Hold on. Your feet need to be apart." He approached and stood behind her, close enough for him to breathe in the sweet scent of jasmine.

He needed to focus on his job. It was just that Amanda was so appealing.

Her head tilted until her gaze absorbed his stance near the chalk line. "Got it. By the way, I worked as a camp counselor for two summers so I'm pretty good at this."

Amanda nocked the arrow until it snapped in place. Then she hooked her fingers around the string, her index finger above the nock, her middle and ring fingers below. Extending her left arm to shoulder height, she aimed at the target, drew the bow and released the arrow, which flew through the air until it connected in the center. Bull's-eye!

The remaining five arrows landed in the yellow zone, the innermost ring.

Seth whistled at her accuracy as the gang cheered and then asked Amanda for pointers. Soon, a friendly rivalry emerged and a contest began. Seth noted all the good-natured teasing and smiles. It seemed like everyone was enjoying themselves. In the end, the four *M*'s were declared the ultimate winners and Seth offered them a drink on the house later on in the bar.

As the group moved on to other activities, they thanked him and Amanda for an excellent hour of archery training.

Amanda lingered and together they tidied up. Once the supplies were put away, she Amanda bumped his arm. "I haven't done that in ages. It was fun, and I was paying you a compliment— you're a huge part of why this ranch will thrive in the future."

He let her optimism seep into him. "Thank you." He liked the feeling, almost as much as he liked her.

"I'm going to call my Realtor and find out if my counteroffer was accepted. See you later."

She gave a little wave and started toward her cabin. He kept watching until she faded from view. Could Amanda be right? Could the ranch succeed on its own merits with its own brand of unique flair? It had come through other hard times in the past ninety years. When had he become convinced it was destined to fail?

He took a deep breath. He'd lost the feeling of

hope the moment he watched Felicity drive away, bound for Wyoming, never to return.

Ever since then, he'd fallen into the role of jovial manager, skimming the surface of his guests' lives, without giving of his whole self, knowing a new group would arrive the following week.

Somehow, he'd distanced himself from living.

What would it be like to have someone who loved this ranch the same way he did? With someone who loved him and wanted that life?

Amanda's shining face popped into mind. She was energetic and optimistic without being overly so, full of surprises, enough so he'd always feel like there'd be new areas of her personality to explore.

And yet she had made that counteroffer. To her credit, Amanda had never indicated she intended to stay, only promising to remain in contact online in her professional capacity.

He had a little over a week to find out if this closeness they had could turn into something real, something that might be lasting.

THE HORSES FLEW by in a brilliant display of grace and agility. Adjusting her lens, Amanda centered the frame and snapped a photo of several mustangs, their hind muscles rippling under their gorgeous roan coats. As unobtrusively as possible, she pointed her camera lens toward Seth, who was watching the proceedings with a look of awe.

He must have seen this a thousand times, but he looked as if he was experiencing it for the first time. She clicked the button in rapid succession. Even if the pictures didn't go on the website, she'd want some of the trip just for herself.

Tonight she'd forego the nightly activities and spend time on the presentation. Between the duck derby publicity push and the dog wedding arrangements, she'd fallen behind on her actual job duties. She intended on burning the midnight oil to impress the Virtue family. She owed it to Grandma Lou to put her best foot forward for Bridget. And Seth...

Amanda wanted this presentation to shine simply because he was Seth, the consummate cowboy.

This ranch was the center of his life, and he loved this place. When he eventually fell for someone, he'd love deeply and forever. Not that he loved her. Although the undercurrent between them was fast becoming an undertow, she was struggling to swim away from it. Despite her growing feelings for him, she wouldn't give up everything she'd worked for these past three years on a whim. She wouldn't be like her father.

Even if that meant tamping down her romantic nature.

While she usually trusted her gut instincts, she ignored the voice inside her shouting this ranch held the possibility of real roots, real love.

The last time she intertwined her personal and

business life, she'd fallen for Blake, her boss's adult son, only for him to betray her after a deal went sour. Her boss confronted them about their relationship, and Blake claimed she used him for her advancement. She was immediately terminated and left to pick up the pieces of her heart. On top of it all, her boss refused to give her a reference. Despite that, Pamela hired her anyway. That alone was a reason for loyalty...

The sound of the horses' hooves and jingles on their harnesses drew her back to the ranch. Turning around, she bumped into someone with her camera lens. "Sorry. It's my fault. I hope you're not hurt."

"Those are your first words to the sister you haven't seen in ages?" Sami's sweet voice registered, and Amanda's jaw dropped. "How about I suggest something better? 'Hey, sis, I'd love a hug.'"

Amanda closed her mouth and let go of the camera, the strap ensuring it didn't fall to the ground. "Sami!"

Her sister had only grown more beautiful since Amanda had seen her last. Lustrous blond hair hung down her back, offsetting those bright blue eyes, almost as violet as the lupine growing wild in the meadow. A couple of inches taller than Amanda, Sami was willowy and graceful. She could easily be a model in her white pants and off-the-shoulder red silk shirt.

Amanda adjusted the camera so it wouldn't

poke Sami in the chest and embraced her sister. Afterward, questions tumbled out of both of them. Amanda held up her hand and proceeded with the most obvious. "What are you doing here?"

"I'm the perfect spy." Sami showed off a perfect manicure, the bright red matching her shirt and lips. "I have the full scoop for you."

"Spy? Scoop?" Amanda's tone reflected her confusion.

Seth approached, and Sami squealed. "Is this the cowboy you've been talking about?" Sami grinned. "You're Seth, right? I'm Sami, Amanda's sister. I hope you don't mind that I dropped by like this, but Amanda made this place sound so wonderful I didn't want to spend another minute in Phoenix."

Seth looked stunned and confused as though a bull had stampeded over him. "Welcome to the Lazy River Dude Ranch."

He seemed to collect himself and returned Sami's smile.

Amanda felt a pang that seemed like, but couldn't be, jealousy and faced Seth. "If it's okay, she can stay in the Bluebell with me."

"Of course. You're part of our family since you're Amanda's sister." Seth tipped the brim of his Stetson in Sami's direction. "You're just in time for dinner. It's in an hour. After that you can either relax or enjoy the ranch's amenities. Saturday's when the real fun begins with the big fundraiser, the Ducks for Dogs Derby, followed by our special cowboy entertainment night."

"Good thing I brought a special dress that'll be perfect." Sami hooked her elbow through Amanda's. "After dinner, Amanda and I have so much catching up to do."

"We'll miss her at tonight's knitting lesson." Seth winked, and a most unsettling feeling jolted Amanda.

Seth startled as though he felt the same electricity in the air. He made a hasty retreat, and Sami cleared her throat. Amanda noticed bemusement on her sister's face. "Hmm, good thing I like Violet Ridge since you're obviously in love with that cowboy. Spending a year here before moving onto greener pastures will be a pleasure."

Love? Huh? Amanda wasn't in love with Seth. She searched for something bland and neutral to focus the attention off of herself. "How was the drive?"

"Cacti, bison, tumbleweeds, you name it." Sami's eyes sparkled. "Did Seth mention dinner? I haven't eaten since breakfast."

"I'll show you the dining hall after we stow your luggage and my camera in the library." Amanda and Sami transported their gear to the lodge.

At dinner, she introduced Sami to Martin, Bridget and the guests. The meal went by too fast but, at last, Amanda stuck the key into the front door of the Bluebell Cabin. She struggled for a second, the lock in obvious need of a few squirts of WD-40. Finally, she held the door open for her sister, already feeling like this cabin was the home she'd never had before. Sami rolled her suitcase into the living area.

"My things are already in the master bedroom." Amanda hesitated but wanted to start off this new time in their life on a positive note. Her sister made the first move and deserved a concession for it. "But I'll move into the smaller bedroom if you'd like, especially since the bathroom is a dream."

Sami's shoulders relaxed, and she collapsed onto the sofa. "Amanda, you don't have to sacrifice anything for me." Her face grew pensive. "Although I've come to suspect you've done just that throughout my life."

Amanda settled next to Sami, grabbing a pillow and hugging it to her chest. "What do you mean?"

Sami reached out for Amanda's hand and rubbed a rough patch with her manicured finger. "You have to try my hand lotion. It does wonders with callouses and dermatitis." Sami gave a wry laugh and retreated back to her side of the sofa. "I found something I love, so stop me if I get overzealous about skin care and hair products."

"I'm confused. How do you find time to work at a hair salon and go on acting auditions?" Just last month, their mother gushed about Sami's newest opportunity. "After all, I just transferred five hundred dollars to Mom for your headshots."

"What?" Sami bolted upright, consternation written all over her gorgeous face. "I haven't had headshots taken in forever, not since I started cosmetology classes. I didn't know she took money from you."

"So Mom lied?" Had her mother really sunk so low as to steal from Amanda? Sami hadn't known about the transfer until now, and Amanda believed her. She'd never see the money again, but she also wouldn't fall for any more of her mother's requests.

"She must have. I haven't been on an acting audition in some time. I've been working steadily as a hairdresser for the past year."

Guilt about being in the dark this long passed through Amanda. "Why didn't you tell me sooner about your career change?"

"I thought you'd be disappointed in me." Sami looked sheepish. "You went to college, and I work in a salon. Not that I'm embarrassed about that. I love what I do! Acting and modeling was Mom's dream for me, not mine."

"I've only ever wanted for you to be happy. I'm glad you're here." This time Amanda reached out for her sister's hand. "We need to get to know each other again."

Sami moved the pillow and hugged Amanda. "So am I." She scooted away and wiped a tear off her cheek. Then she waved her hand around the living area. "This place is so much bigger than last night's room."

Amanda winced. "I know my apartment's small…"

"I wasn't there. I spent last night at the Rocky Valley Guest Ranch. I'm a spy, remember?" Sami's eyes sparkled, and she moved off the couch. She returned with a small cosmetic bag, which she handed to Amanda. "The hotel has its own signature line of soaps and shampoo products, each with a light botanical woodsy scent."

Amanda unzipped the bag and pulled out a teensy perfume bottle, a trial size of shampoo and a circle of soap wrapped in tissue paper sealed with the guest ranch's logo. She held it to her nose and didn't care for the smell, placing everything back in the satchel. "The room was small?"

"Minuscule," Sami confirmed before launching into a full report. "The staff seemed discontent, and the management wasn't as sweet as Martin and Bridget. If you want a luxury experience, it's great, but this place seems more like a real home with family you'd like to be around for a week or more."

That concept was exactly what Amanda wanted to capture in the revamped brand and slogan. Something along the lines of "Let this family be your family for a week."

"Speaking of homes, I'm waiting to hear about the counteroffer."

Amanda found her phone and showed Sami pictures of the house. "Best of all, there are two bedrooms. You're more than welcome to stay with me."

Sami launched herself at Amanda, delivering another hug with the ferocity of a leopard before pulling away once more.

"Just for a little while." Sami crossed her heart and grinned. "I have a lot of living to do, but I'll pay you rent and stay until I earn enough money to see the world. Paris, Sydney, Galveston."

"France, Australia and Texas?" Amanda didn't quite understand the connection linking those three destinations.

"Grandma Lou lived there." A huge yawn came over Sami. "I've put a lot of miles on my car this week, and I need to go to sleep."

Sami rolled her suitcase toward the smaller bedroom. Amanda cleared her throat, convinced she needed to do something for her younger sister. "Would you like a cup of herbal tea? Decaf coffee?" Amanda asked.

"Thanks." A soft smile came over Sami. "Maybe tomorrow night."

Amanda nodded. "Thanks for being my spy."

Sami just winked and closed the door behind her.

So many converging thoughts swirled in Amanda's mind. Sami, the counteroffer, Seth. Why did all roads seem to go back to Seth?

Amanda went to the master bedroom and opened her laptop. She pulled up the palette of colors she was considering for the ranch logo, hoping work would distract her, but that brown matched Seth's Stetson and that red was the color of the plaid flannel he wore tonight at dinner.

She might not live on the ranch, but this place provided respite and relaxation to so many. It needed to stay fiscally viable. After she made herself a cup of lavender tea, she set out to create a logo for a brand that would help the ranch thrive even if she wasn't here to see it for herself.

CHAPTER NINE

Friday

A CHANGE OF plans wreaked havoc with Seth's Friday morning schedule. Daisy had graciously arrived early and helmed an art lesson in the rec center as the paddleboard yoga, along with all other pond activities, was canceled. Buck, however, had grumbled about taking over the mountain hike since he preferred horses to people.

Now Seth found himself at the duck pond instead of at the stable. Immediately nine angry ducks waddled toward him, wings flapping as if they knew he was the one who okayed the disruption to their pond. He sidestepped them and found Ben, who was discussing something with one of the derby organizers.

"I thought you were going to install the duck-lowering apparatus at the other side of the pond," Seth said, rather exasperated.

Ben winced. "So did I." He turned back to the man. "I chose the other side to be the least disruptive to the wildlife."

The tall man removed his hard hat and swiped at his forehead with a bandanna. "We couldn't get our equipment around the gazebo. We have to put it here."

More ducks came over and quacked their protests. Ben and the man both looked at Seth. "It's your call, Seth," Ben said.

"Just watch out for the living ducks." Seth nodded his approval.

Over the next few hours, he directed the positioning of the apparatus that would lower over a thousand ducks into the pond. Still, one real duck gave him a fierce look of disdain before it set off for the other side.

Seth scooted out of the way of a UTV carrying picnic tables before it came to a screeching halt.

An older man hopped out of the vehicle and approached Seth. "Who's in charge here?"

Seth pointed to Ben. "The mayor is over there, and I'm Seth Virtue, the ranch manager."

"Only tables were delivered but no chairs or benches. What good are tables without seats to go with them? Do you still want me to set them up?" The man looked at Seth as if he expected him to have all the answers. So much for minimal involvement on Seth's part.

Seth texted Ben, who assured him he was on his way. Seth relayed the message and headed toward the lodge for breakfast, more like brunch now, when a text from his grandfather said Rosa was set to have her foal soon.

Leave it to Rosa to have finally gone into labor now. While most mares gave birth at night, Rosa started labor in the wee hours near dawn, her foal due any minute. Grandpa Martin found staffers to replace him in his scheduled activities and was monitoring his wife's beloved mare.

Seth detoured toward the stable when he spotted Amanda throwing lettuce to the ducks, now swimming on the opposite side of the pond.

She was a sight for sore eyes in jeans and a bright pink flannel shirt that complemented her honey-blonde hair. Somehow, his heart rate had a way of speeding up whenever she was close by. Should he tell her about his burgeoning feelings? No. They were adults and long-distance dating rarely worked out.

As hard as it might be, he had to manage this temporary crush until she departed.

Still, if Rosa was going to deliver her foal, Seth wanted Amanda by his side. He reached her as she was ripping a leaf of romaine in two before offering him one of the pieces.

"We have to stop meeting like this," she said.

His heart thudded until he caught sight of her huge grin. "What do you mean?"

"Feeding Winnie and now feeding the ducks." She threw the lettuce and a brace of ducks emerged from the water and surrounded her, quacking for more. She obliged. Seth glanced in the direction of the rec center. "I thought you were signed up for the hike. Shouldn't you be halfway to the mountaintop by now?"

"Sami took my place after one of the local news channels called me about the duck derby. They're going to mention it tonight on their newscast and send a reporter tomorrow. Then a client from Arizona texted me about an issue that had to be handled immediately on top of some other work-related projects. I thought I'd feed the ducks on my break." Frustration came over her pretty face as she shredded more lettuce leaves. "Some sister I am, leaving Sami to herself the first morning she's here."

"I'm sure Sami is enjoying the hike as much as these ducks are enjoying their treat." Each day was a different trail, and Friday's was, by far, the most breathtaking.

Maybe this ranch did appeal to a different clientele than people seeking massages, stylish lounges and champagne. Nature was a great outlet for stress management. After all, here was Amanda on her break, relaxing, spending time with the ducks. Was he wrong to turn the ranch into something it wasn't?

"I just wish I was with her." Amanda glanced at her boots, and so did he. They were dusty and looked like she'd owned them forever. "We haven't seen each other in so long, and here I had to finish social media updates for two clients and organize focus groups for three others. I promise, though, the marketing presentation will capture the essence of the ranch."

This wasn't a vacation; this was pure work.

He couldn't believe he'd been so quick to assume she was out to scam his grandmother. Six days ago, he'd have sent her home in a heartbeat. But now? Her professionalism won him over. Her ideas were in line with the ideals of the ranch, and he looked forward to her campaign bringing customers back to Lazy River.

He was about to say something to that effect when a slight whinny caught his ear. It must be near time for the foal to be born. While the stable was off-limits today to the other guests for obvious reasons, Amanda was more than a guest. She was his friend, even if he was beginning to want something more.

He grabbed her hand and tilted his head toward the stable. "Want to see something extraordinary?"

Because no matter how often he saw a foal born, it always took his breath away. Moments like these were why he couldn't live anywhere else. Sharing them with her? Maybe someday she'd consider moving here.

She nodded, and Seth motioned with his finger for Amanda to remain quiet. He led her inside the stable, locating Grandpa Martin near Rosa's stall.

His grandfather acknowledged them with a nod of his head. "It should be soon. She's doing great." Pride laced his whisper, and the older man gazed at the mare with admiration.

Rosa walked in a circle around her stall and then lay down, a sign the foaling was imminent. Amanda's sapphire eyes sparkled, and their gazes locked on each other. Seth nodded. "It's almost time."

A slight nicker from Rosa gave Seth pause. Many mares preferred to give birth to their foals in solitude, but Rosa shared a bond with Grandpa Martin, who wouldn't budge from his spot. Still, she wasn't close to Amanda. He motioned toward her, and they moved to a place where they could see Rosa, but she couldn't see them.

In the darkened stable, Rosa lay on her side, and Seth reached for Amanda's hand, reveling in the warm comfort. Minutes later, Rosa's foal made its appearance, and Amanda squeezed his hand. They continued their silent vigil while Rosa cleaned up her foal, a fine-looking colt. That familiar awe in seeing the foal wobble before standing for the first time swept over Seth.

This time, though, there was something different.

Amanda was by his side.

That made this morning's struggles seem manageable. Having her near him reassured his innermost core. When she was nearby, he felt like everything would work out for the best. Her mere presence strengthened his commitment to face the ranch's challenges, one at a time.

His phone vibrated. He released her hand and excused himself. Once outside, he read the text from one of his best housekeepers. Even though he understood Shaylynne had to leave to check out her daughter from school, that meant they were that much more shorthanded. He acknowledged the text with a reply to keep him updated on Asia's not feeling well. He'd met the six-year-old at the last employee picnic lunch, and the child was a sweetheart.

He pocketed his phone and accepted the responsibility of a late shift. First up was swinging by the barn, the location for tomorrow night's dinner and cowboy entertainment show. Doing a quick inventory would show him if any extra supplies were needed. Red, white and blue bunting. Check. Centerpieces. Check. Microphones and riser. Check. A popular country music singer would perform his original tunes on his guitar, and the town's clogging quartet would provide a demonstration and offer a lesson to anyone wanting to try the technique. After a rich steak dinner or tasty pasta alternative, there would be a square dance. The guests would promenade around the decorated barn, learning the terms and hopefully having a laugh while they tried something new. The affair was the culmination of the week's events. Many guests cited the evening as the reason they'd returned to the Lazy River.

Amanda joined him. "That was beautiful. Rosa did great." He turned and met her gaze, the morning sun lighting her face, her inner glow matching this outer one. "Thank you."

His phone buzzed with another text.

The peaceful aura from the foal's birth dissipated like that.

"I've got to go," he said.

She reached out and held him in place. "If it's something to do with the duck derby, maybe the two of us can handle it together? Like earlier." This ranch was all he'd ever wanted for so long, yet now he wanted more, like a certain marketing professional who seemed to always know the right things to say.

"It could be about the ducks. I'm sure they'll have something to say about it if it is. Sure, come with me."

Seth slipped his hand into his pocket for his phone, found it, and also found a hole. His heart froze, and he felt around for the silver dollar that was gone.

He couldn't have lost it. Anything but that. He quickly checked his other pockets and his shirt pocket.

"Seth, what's wrong?" Amanda's voice was full of concern.

"I have a hole in my pocket."

"Oh-kay." She drew out the syllables enough that Seth finally heard a faint trace of a Texas accent. "I wouldn't have pegged you as a person who'd be concerned about that, but I'm sure someone can mend it."

"That's not the real problem." Where had he been this morning? He groaned. Where hadn't he been? The horse pasture. The pond. The setup for the derby. Each cabin. His shoulders slumped. The chances of him finding the silver dollar were slim at best.

"Then what's going on?" The same concern that laced her voice showed on her face, more than he'd expect from a casual guest or even the other employees.

Could she be starting to care for him, too?

As much as he wanted to ignore it, there was something special between them. If he shared how important the silver dollar was to him, together they could cover more ground, especially since he had a maid shift to tackle, a dog wedding to officiate barn to decorate and a ranch to manage.

Yet he had to search for the last present his father ever gave him.

Another wave of panic washed over him before her cool collectedness reassured him. She might be able to manage the impossible and find the coin in a haystack.

"I lost my silver dollar from the year I was born," he told her. She kept her gaze focused on him, a rapt listener who was hanging on for more of an explanation. "It was a present from my father on my tenth birthday. He died a few months later."

"We'll find it." The huskiness in her voice echoed the determination in her eyes.

She started for the stable, but he shook his head.

"It couldn't be in there. I've been all over the ranch today, and it would have fallen out before now." On a normal day, he rubbed that coin at least twenty times.

Then again, none of his days had been normal since Amanda arrived.

"We won't know until we look." She sent a confident grin, and he put his finger on what she brought back to his life: hope. "Besides, if it's not there, you'll have one less place to search later."

There was something about pointing out the obvious that anchored him.

He brought his finger to his lips. "We have to be quiet, though. Rosa and her foal."

"It'll be like we're not even there." She made a tiptoe gesture with her fingers, making it easy to imagine her as a precious little girl, sneaking into the living room on Christmas morning.

Would her daughter have her blue eyes?

True to her word, she walked with stealth and paused, pointing toward a sleeping Grandpa Martin, his snoring snuffles soft enough so as not to disturb Rosa and the colt. Despite his despair at losing his silver dollar, Seth managed a smile at the peaceful sight before him. A glance at the mare and colt bonding in the stall lessened the deep ache within him. The ranch endured, and somehow so would he.

Amanda crept onto all fours like one of the stable cats and whipped out her phone, turning on the flashlight. No silver glint, and the loss crashed down on him. If it had fallen out of his pocket by the pond, it could get swept into the water or someone might find it tomorrow and keep it without knowing its sentimental value.

He lowered himself next to her and brushed her hand. Something stirred in him, and he tamped down the unwanted feeling.

But his grandmother had instilled manners in him, and he owed Amanda something, even only if a mere word, for her presence. She didn't have to be here, yet she was on her hands and knees looking for the coin.

"Thanks." He mouthed the word so as not to disturb his grandfather or the horses before motioning to the exit. "Ready to go?"

She gasped, and hope flickered in him. She waved the silver dollar under his nose and jumped up, heading for the exit.

Once they were outside, she clutched his silver dollar with a hint of victory in her eyes. "Do I get a finder's fee?"

One thing came to mind. Her lips looked so pink, like a breath of spring. What would it be like to kiss her? She looked so happy and carefree, the same way he felt on the inside at this moment. Joy poured out of him. He picked her up and twirled her in a circle. She squealed. As the sound registered, so too did his good sense return. He lowered her to the ground. Kissing her would have been a huge mistake. They had to work together for the good of the ranch. He wouldn't do anything to jeopardize its future, his grandparents' livelihood, especially when he wanted to remain in Grandma Bridget's good graces now that she'd forgiven him.

"Thank you." He held out his hand. "I'm in your debt."

"I was thinking of something else for a finder's fee." She was flushed, and her breath came out in short spurts.

Her face was close to his, those pink lips still tantalizingly plump and kissable. *Grandma Bridget, Grandma Bridget, Grandma Bridget.* The third time was the charm, and Seth could think more clearly again. "I could see if Ingrid could whip you up a goodbye package of sweets."

Instantly, her face fell. "That wasn't what I had in mind," she said.

Had she wanted him to kiss her? But one kiss might lead to another, and he knew himself. He'd fall for her, and this time, his heart might never recover. Besides, he was awful at keeping secrets. The whole guilt thing. He'd tell her everything about his life and the ranch, including the mortgage, and that would make everything awkward between them. And she was the person who could help bring guests back to the ranch.

He searched for something light, something to restore the easy rapport of that first truck ride and a few minutes ago while they awaited the colt's birth. "How about I promise I won't sing tomorrow night? That's a favor to everyone."

"Hmm. I think this deserves something more than that." She squinted at the coin and looked at him. "You're thirty-three?"

He held out his hand, and she deposited the coin into his palm, the jolt from the contact almost sizzling. "Thirty-two. My birthday's in November. I wanted a saddle and didn't appreciate this at the time. Now I wouldn't trade the silver dollar for anything."

"I can see why you value it."

Seth was about to return the coin to his jeans when he remembered the hole that caused the problem and deposited it in his shirt pocket instead. "How about a dance tomorrow night?"

He blurted it out before he could stop himself. Too late to take it back now. He offered his hand to seal the deal.

"Ooh. There's dancing tomorrow night? Sami will be beside herself." She jerked her hand back before they could shake on the bargain. "Ask my sister to dance with you. That's my finder's fee."

With her striking looks, Sami would have no problem attracting men to dance with her. While Sami was classically beautiful, there was something about Amanda, though, that impacted him deep down to his soul. Her inner glow and composure appealed to him in a way Sami didn't.

"I'll ask Sami for a whirl around the floor, but only after we've already shared a dance." He kept his hand outstretched.

She considered his offer and accepted his hand. "I just want to make sure Sami doesn't feel left out."

He motioned toward the barn. "If I don't decorate that space, there won't be a cowboy dinner tomorrow night."

Decorating first, and then he'd cover Shaylynne's shift in housekeeping before he supervised the finishing touches for the canine nuptials. He strode in the direction of the barn and found Amanda by his side, matching his pace. "Since I'll be taking pictures, I'll help. That way, it'll be as photogenic as possible."

A dog wedding, a duck derby and the famous cowboy dance in twenty-four hours. How would he get everything done in time? One look at Amanda, and he knew. It was about having fun on the journey as much as the destination itself.

Once in the barn, they agreed that Amanda would work on the table decorations while he strung the fairy lights. He started climbing the rungs and glanced at Amanda.

If he'd experienced a whirlwind of emotion when he believed his silver dollar was lost forever, how would he feel if she left Violet Ridge without knowing he was beginning to fall for her?

WITH THE BARN decorated and the social media accounts for her clients updated, Amanda had the rest of her Friday afternoon free to attend the big wedding. It wasn't every day one went to such an event. She'd take photographs and capture the moment for the owners and for future publicity campaigns. She changed into a cute pink shirt paired with her best jeans but kept her cowboy boots on and took the path that led to the paddock. Rosa and her foal had bonded well enough for Seth and Buck to lead the horseback excursion that would deliver the guests to the special location chosen by the dog owners for the ceremony. She had tried to convince Sami to join her, but Sami shooed her away, insisting she'd already made other plans.

That gave Amanda pause. What could Sami be doing by herself at the ranch that superseded a dog wedding? Part of her was hurt it didn't involve her. *Stop that, Amanda.* So many years of failed communication were finally at an end. Being in the same place now was a bridge to a more hopeful future. Besides, she'd be sharing this time with Seth.

With that new attitude, Amanda approached the

paddock where a group of saddle horses waited for their riders.

"This is even better than a scavenger hunt," Trevor said before mounting his horse.

"I'm getting pictures for my little girl." Michelle, one of the four *M*'s, announced. She snapped several photos with her phone and smiled at the dogs snuggled alongside their owners, who were now astride their horses. "That is the cutest veil."

Amanda did have to admit the dogs looked sweet. Even from this vantage point, Romeo's little bow tie was adorable, and Juliet's delicate lace veil was sitting between her perky ears.

Brian and Colleen Carr were near Buck, who was helping Mabel mount a roan mare.

Once she was upright, Mabel patted the mare's mane. "Hi, Strawberry. We're going to be best friends, and you get to be a guest at a wedding. I love my honeymoon!"

Amanda smiled at Mabel's exuberance while Buck guided Brian and Colleen to their respective horses. She approached Seth, who stood next to a gorgeous flaxen chestnut Tennessee walking horse with a star of white on her forehead.

"This is Cybill," he said, holding out the reins to Amanda. "From what you said about Roxie, I thought you two would be a good match."

Seth remembered. Her heart swelled at his gesture almost as much as at the sight of Cybill standing there as if impatient to be on the trail ride already. On a day like this with the sweet smell of pines and a blue sky that went on forever, Amanda understood why Cybill wanted to be underway.

"I thought you'd be cleaning cabins," she said.

"Shaylynne arranged for someone to cover her shift. Good thing, too, as I'm the officiant of this shindig."

She accepted the reins from Seth and mounted the beautiful horse, murmuring sweet nothings to her.

After everyone was ready, Buck and Seth led the group toward the mountains. As they climbed in elevation, Amanda gripped the thick leather of the reins and adjusted her weight in the saddle, discovering Cybill's mannerisms. When the Tennessee walking horse finally relaxed her ears and lowered her head, Amanda knew they were bonding. Seth nudged his mustang, Mocha, into position, riding alongside her. "You and Cybill seem to have hit it off."

"Cybill's about nearly perfect." The only thing that would have made her perfect was riding the Tennessee walking horse daily.

"This was a no-brainer when I was assigning horses to the riders." That type of attention to detail and his guests' comfort was as much a part of him as those charcoal flecks in his deep brown eyes.

Amanda studied Seth, who seemed as if he was one with Mocha, perfectly at ease on the trail.

She turned her concentration back to Cybill and flicked the reins. The horse didn't need a second command and started galloping. The soft breeze caressed Amanda's cheeks. She felt a peace unknown since riding Roxie. No matter her schedule in the future, she had to make time for this. Even better she'd ask Sami to join her for an afternoon of sisterly horseback riding.

Around the one-hour mark, Buck and Seth guided the horses into a sheltered alcove. Everyone dismounted and tethered the animals to the nearby rail. The watering trough provided welcome respite for the horses.

At last, it was time for the ceremony. Everyone gathered while Seth took his place beneath a bower of flowers, perfect for such an occasion. Buck produced his phone and soon strains of classical music filled the air. Romeo's owner escorted the Pomeranian down the makeshift aisle with everyone grinning and taking pictures. Then his wife escorted Juliet down the aisle, the dog seemingly lapping up the attention.

Amanda captured the moment. Once Seth declared the couple to be doggy mates for life, the crowd burst into applause.

Seth and Buck passed out snacks and slices of wedding cake to the guests and they mingled and relaxed.

Seth made his way toward her, a slight smudge of dirt on his jean cuffs and a matching one on his shirt. Always rumpled, he was living proof of how much he loved being outdoors.

He offered her a choice of a protein bar or a bag of trail mix to go along with the slice of vanilla cake with lemon frosting. Amanda selected the latter and thanked him. After they enjoyed their cake, she unzipped the bag and selected some peanuts. "This ride with Cybill is the highlight of my trip so far, along with Rosa's foal. You did a great job today. Five stars. Would highly recommend."

Seth placed the rest of the snacks into the satchel on Mocha's saddle. "Aw, shucks. So much for bestowing that honor on me."

She laughed. Already it was hard to believe they'd gotten off to such a bad start. He'd ride an extra mile for any of the guests at the ranch, especially her. "Of course, I'm looking forward to the duck derby, even if the real ducks are rather upset about their turf being invaded. Guess I'm like you in that animals will win every time. You'll have to take a back seat to them."

Seth plopped onto the picnic blanket with a thud. "I will accept my defeat with more grace than my attempt at sitting."

"You give up too easily." She scoffed and plucked out some of the raisins. Their sweetness was the perfect contrast to the peanuts' saltiness. "Besides, you have two more days to top Romeo and Juliet, not to mention Cybill and Rosa."

"They set a pretty high benchmark." Seth peeled back the paper surrounding his protein bar.

"So do you." Amanda's breath caught at her admission.

"I'm just your family for the week."

A reminder that this was the vacation weaving its romantic spell, not her. She sought out anything that might salvage her heart before she lost it to the winsome cowboy. That wasn't a difficult task considering the beauty all around her: the mountains standing guard, the tops of the aspens swaying in the slight breeze, the horses at the rail. Nearby a creek lent a peaceful melody to the buzzing conversations around them.

"I can't imagine seeing this every day. No wonder you don't even want to venture to Violet Ridge unless you need to do so."

"Anything not to miss the great outdoors. Even a wedding for dogs."

She chuckled. "I'm glad I got those photos. Everybody had a good time, even the scavenger hunt guests. You might want to consider incorporating a family version of that type of activity, by the way. And I hope the duck derby stays here from now on. That's a classic that'll make my marketing job so much easier."

Going home with her heart intact began with steering the conversation back to business and away from anything personal that would appeal to her romantic nature. She launched into an explanation of her social media posts and press releases for the duck derby. Seth reached for her hand until she stopped talking and looked at him.

She shouldn't have done that. Right now he was the epitome of the caring cowboy with his Stetson tilted at an angle, his eyes warm and compassionate. You didn't have to hang around Seth for long to know that was his core nature. He cared for his family and everyone on the ranch, dogs and horses alike.

She was a goner.

"You don't have to defend yourself. I know how hard you've been working." Seth chewed a bite of his protein bar. "You're more popular with the staff than I am."

"Don't sell yourself short." Seth treated his employees with respect, same as Martin and Bridget, and was held in high esteem. "They like you."

"You should have met my father." Seth finished his protein bar in two bites. "Everyone on the ranch loved him."

"You're also quite special. But what happened to him and your mother?" Amanda wanted to know that and so much more about Seth. "You were really young when he died."

Seth pulled the silver dollar out of his shirt pocket. "I was ten." He regarded the coin with a wistful smile and then carefully returned it to his pocket. "A few months after my birthday, Jase came down with a cold or something. Mom and Dad arranged for the rest of us to stay with Grandma and Grandpa for the night. They were heading home when they swerved to avoid an animal. Jase was the only survivor."

As a boy, he'd suffered a loss of unimaginable consequence. No wonder he found solace in this ranch, the only home he'd ever known. That was what she wanted. A home of her own. Growing up with parents who moved residences more often than she celebrated her birthday, she craved that type of solidity, a haven of rest when everything was at its worst.

"Is that why Jase left the ranch?" An accident of that magnitude impacted each Virtue sibling, but being in the car would explain why Jase wanted to move away from the area.

Seth nodded, a look of admiration filling those brown orbs. "The three of us are still waiting for Jase to realize that."

"Have you talked to Jase about it?" Amanda asked. "Is there any chance he'll return to Violet Ridge?"

Seth jammed the wrapper into his jeans pocket. "Jase moved to Denver and loves his job." His shoulders stiffened, and his brown eyes darkened to black like a cloud blocking out the sun.

"I'm sorry I pressed the issue."

"Actually, I was thinking of someone else who worked at the ranch and left anyway."

The hairs on the back of her neck prickled in

something that almost felt like jealousy, which was preposterous considering she and Seth weren't a couple.

"Who?" To her dismay, her voice came out like a chirp.

He faced Amanda, a sigh written over his expressive features. "A couple of years ago, I fell in love with a fellow employee. I thought Felicity loved this ranch as much as I did, but she loved Wyoming more. She moved back home and married someone else."

No wonder he guarded himself around her. At first she believed he was protecting his grandparents, which he was, but now she knew. He was preserving his heart from harm.

"Did you consider moving to Wyoming to live with her?" She finished the rest of her trail mix, the chocolate chips tasting bittersweet since she already knew the answer.

"Everything I love is here. This land. The horses. My family." He glanced over his shoulder at the surrounding scenery. "How could I ever leave?"

Her stomach sank. Sparks without fuel were bound to dim and fade away. Whatever was happening between them didn't have anything substantial behind it. That thought brought a deep ache inside her. She popped up and handed him the empty Ziploc bag.

"I can't blame you." Their fingers brushed each other, a zap of energy flowing between them. She hurried and cut off any contact before either could acknowledge what was happening. "The dude ranch is special just the way it is. Embrace that."

The dogs yipped, a sign it was time to go back. Others started rising, and the horses nickered as though they also sensed they were once again about to feel the ground move under their hooves. Amanda fed Cybill a carrot before Seth helped her mount. She held the reins so she could feel something solid under her shaking fingers. Cybill gave a slight whinny as if to make sure Amanda was okay.

She patted Cybill's flank. "This could have been the beginning of a beautiful friendship."

At least she had the satisfaction of this lovely day and an unforgettable event with more in the waiting before she was set to head back home.

It would be easy to just let herself be carried away, allowing the present dictate her future. As long as she kept her eyes on what she had in Phoenix, though, she could savor this experience, then move forward.

As if life was ever that simple.

CHAPTER TEN

Saturday

SETH REELED AT all of the last-minute snags for the Ducks for Dogs Derby. The parking lot near the front gate was full, and he'd had to designate an area for overflow. All of the ranch's UTVs were now in use shuttling attendees to the drop-off point at the lodge. Seth must have talked to every resident in Violet Ridge and quite a number of tourists. Every time he had spotted Amanda, she was heading in the other direction taking photographs of the preparations and chatting to people.

His walkie-talkie squawked with one of the volunteers requesting his immediate presence where the food trucks were congregating.

Seth rushed toward that meadow and stopped short. Winnie the goat was chewing contentedly in the spot where one of the trucks was set to park. There was only that space left.

"Every time I approach her, she bleats and paws the ground," the volunteer said.

Seth headed to the food truck, and the driver

rolled down the window. "Do you happen to have a carrot and possibly a length of rope?"

"Sorry. We sell snow cones." The driver shrugged.

Seth searched out the trucks already parked and hurried to the one featuring vegetarian offerings. After procuring the necessary items, he approached Winnie, who chomped on the carrot while he formed a slipknot and attached the rope.

He led Winnie away and waved at the snow cone driver. Once in her pen, Winnie seemed more content away from the noise and people. Seth double-checked and made sure the fence was secure before he rejoined the crowd.

Energy buzzed around him. Tents with children's face painting and games occupied space near the pond. Long lines greeted him everywhere he looked with lots of people queued for buying tickets for the ducks, while others checked out the sponsors' baskets or the silent auction items.

Seth patted his phone, which now contained four new employment applications. Later tonight after the cowboy dinner and entertainment show, he'd review them with his grandparents and schedule interviews for Friday afternoon.

Amanda's publicity pushes seemed to have brought results.

As he scanned the area, he saw everyone but Amanda. Over by the canoe shelter was the town's former mayor, Zelda Baker, always easy to spot with her bright green pixie cut. Zelda had been one of the first arrivals this morning, lending a hand to assemble the game booths. She stood next to her identical twin sister, Nelda, who wore her silver hair in a long braid. He still remembered Nelda babysitting him and his three siblings on rare occasions. They heralded him and approached.

"This might be the best duck derby yet. The animal shelter should exceed its fundraising goal from the looks of it," Zelda said, conveying her admiration for the event's success.

Nelda tugged on her sister's arm. "Come on. I saw the baskets for the winners. The owner of the rubber duck that comes first wins front row tickets for the Evalynne concert taking place at the Irwin Arena on July Fourth! I want to buy extra ducks before my shift at the ring toss booth."

Zelda before she followed her sister to join the long line to buy a duck.

As hard as he tried, he still couldn't find Amanda. Instead, he located Aspen, his rambunctious nephew, spending time with his stepfather, Ben, while Daisy was in the snow cone line with her two daughters. As always, his niece Lily's nose was stuck in a book. She was the spitting image of her uncle Crosby.

Seth moved from person to person, murmuring greetings and other pleasantries, still on the lookout for Amanda. Had he said something to scare her away? Yesterday he'd come close to kissing her on two separate occasions.

What he was starting to feel for her went deeper than surface stuff like shared likes and dislikes. She was the calm to his constant motion, the rock behind his being pulled in so many directions. Was all of that enough to translate into a forever type of relationship, the same as his parents and grandparents had? Not only were his grandparents close to marking their sixtieth wedding anniversary, but they'd also survived the immeasurable loss of their son and daughter-in-law in one fell swoop, becoming guardians to their four grandchildren.

But pouring the foundation for love, something as scary and exciting as riding a bucking bull, required patience and attention. Living in the same area was a prerequisite as far as he was concerned, and Amanda wasn't staying.

How long would it take for his heart to finally receive that message?

After a mere week with her, his world was topsy-turvy, the spark between them close to combusting. When he'd faced himself in the mirror this morning, he'd combed his hair and trimmed his beard. He'd even donned his best flannel shirt and jeans. She made him want to look a little nicer, do a little better.

Stop it, Seth.

There was no use dwelling on what could never be.

Not with that attitude, he couldn't. If he didn't say something before Amanda departed, he'd never know if he had lost something even more precious than his silver dollar. The way she'd told him he was special yesterday? There was something between them. He was sure of it.

"Mr. Virtue! Well done." Seth stilled as he recognized that voice. It belonged to Killian Wilshire, the CEO of the company behind the fancy new Rocky Valley Guest Ranch nearby.

Seth turned and faced the only person here in a charcoal black suit and red power tie. Fit and tanned, Wilshire could pass for a man in his fifties although his white hair and fine crinkles around his eyes were proof he was older.

"Mr. Wilshire." Seth mimicked the man's more formal tone. "Welcome to the Lazy River. I didn't take you for someone who would want to see rubber duckies race to the finish line."

"I'm not." Wilshire's gaze wandered to the mountains before settling on the boat shed, which needed repairs and a good pressure washing. "I'm here with an offer on this property. This site would be a nice complement to my hotel. I can see my name and brand on top of that front gate."

"Sorry you came all this way for nothing, but the Lazy River's not for sale." Even though he was only the manager, Seth had no trouble speaking for his grandparents about this.

"My sources at the bank say this is the prime time to entertain an offer." Wilshire reached into his inner suit pocket and pulled out a card. "Here's my initial bid along with my direct number."

Seth resisted the urge to tear up the card. "Don't hold your breath." Seth pocketed the offer next to his silver dollar. "I won't be calling."

"Talk it over with your grandparents. This figure will help with future medical bills and provide nest eggs to you and your siblings. You could own your ranch instead of managing this one." Wilshire tapped his black loafer on the ground.

Seth already knew the four Virtue siblings would own this ranch together someday, a far-off someday, he hoped. "Thanks, but no thanks."

He reached in his pocket to return the card to Wilshire, but the odious man had already taken his leave. Seth rubbed his beard, the bristles thick and coarse. Should he convey Wilshire's offer to his grandparents and risk ruining their day? Or should he warn them to stay away from Wilshire? Grandma Bridget was too perceptive for the latter. She'd want to know why, and Seth wasn't about to keep anything of this magnitude from her again.

No matter what, though, he intended to talk to Mateo on Monday and find out if the new bank manager was the source who revealed insider information to Wilshire. While Seth didn't want to believe his high school friend would do something like that, he wanted the confirmation for himself.

His gaze landed on his grandmother approaching her great-grandchildren, all the triplets launching themselves at her side. Daisy's children had come through so much that had happened in their short lives, but their mother's newfound happiness had helped them blossom over the past year. Rosie, Aspen and Lily now had two families to guide and care for them. The love radiated off the group, and Seth smiled despite the turmoil within him.

"That's a pretty sight, isn't it?" Coming from behind, his grandfather surprised Seth. "Bridge and the triplets always bring me joy. So does seeing all these families having a happy time. The animal shelter will do a lot of good work with the proceeds."

Grandpa Martin's eyes softened the way they always did when he called his wife by his special nickname for her.

"Not everyone here today has a worthy motive." As much as it pained Seth, he handed the card over to his grandfather. "Wilshire made an offer on the ranch. Said you could help Daisy, Crosby and Jase with the money."

"We taught all of you to be self-sufficient. None of you need the money." Grandpa Martin ripped the card in half. "This is your home. All of you need this place, even Jase."

Seth scuffed the ground with his boot. "I already told Wilshire the answer was no."

"Good. I promised change was coming, but that's not what I meant. Put Wilshire out of your mind and enjoy the day with someone special."

Grandpa Martin's gaze went to the line near the food truck. "Go have a snow cone."

Seth's attention wandered to the line and caught sight of Amanda, a vision in a bright yellow sundress and white sweater paired with cowboy boots. His heart did a somersault, and he tipped his hat in his grandfather's direction. "Don't mind if I do."

On the way toward the snow cone truck, he passed the Carr family. Mabel insisted on giving him a hug and telling him all about her morning.

"This is the best day!" Mabel shouted with glee. "And this might be the bestest honeymoon ever!"

"I agree, but I'm sure Seth is busy and has other people to see." Mabel's stepmother, Colleen, placed her hand on Mabel's shoulder.

Mabel pouted before beaming. "We can come back next year, right? I have to find out if Strawberry missed me."

Colleen shared a smile with Brian, then faced Seth. "We've already decided we're coming back since the atmosphere and amenities played such an instrumental part of bringing the three of us together as a family. This place will always mean the world to us." She hugged Mabel and tweaked her chin. "Come on, Mabel. Let's go buy a rubber duckie."

Family atmosphere. Having Colleen boast about that seemed somewhat ironic as his four siblings were on such different paths. When all was said and done, the ranch wasn't enough to bind his family together. With a sigh, Seth watched the Carrs walk away before searching for Amanda, but she was nowhere in sight.

Time was running out for him to tell her that he was beginning to care for her. Despite his grandfather's command, Seth couldn't help but think about Wilshire's offer. Selling the ranch would give him a fresh start, maybe even in another state. After all, there was land for sale in Arizona.

Stop it, Seth. This is your home. It's where you belong.

Over the years, his grandfather had done what was best for their home and his family. With the recent exception of not informing Grandma Bridget about the mortgage, his grandfather was a wise man. It was time to listen to Grandpa Martin and enjoy this day.

SETH VIRTUE WAS a hard man to pin down. Every time her gaze had honed in on him, he was talking to someone. Still, something about him seemed different today, but what? She caught her breath and stopped short of splattering her precious cargo on the ground. There was nary a trace of any dirt on the man's clothes, nor any lost buttons. His red plaid shirt was tucked into a pair of jeans with a gold rodeo belt buckle, and his beard was neatly trimmed. Even his thick, shaggy brown hair was combed.

She wasn't sure which was better, the slightly off-kilter cowboy or the cleaned-up version. Both sides of him were equally devastating.

Had he done that for the crowds?

Or for her?

She brushed that aside, the delivery of what she held in her hands of utmost urgency. He was finally within arm's reach, and she closed the gap before he got away again.

"Root beer or strawberry lemon?" Amanda presented two snow cones, each starting to melt. "Eating both would give me a stomachache."

"I'd hate for the prettiest woman here to be sick on my account." Her stomach did a funny flip at him calling her pretty. "I'm good with whatever."

That was the Seth she was getting to know. Sacrificing what he wanted for others. He deserved more than that. She handed him the root beer snow cone. "You drank two glasses at Brewer Brothers so I guessed this was your favorite."

"You guessed correctly." He reassured her with a wink, and she handed over that one.

She licked the strawberry syrup dripping off the paper rim. "A beautiful day and a container full of rubber ducks about to be dumped into the pond. What could be better?"

He munched on the shaved ice and gazed out at the pond ripples. "A long horse ride without all these people around. That's my idea of perfection."

That was her perfect vacation day, too, except

he got to live that every day. She slurped more of the sweet syrup. "Followed by an evening in the library with Hap and Trixie, knitting with Grandma Bridget."

"While I tip my hat over my eyes for a catnap." He glanced around at the crowd and began walking to the edge of the pond, motioning for her to join him. "Thank you for raising awareness of the event. The folks at the animal shelter are over the moon at how many people showed up and bought ducks for the derby."

They found a spot, perfect for two, and she tried to hide her cheeks, warm at his compliment, from him. "Just doing my job."

"You're being too modest again." Seth slurped the root beer liquid. "Why?"

She transferred her gaze to the pond, the warm breeze casting ripples where the rubber duckies would soon be floating. "I make my living at bringing the best out in the products or services I represent. I prefer to let the marketing speak for itself."

"How many hours did you work this week?" Root beer flavoring spurted out of the paper cone and beaded on his beard.

She handed him a napkin from the pocket of her short-sleeved white sweater. "I lost count."

"I thought this was your vacation, aside from working on our account." He blotted his beard with the napkin. "Why didn't your boss cover for you?"

Amanda outlined their different roles in the company. "We agreed to those terms when she hired me." Without a reference or any offers in her inbox. Those weeks of unemployment were too much like what she'd seen over the years from her father, and she'd jumped at Pamela's offer.

"Seems one-sided to me." Seth glanced in the direction of the stable. "I've done pretty much every job on this ranch, and I'd do any of them tomorrow if need be. If she owns the company, she should do the same."

She believed Seth for she'd seen him deliver towels to guests and then weed the flower beds.

"Every client and industry is different," Amanda explained. "Pamela excels at converting potential customers into permanent clients. You'll see when she arrives later next week."

The division of labor at the firm had been the same for three years. Amanda worked the back end while Pamela was the face of the company.

Fear crept to her toes at the thought of revealing why she'd been fired at her previous job to Seth. What if that changed the way he felt about her? The friendship she and Seth formed over the past week meant a great deal to her, especially after such a rocky beginning.

Truth be told, no one had ever made her toes curl the way Seth did.

Her stomach clenched. He confided in her about

Felicity; he deserved to know the truth about her greatest failure

Telling him about her past was a risk she had to take if he was a true friend. "The job I had before I worked for Pamela didn't end well."

"Anyone would be lucky to have you. You're industrious and creative. After today, I'm sure Ben would recommend the town hire you in a second. He's been diligent, trying to match the right people to opportunities to benefit Violet Ridge." He smiled while something close to admiration lit up his face.

She hoped he felt that same way in a few minutes. Having a crowd around gave her enough strength to confide in him. She inhaled and exhaled a deep breath. "At my former position, I was assigned an account with the owner's son. We became romantically involved but kept it a secret. We lost a major client, and Blake blamed me. He told his father I'd come on to him, urging him to use my ideas so I'd get a big promotion, none of which was true. His father confronted me and fired me. I asked a potential employer why they didn't hire me, and he said the company gave me a bad reference. Pamela was the only employer willing to give me a chance."

Getting fired had been too much like her father's constant job turnover for her liking. With every box she packed after the Blake debacle, she remembered the constant moves where she'd have to start at another school, never feeling like she was good enough to have friends or a home. For a while she even stopped trying, knowing they'd just move again in a few months.

Seth squished the paper cone, anger blazing in his eyes. This type of reaction was why she hadn't confided this to anyone, including Sami.

She gazed at the pond and nodded. "I understand if that changes the way you feel about Parkhouse Promotions." *And about me.*

He faced her with an incredulous look. "Of course it changes how I feel about Parkhouse Promotions."

Her hand was a sticky mess, and she wanted to clean up before packing to return to Phoenix. "I can't refund the money your grandfather paid up front to Pamela, but I'll pay back the fee you would have received if someone else had stayed in the cabin."

"What are you talking about?" Seth placed his hand on her arm. Despite how his opinion of her had changed, tingles still spread along her skin. Through all of her, really. "Pamela is taking advantage of you. You're incredible, and she knows it. I'll listen to the presentation, but I can tell you right now any future business we do with your firm will be conducted through you and not her."

His praise went straight from her ear to her heart. He found her incredible and pretty? Those chocolate flecks in his brown eyes grew darker, a signal he was telling the truth.

Maybe it was time she believed she was good enough for her job and deserved that raise and promotion.

And just maybe it was time to embrace the fun all around her. This ranch recaptured the joy of marketing for her. It was more than the ranch.

It was Seth.

With his hand still on her arm, she stepped toward him. Would the taste of root beer linger on his lips? How would it taste mingled with strawberry lemon?

A loud squeal of electric feedback reverberated through the sound system. She jumped, and he stepped away.

"Good afternoon. Welcome to the tenth annual Ducks for Dogs Derby!" The announcer directed everyone's attention to the platform where a thousand rubber ducks were about to be released into the pond.

Martin and Bridget Virtue joined Mayor Ben Irwin at the release lever. The countdown began, and the crowd shouted the final seconds until the three of them pulled the lever and did the honors. The rubber ducks cascaded out of the dumpster and splashed into the pond. Everyone cheered and clapped. They surfaced and floated toward the finish line, barriers guiding their way toward rodeo star Ty Darling, who was waiting on the other side of the pond to pluck out the first three to cross the finish line.

The electricity in the air compelled Amanda to squeeze Seth's hand. She managed a controlled breath, long enough to free her ticket from her sweater pocket. He laughed when he saw her clutching it. "Your chances of winning are a thousand to one."

"It's not about winning anything—it's about supporting a good cause." She stared at the numbers on the side of the blue ticket. "Did you buy a ticket?"

He shook his head. "It would look suspicious if the ranch manager won first prize."

"I see your point considering you own the ranch and all."

It was his turn for his cheeks to become ruddy through his beard. "It's my grandparents' ranch, not mine."

Suddenly, a real duck flapped its wings and splashed down right in the middle of the sea of rubber ducks. It quacked and shook off water from its wings with several of the rubber ducks flying every which way.

People laughed at the real duck's antics while others rooted the ducks on as they started approaching the finish line. Amanda cheered along with the rest.

Her gaze went around the crowd, picking out the guests getting into the spirit of the occasion.

She saw Kevin, Todd and Trevor near the edge of the pond, waving on the ducks, their excitement evident.

Before she could shout out a warning, Trevor slipped and fell into the water, sending up a large splash. Luckily the pond was very deep and Kevin and Todd fished their soaked friend out of the water with nearby bystanders checking on Trevor. Coughing, he wrung his shirt and waved to everyone, presumably to relieve any concern.

Finally, the ducks were close to the finish line, several bunched together. They all arrived at the same time and the rodeo star bolted into action, scooping the three rubber ducks closest to him.

"We love you, Ty!" his fans called out as the cowboy kept calm and handed the three winners to Mayor Ben, who joined him.

Before she could ask Seth to elaborate, the announcer spoke again over the intercom system. "It's time to check those tickets, folks!"

The announcer reeled off the number for third place. A shout of joy sounded.

"That's Jenny Olsen. She's a firefighter and has done first aid for us from time to time." Seth neared, and his breath tickled her cheek.

"I saw all the baskets. They had great prizes." Amanda tried to concentrate but found it hard when he was so close.

The crowd clapped, and the announcer launched into rattling off the next number.

"Congratulations." His voice startled her, and it was only then she realized she possessed the winning ticket.

One of the real ducks must have wanted to get in on the action, since it left the water, wiggled its bottom dry and plopped itself in front of her. Another one followed suit.

She and Seth laughed at the ducks' antics. She turned and gazed into his eyes. Her stomach flipped, not because her duck had come second, but because Seth was sharing this moment with her. She threw her arms around him and embraced him. He held her tight and she reveled in the joy of it. This felt like coming home on a cold night to a warm fire and a cozy blanket.

If she let herself, she could stay like this forever. If she let herself, she could fall for Seth. Who was she kidding? She was already falling for this cowboy who protected his family, and this ranch, with every fiber of his being.

Reluctantly, she broke the contact. "I'm going to claim my basket."

Amanda backed away until he grabbed her arm. "You were about to step in the pond. It might be a shortcut, but it's not worth the trouble." He pointed toward the path. "You'll stay drier if you take the longer way around. We've already had one person get wet today."

She blushed, embarrassed. "Yep."

Amanda walked toward the prize tent when

the announcer asked the crowd for a drum roll. She stopped as several people started trilling their tongues and tapping their thighs in response. The announcer read off the number of the first-place duck. There was silence as everyone waited.

Trevor, one of the scavenger hunt guests, raised his arm in the air and shouted, "The ticket's wet, same as me, but I won!"

The crowd cheered. Todd and Kevin patted their friend on the back, congratulating him.

Amanda turned, wanting to see Seth's reaction to the announcement. One of his nieces approached and launched herself into his arms for a hug.

He obliged and Amanda's heart went into overdrive. A cowboy hugging his niece? Priceless.

And she knew then that leaving the dude ranch next week was going to be near impossible.

CHAPTER ELEVEN

SETH HELPED THE crew take down the last of the derby tents and load the trucks. He raised the tailgate of the last vehicle and bid a farewell to the driver.

The fundraising event had been a rousing success, but his Saturday wasn't done. Tonight was the last gathering for this week's guests. The Cowboy Dinner and Entertainment Night was his grandmother's favorite amenity, ending with singing and dancing.

Seth made his way to the barn, wanting to check on the last details for the festivities. He was almost there when two of his maintenance workers, Nancy and Al, found him.

"There was an issue in the Blanketflower Cabin," Al said. "One of the guests reported the air conditioning wasn't running. We swapped the unit out, which meant we didn't have time to finish setting up the barn."

"If you and Nancy get the centerpieces, I'll take care of the rest." Seth slid the heavy barn doors open until sunlight flooded the interior. His breath caught at how much still needed doing. Chairs and tables were stacked against the wall, decorations needed to be hung and important last-minute touches applied.

This required backup. Could he call on Amanda again? Was he taking advantage? He hoped she wouldn't see it that way. Who better than Amanda to help him get things right? He texted her and she replied immediately that she'd be right there.

Quickly, Seth leaped into action.

This dinner might have to be scaled back. Would that be too bad? Losing some of the romantic fittings and fixtures wouldn't be the end of the world. Romance could happen wherever and whenever you least expected it. This morning was proof of that when he'd found romance with Amanda among the ducks and goats. Location didn't matter. Amanda made him happy and confident just by her being near. Holding her by the pond, everything seemed so right. The way she fit against him, the way she smelled so sweet, the way their heartbeats seemed in synch. It had taken all of his willpower to keep from kissing her, and it was a good thing. After the embrace, she looked horrified, so much so she almost fell into the pond.

This ranch needed her. Even if she only worked on the marketing in Arizona, he couldn't afford to mess up their business relationship. He sensed they were fast becoming friends, and even though he wanted more, he wouldn't do anything to ruin her job. She'd already been badly betrayed by her ex-boyfriend.

He shook himself out of his reverie and started snapping together the tiles for the portable dance floor when he heard someone clear their throat behind him.

"Need a little help, cowboy?" He turned and found Amanda at the doorway, sunlight illuminating her, a vision in a pink flannel shirt and worn jeans. She held a basket in hand as her gaze took in the messiness. "You texted at the perfect time. I was on my way to the lodge to look for you so we could open this together, and so I just took a detour."

Little did she know, thanks to a detour, his heart was now on a different path than a mere week ago. Falling for someone else who didn't live in Violet Ridge wasn't how he expected to spend this week, but the best-laid plans...

Maybe he wasn't falling for her. Maybe she was only waking him up to the possibility of love in the future. Amanda neared, close enough for him to see her slightly damp blond hair, a sign of a recent shower. Her jasmine perfume pierced his senses. The same spring scent had hung in the air whenever his mother threw open the windows, letting in the scent of the garden in full bloom next to the house, now sitting vacant on the other side of the property.

Face the truth, Seth. No pretense or excuses.

Just the plain, simple, hard facts. As much as he'd fought against it, he was falling for Amanda, and she was leaving in a few days.

She waved her hand in front of his face. "Earth to Seth. Do you have an extra set of gloves?" she asked. "Work first, then fun."

"I agree." He left and returned with a pair that would fit her hands.

She thanked him, and they got to work with him installing the dance floor and her setting up the tables and chairs. Every so often, she'd look up and tell a joke, stumbling over the punchline. Then she scrunched her nose at her delivery. He laughed anyway, simply enjoying her company. In kind, he relayed stories about Hap and Trixie, and she chuckled at their antics.

An hour passed in no time. The dance floor gleamed, and the tables were perfectly positioned. Soon, he was assembling the sound system, while she hung lanterns and dried corn husks in strategic locations. He stepped back and let the ambience sweep over him. The dank barn smell was gone, replaced by fresh mountain air and the faint whiff of jasmine. Tonight would go on as planned.

"I couldn't have done this without you." Seth smiled, then took a long swig of water.

"Of course you would have." Amanda followed suit and then nudged his side with her elbow. "It wouldn't have been as fun, though."

What would it be like if she lived here? Would

they have this much fun while he renovated the dude ranch and brought it into the current century with automatic gates and digital key cards? Was it fair of him to ask her to move to Violet Ridge when they'd only known each other for such a short time?

More questions popped into his mind. How would he feel if he didn't put up a fight this time? Perhaps long-distance dating was worth a try until they were both sure of their emotions.

Talk about putting the cart before the horse. He hadn't even told her he was developing feelings for her, and Amanda had given no indication she cared for him as anything more than a friend.

He decided to keep it light and reached for the basket. "What did you win?"

She ripped off the cellophane, a loud, crinkly noise filling the air. She peered into the basket. "Um, gift cards to downtown businesses. Rocky Mountain Chocolatiers. Lavender and Lace." She tapped her ears. "I'll buy a pair of Daisy's earrings."

"We sell those in the gift shop." He hadn't considered donating a gift card to the baskets. There was always next year.

Except Amanda wouldn't be here.

Tell her, Seth. Ask her on a date. See if she'd be willing to keep this going long-distance.

Amanda glanced around the barn. "Look at how well this place cleaned up when we worked together. Almost as nice as you looked today." Her cheeks grew pink, and his heart soared at her noticing his appearance.

"Thank you. We aim to please." He almost groaned at sounding so corny.

She smiled at him, and it was as if the dark cloud hovering over him dissipated and cleared to reveal the sun's bright rays. His collar tightened against his neck. They were alone. This was the perfect time to tell her about his growing affection.

She returned her attention to the basket, digging toward the bottom while he struggled to find the words to express what was inside him.

Here went nothing, and everything.

"This year's calendar and a pen from the bank." She spoke before he could, and the moment passed by once the bank's logo reminded him of the deep financial hole the ranch was in. He wasn't sure where he'd be a year from now. It would be unfair to ask her to tie herself to a sinking ship. She faced him, her eyebrows raised. "Why did you just sigh?"

"Did I?" he asked.

She reached for his hand and led him over to the hearth surrounding the old forge in the corner of the barn. They sat next to each other, their legs touching. He shivered with her so close. With little room separating them, his coherent thoughts went out the sliding doors.

"Sorry. I overstepped my bounds," she said.

He was right. She only thought of him as a client, and possibly a friend. Thank goodness, he hadn't made a fool of himself.

Then again, she'd also warned him before he had a tendency to assume. He wouldn't make that mistake now. "Why do you say that?" Seth asked.

"You shivered. Not exactly a sign you want me here." Her muscles tensed as if she was about to rise.

He hurried and placed his hand on her arm. "I want you here. You're exactly where you should be."

Tension coated the air between them, and she stilled. Her lips were so pink and kissable. He moved near her when she lost her balance and fell off the hearth, landing with a thud on the dirt.

"Oof." The groan turned to a wry chuckle after she regained her balance and sat next to him again. She brushed away his concerns while wiping dirt off her jeans. "I'm fine. It's just my ego that's bruised."

If anyone could understand a bruised ego, he could. "That seems to be the case for everyone this week."

"How so?" She reached for his hand, and he tucked his fingers into hers. It was almost as though her inner calm flowed out of her and into him, buoying his spirits from even this, the smallest of gestures. "Does this have to do with the bank? That was your errand before we met Crosby for lunch, wasn't it?"

He nodded and considered whether he'd be breaking any family confidences if he told her everything. She'd opened up to him at the pond, and so he decided to do the same.

"Your marketing campaign is more important than ever. There's a mortgage on the ranch. Our coffers are dry since we haven't been booked solid since Wilshire opened his guest ranch." He scuffed the ground with his boot. "There's no money for anything until your marketing campaign takes effect."

"And if we're a bust, you won't be able to fill those cabins." She finished his thought for him.

"Today's duck derby was a success. People heard about it thanks to you." He patted his pocket, his phone nestled above his silver dollar. "And I have four new employee applications."

She cheered and threw her arms around him, that jasmine scent twisting his chest into a tight vise. "Little steps." Her voice was a breathy caress against his skin. "I'll do my best to bring back former customers and draw in new guests."

That almost sounded like a promise. Seth held her, the emotion running through him foreign and new. He'd never felt like this before. Here went nothing.

Commotion outside the barn doors caught his ear, and he jumped to his feet. Whistling, Ingrid pushed a cart with the floral centerpieces inside the barn, Hap and Trixie at her heels. "Nancy and Al said you were ready for me to deliver these."

Hurrying to help, Seth reached for the handle and pushed it to the first table.

He caught sight of Amanda, her cheeks flushed, scooping everything back into her basket.

"Tonight." She mouthed the single word toward him, the air thick with anticipation. She said something to Ingrid and then exited, basket in hand.

Seth stood there, and Trixie nudged his hand. "How do I tell her I'll miss her?" he asked the dog, who had no answers.

Instead, Seth helped Ingrid while he tried to muster an answer of his own.

AMANDA CARRIED THE basket on the trail back to the Bluebell Cabin, her mind preoccupied with everything that had happened in the barn. Had Seth been about to kiss her? Or had she been about to kiss Seth?

That wasn't the only charged moment between them today. Earlier at the derby, she thought they were finally going to take the plunge and kiss. Instead, she'd almost ended up taking a swim, same as Trevor.

Lost in thought, Amanda found herself at the pond, having overshot the cabin by a good half mile. Shaking off her reverie, she ventured over to a nearby bench and placed the basket on the ground. She stretched her arms when her phone vibrated with an incoming text.

She gasped. The house was hers! Even though it was Saturday, her real estate agent wanted to let her know right away the owners had accepted her counteroffer. Amanda waited for something inside of her to burst from the good news. Instead, there was nothing. She caught sight of the sun's rays rippling along the pond's surface and considered the friendships she'd made over the past week. When she presented her ticket to claim her basket, Ben and Daisy had congratulated her by name. Their genuine smiles had brought her a joy she usually only felt when she was riding or deep in a new marketing campaign.

You're exactly where you should be. Seth's words came back to her. Did he mean her location at that exact moment? Or was he referring to a future in Violet Ridge?

"There you are!" Sami heralded her, and Amanda faced her beaming sister. "I've had the best day, and I've been looking for you to tell you all about it."

"Where else would I be?" Amanda cringed as a sisterly relationship was exactly what she'd been missing in her life.

"With me. Like we are now."

If only there was a way to have a bond with Sami and a relationship with Seth at the same time.

Guilt at wanting to stay in Violet Ridge flitted through her. For years, she and Sami hadn't communicated with each other although it now seemed as though their mother was the major reason for that. Now that they were in touch with each other, she needed to be a good big sister. She needed to look out for Sami. "Luckily we found each other at the perfect time."

The white lie bit at her heels. A week ago would have been perfect. *Now?* She couldn't help but wish they both could have stayed in Violet Ridge longer.

"And now I have my sister back in my life." Sami came over and hugged Amanda.

"My real estate agent just texted. The owners accepted my offer. The house is mine!"

She expected another hug and kept waiting.

"In Phoenix?" Sami hesitated, a wobble in her voice, before a smile flickered and faded. "I'm happy for you, Amanda."

"Wait a minute." Amanda frowned. If she wanted to be a good big sister, she needed to focus on Sami. "Tell me about your day."

"I love it here." That Sami enthusiasm was back before a puzzled expression came over her. "Hold that thought, Amanda. I'll be right back."

What had captured Sami's attention? The only person coming their way was Crosby Virtue, his nose stuck in a book like always, his black glasses slightly askew. Sami made a beeline in his direction, and Amanda followed her sister.

"Excuse me." Sami approached Crosby and planted herself in his path. "Did you lose a pair of glasses today?"

Crosby glanced at her, his eyebrows furrowed. "How did you know?"

"I found them for you. How did you not notice you've had two pairs of glasses all day?" Sami plucked the second set off his head and handed them to him. She peeked underneath at the title of his book. "The movie was better."

"Thanks, I've been looking for these. I thought I'd lost them." Crosby pocketed the glasses and sent a withering glance in her sister's direction. "The book is always better."

Sami laughed off his statement. "Look at this gorgeous scenery. Green mountains, silver aspens, soaring hawks. Get your nose out of a book every once in a while. When was the last time you lived a little?"

He squinted and pushed his glasses up on the bridge of his nose. "Do you know you have a colorful smudge on your cheek? It looks like a butterfly." He pulled a bandanna from his pocket and extended it toward her. "I don't need it back."

"I painted faces at the duck derby. I'm keeping my temporary tattoo for tonight." She nudged his hand away. "There's going to be a dance for guests. Are you going?"

"I wasn't planning on it. This book is fascinating. It's about the history of the Violet Ridge Silver Mine." Crosby positioned the book under his arm and then shoved the bandanna in his pocket.

"Dances can be fascinating, too. When was the last time you went to one?" Sami opened her mouth as if to offer and then closed it again. "Then again you might have a wife or girlfriend for that."

It was Crosby's turn to laugh. "I'll stick to books. They're safer, too."

"But they don't return texts or hug you." Sami folded her arms and seemed to be waiting for his comeback.

It was fun to watch the fireworks between them, but Amanda decided introductions were in order. "Crosby, this is my sister, Sami Fleming. Sami, this is Seth's brother Crosby Virtue."

"Sami. That reminds me. I have a message for you." Crosby cleared his throat. "My grandmother is looking for you. She says she's ready for you now. Whatever that means."

"Thanks for letting me know. I hope you'll reconsider about the dance. It'd be fun to run into each other. Just you wait and see if I'm not more interesting than that book of yours, Crosby." Sami waved. "Amanda, let's catch up later." She disappeared from sight, and Crosby stood there as if shell-shocked. "Wow. Sami's nothing like you. She's a force of nature."

"Gee, thanks." Amanda already had one Virtue male mess with her emotions today. Now here was Crosby doing the same thing, but with different feelings.

He blushed a deep red. "I just meant you're calm and steady, the eye to Sami's hurricane. That's why you're perfect for Seth."

Now it was Amanda's turn to feel heat spread to her face. "Seth's not my boyfriend."

"Even I can see there's something between the two of you." Crosby opened his book once more. "I didn't know there was a movie version of this. I'll have to check it out."

He wandered down the path, and Amanda retrieved her basket from beside the bench.

She glanced at the pond, taking note of the ducks gliding along the surface. Whatever was going on between her and Seth had the potential to be deep and meaningful. Even Crosby, who seemed to always have his nose buried in books, recognized that there was something between her and Seth.

Now, Sami wasn't the only Fleming sister looking forward to the dance. Tonight, Amanda intended to get to the bottom of whatever was happening between herself and her cowboy before she signed any house-owning papers and the Lazy River Dude Ranch became another place in the rearview mirror like so many others in her past.

CHAPTER TWELVE

DUSK SPREAD OVER the valley, and Seth soaked in the deep orange and purple hues surrounding the mountains. Soon the stars would twinkle brighter than the fairy lights in the barn. He brought his hand to the metal clasp—a silver oval with the ranch's river logo—of his bolo tie, the one that had been his father's. He'd wanted to look his best tonight, donning a crisp linen shirt with his finest jeans. All seemed for naught as Amanda was nowhere in sight.

The musicians began tuning their fiddles and guitars, a sweet cacophony that echoed in the barn's rafters. Paper lanterns and the fairy twinkle lights gave it a festive air and showed off the parquet floor, burnished and ready for some serious square dancing. Mason jars wrapped with strings of tiny lights, holding sunflowers, provided added color. The barn looked better than it had in years, a reminder that a little effort went a long way.

Seth considered searching for Amanda. She'd missed the dinner, while Tiffany had shown him pictures of her cats and Kevin raved about the steak and potatoes au gratin. Seth had made the rounds, chatting with each guest, but now it was getting late and he didn't want Amanda to miss the dance, too.

Perhaps Amanda was onto something by insisting the new marketing campaign should revolve around family while adapting to whatever eclectic requests came their way like dog weddings and duck derbies. Perhaps he and Amanda could brainstorm together. Focusing on families of all kinds, however it was defined, like college friends or buddies on a guy's trip, was the ranch's strength and might be what set it apart from that snooty place not so far away.

As if out of nowhere, Crosby arrived and joined Seth. "I'm late for dinner, aren't I?"

"You remembered to make it for the dancing and singing." Seth was impressed Crosby came at all. "How's the dissertation coming along?"

"Almost done." Crosby crossed his fingers. "I go before the panel next month."

"Dr. Virtue." Seth choked on the words. "Mom and Dad would have been so proud."

"I'm proud of you." Crosby removed his glasses and wiped at the corner of his eye with his suit jacket sleeve. Then he returned his glasses to their familiar position. "You keep this family together."

Seth swiped at the dirt with his boot. "Hardly. Jase is in Denver, and you and Daisy live in town."

Crosby shook his head and placed his hand on Seth's shirtsleeve. "We all know. You're terrible at keeping secrets."

Seth's pulse raced. He thought his siblings didn't know about the mortgage yet, but it was better everything was in the open. Secrets never served anybody well. "How did you find out?"

"It was obvious, wasn't it?" Crosby gave a wry laugh.

Seth glanced at the hay covering the dirt in the barn. "Grandpa Martin did what he had to do."

"There you go being humble again. You put in the hard work." Crosby squeezed Seth's arm. "Take the credit every once in a while."

"Are we talking about the same thing? You're referring to the mortgage Grandpa Martin took out for Grandma's medical expenses, right?" Seth asked.

Crosby gasped. "Mortgage?" He gave a low whistle. "You'll have to fill me in on the details later. I was talking about you. The three of us knew you were having trouble with your high school classes, but you kept at it so you'd be a role model for us."

Here he was thinking he'd done a good job hiding how he'd struggled with trigonometry and physics when his mind was at the ranch wondering how Grandpa Martin would get everything accomplished without him.

"It's not a big deal." His voice came out husky

and deep. His father had been so much better at the deep conversations. "You're getting your doctorate. That's a huge accomplishment."

Crosby patted Seth's shoulder. "Don't underestimate yourself. You led the way, doing what you loved and letting us do the same. Daisy loves fashioning jewelry and silversmithing, and Jase?"

Their gazes met, and the nervous tension broke. Laughter bubbled to the surface.

"Jase is even more independent than I am," Seth said.

Crosby nodded. "He's got time yet to figure out he needs us as much as we need him. There are plenty of cases in Violet Ridge."

"For a little brother, you're awfully smart." It was Seth's turn to nudge Crosby's arm.

"I learned from the best." Admiration danced in Crosby's blue eyes. "You don't believe me, but you know so much about this ranch and animals and the land. Don't cut yourself short."

"Excuse me." Amanda's sister, Sami, approached them. "You two look like you're deep in conversation, but my new friend here promised me a dance."

Seth turned to see if Amanda was with her, but he was disappointed. Then he remembered his promise to her. "Will you save me a dance?"

Sami flashed a smile in Crosby's direction. "Later, thanks. Right now, I think your brother needs to start living and stop hiding behind books."

A scowl crossed his face. "Books contain facts and are dependable," Crosby defended himself.

Sami tilted her head, one way then the other. "I've never claimed to be dependable." Then she winked at Crosby. "Everyone needs one friend they can't count on."

Seth pushed his brother in Sami's direction and laughed. "Don't worry, Crosby. I'll always have your back." Even now it was obvious Crosby needed this.

Seth watched Sami lead Crosby toward the wooden dance floor. It would have been nice to take a twirl with Amanda, but it was for the best they never had the chance. She was leaving, and she didn't need to take his heart with her.

He jammed his hands in his pockets and headed out of the barn toward the lodge. Tomorrow would be a busy day with ushering out one group of guests and checking in the next.

Then his chest clenched when he saw the vision that was Amanda, her blond hair falling in soft waves around her shoulders. She was in a yellow halter top dress with a long orange floral skirt that brushed the path. She paired it with a short brown leather jacket.

He was a goner.

"I missed dinner, didn't I?" Her soft voice was breathless. "Sami's going to be upset with me."

"She looked quite content when I left her." He tilted his head toward the barn, the music from the band reaching them along with the nickers of the horses in the pasture. "Your sister is a miracle worker. She got Crosby to dance."

"I'm not surprised. They hit it off this afternoon." Amanda grasped a bright orange purse in her hands and twisted the gold chain around it. "I borrowed this dress from Sami. The clutch, too."

"It's beautiful." But not as beautiful as the woman wearing it.

She dipped her head in acknowledgment. "Sami also styled my hair." She stopped fingering the clutch chain and stroked the curls near her shoulder. "Then I got lost in my work, but I finally came upon the right color palette for the website's landing page."

For one night, Seth didn't want to talk business or worry about the ranch. Well, he'd always be concerned about the Lazy River, but tonight was his night with Amanda. He closed the distance between them. "We can discuss that tomorrow. May I have this dance?"

She crooked her arm and led him into the barn, setting the clutch on a table. "Don't forget. You have to ask my sister to dance with you."

"I did, and she chose Crosby." He swept Amanda into his arms. "And she's not the Fleming sister that I want to dance with."

"But Sami's always the sister who…"

Seth closed the distance between them and met

her gaze, the charge between them electric. "I want to dance with you, Amanda."

The world swirled about in slow motion. She nodded, and he placed his arm around her waist. He didn't know what song the band was playing; he just didn't want them to stop. Her head snuggled into his neck, and he closed his eyes, swaying in time with the music and her. The smell of jasmine would always take him back to this minute.

The moment he knew he was in love with Amanda Fleming.

THE SONG ENDED, and the band segued into a reel. Everyone started clapping, and Seth broke contact with Amanda. She stood there, breathless, her mind in shock. How could one week change everything? How could one dance change everything?

Amanda wished it was easy to quell the storm raging within her with Seth so close.

She searched the area for Sami and found her heading her way with Crosby. "Where have you been?" Sami clucked her tongue. "Never mind. You finally arrived."

Sami hugged Amanda and then faced Seth, pointing toward a back table where Seth's grandparents sat together, their heads touching, their hands entwined. "Your grandmother is a darling. We had the best time this afternoon."

Bridget seemed different, and Amanda realized

she wasn't the only one who'd received a Sami makeover today.

"Let's join them." Seth headed toward Bridget, and Amanda followed with Sami and Crosby tagging along.

Seth halted in front of the table. Martin smiled at Sami while continuing to hold Bridget's hand. "What's your secret, Sami? You got Crosby dancing and made my Bridge even more beautiful, something I didn't think possible."

Amanda didn't know whose smile was bigger: her sister's or Bridget's.

"It was my pleasure on both fronts. I already feel like I've known Crosby forever." Sami gave him a blinding smile.

Bridget touched her hair, a pretty silver that suited her features, cut into a flattering style. "Thank you, Sami. I haven't had my hair done by a professional since my stroke. I feel wonderful."

Martin swiped at his eye and then looked straight at Sami. "You have a permanent job here whenever you want one."

Sami laughed and waved away his offer. "I'm keeping my options open for now. Wherever I end up, it won't be for long. I want to see and experience everything while I'm young."

That might be what her sister wanted, but that type of life wasn't for Amanda.

Seth gestured to his grandparents. "You two sure look happy."

Martin released Bridget's hand and placed his arm around her shoulder, pulling her close to his side. "We've had a long talk."

Martin nodded as if emphasizing that was all he needed to say.

"We cleared the air between us," Bridget finished for him. "The night is young, and so are all of you. Go enjoy yourselves."

Sami led Crosby back to the dance floor, but Amanda wanted to talk to Seth. There was so much she wanted to say to him. From the look on his face, there was much he needed to confide in someone else, too.

She was more than willing to be that person.

Amanda reached for Seth's hand. "I think I need another astronomy lesson."

He extended a farewell to his grandparents, and together, she and Seth walked outside. The night air was sweet, and the frogs and crickets provided as much of a symphony as the band. They took their time and sashayed toward the pond, the ducks and geese floating with all vestiges of the earlier duck derby gone.

Would it be like this a week from now when she had departed? Would all traces of her melt away?

Would he forget her?

She pushed that out of her mind and squeezed his hand.

They both started speaking and then laughed.

"Ladies first," Seth said.

She settled for the easiest topic first. "Is everything okay with you and your grandparents?"

They proceeded along the trail, the scent of the wildflowers combining with the spicy aroma of Seth. "Day by day, the trust is coming back."

Funny. She could say the same about her and Sami.

A comfortable silence descended while she relished being in his company. She glanced at the night sky, the stars gleaming, their presence a steady light. "Do you think Leo the lion wishes there was a lioness constellation?"

"Everyone needs someone, even lions." His voice grew husky.

The dance, the night, Seth. Here he was, the epitome of a cowboy with the bolo tie and boots. All of it was too much to resist, so she didn't. She reached for him, pulling him closer.

She was falling for the rancher.

"I changed my mind about my finder's fee. I want a kiss instead." Amanda held onto him and smiled.

"This kiss is freely given. No strings attached."

With those words, he leaned toward her. Their lips connected, and the kiss was everything she'd ever wanted. His beard tickled and caressed at the same time. The dance would always possess a sweet corner in her memories, but Seth and this kiss were the cornerstone of her heart. This moment was right. Every atom of her was on full alert, tingles shooting down to her toes.

She entangled her hands in his hair, the curly strands thick and full, his lips still warm on hers. Time stood still. She was right where she belonged, where she was good enough to be an integral part of something that meant so much to so many.

"Hello? Excuse me." A familiar voice cleared her throat behind them. "My niece and I have been looking for someone to help us for the past twenty minutes. Do either of you work here?"

Amanda jumped away from Seth as recognition of who belonged to the voice shot through her. Her gaze went to the shocked expression gracing her boss's face. Pamela Parkhouse had arrived early.

And she'd found her employee kissing a client.

CHAPTER THIRTEEN

Sunday

AMANDA CLOSED HER laptop in the privacy of her cabin. She was alone as Sami had departed at sunrise for paddleboard yoga. If only Amanda could find the same sense of peace, but she was too upset. Last night, Pamela had insisted on checking into the lodge for her eight hours of beauty sleep. So far, there hadn't been a word about how she'd caught Amanda kissing a client. That felt worse than if she'd blown a gasket on the spot.

But her boss's discovery paled in comparison to what was really bothering Amanda. Namely, how much she enjoyed kissing Seth.

While watching a foal being born was extraordinary, that kiss was earth-shattering. Nothing prepared her for that type of connection with someone, the intensity and emotion unlike anything she'd ever experienced before.

Of all the times for her to meet someone like Seth. Why now when she was set to buy her first house, a real home, something permanent and hers? It wasn't like she could move to Violet Ridge, even if this town did have everything she was looking for. If she lived here, she'd turn into her father, always thinking the grass would be greener around the next bend.

But would she be able to continue living in Phoenix if Pamela fired her?

She groaned and lowered her head until it collided with the laptop's cold metal case. Sitting up, she rubbed the sore spot.

Despite everything, she'd kiss Seth a second time. In fact, the worst part was she wanted to kiss him again. And again. And again.

A knock on the cabin door sent Amanda's already unsettled stomach churning. What if it was Seth wanting to talk about what had happened last night?

But it wasn't Seth. Instead, Pamela and Paisley were waiting on the porch. While there wasn't a strong physical resemblance between Pamela with her chic auburn bob and tall, regal stature and her petite niece who styled her hair into short blue spikes, their facial expressions matched each other.

Amanda ushered them into the main living area, offering them some sparkling water. Pamela asked for a tour, and Amanda obliged. Anything to put off the impending discussion for another few minutes. Then again, if Pamela fired her, that would solve everything.

No, it wouldn't. She'd be just like her father, getting fired from two jobs in a row.

Amanda finished the tour and returned to the table where she'd set up her laptop and notes. "I'm almost done with the preliminary research for the presentation. If you'd like, we can start going through the graphics."

"That's just what I wanted to hear. I know we arrived earlier than expected. My niece deserves a few days of relaxation after graduation." Her boss smiled at her niece before turning her attention back to Amanda. "We need to move up the presentation. There are clients clamoring for you back in Phoenix. I'll introduce myself to the owners and reschedule the meeting."

Paisley plopped herself on the sofa and hugged a pillow. "This is much nicer than our tiny suite, Aunt Pamela."

Her boss sauntered over to the glass window, the one that overlooked the Rocky Mountains. "You're right, Paisley. Plus the view is better." She looked over her shoulder at Amanda. "The beds in our suite were so uncomfortable, and the sheets? I get itchy just thinking about them. I don't want to spend an extra minute in that cramped space."

Her pointed tone gave Amanda pause, and she sought a compromise. "We can work here today. You can bring your attaché case and laptop here."

She turned toward the younger woman. "There's always something happening at the ranch. Perhaps you'd like to go horseback riding or kayaking. You shouldn't be bored while your aunt and I discuss business."

Pamela tapped her fingers on her chin. "Hmm. Aren't the other guests checking out now?" She sent a pointed glance toward Amanda, and she nodded. "Come on, Paisley. We're going to demand a cabin that's better than this one."

Nothing was going as planned any longer. Amanda slipped on her boots and hurried to catch up. She only did so as Pamela approached the reception desk in the main lodge where Seth was assisting Tiffany and Derrick.

"So, you've decided to go home to your cats?" Seth asked while processing their checkout.

Derrick put his arm around Tiffany's shoulders. "Yeah. Tiffany misses Princess and Earl. We're postponing our other adventures for a bit. Thank you for everything."

"We'd love to come back, especially now that we know you're pet friendly and we can bring the cats," Tiffany said.

They waved at Amanda as they passed her and she waved back. Meanwhile, Pamela stepped forward.

"You!" A frown came over Pamela's face. "You're the man my assistant was kissing last night. You work here?"

Amanda's stomach dropped. No wonder Pamela hadn't pressed the subject last night. She hadn't realized who Seth was.

Seth faced Amanda, his hands on a keyboard. "Didn't you tell her who I am?"

Come to think of it, she hadn't. Pamela had been in such a hurry to check in she hadn't waited for an explanation as to Seth's role at the ranch.

A stony silence drew out until Paisley tapped on the counter. "My aunt and I would like an upgrade to another cabin."

Seth glanced at the screen and shook his head. "We're booked solid. Thanks to Amanda's great work on the derby, a family booked the rest of the unreserved cabins for a reunion."

Amanda stepped forward; problem solving was one of her best skills. "No problem. We'll swap cabins. You can have mine. Sami and I will move into yours." Perhaps giving Pamela the cabin would soften the reprimand Amanda was positive was on the horizon.

Pamela turned a frigid eye toward Amanda. "Is there a place we can speak in private?"

Amanda looked at Seth. "Is anyone using the library?"

"Just Hap and Trixie, loving the warmth of the fire. I placed them in there so they don't herd the guests when they leave." His voice sounded too much like the Seth of day one. She searched his gaze, only to find disappointment at her omission lurking there.

A first fight would normally indicate they were transitioning into relationship territory.

Yet that was the last thing that could ever happen between them.

"Thanks for the heads-up. I'll be careful they don't escape," Amanda said.

She ushered Pamela into the quiet room where Hap and Trixie stirred from their dog beds near the hearth.

Hap stretched and rolled on his back for Amanda while Trixie investigated Pamela, who was flickering her hands toward the door. "I don't get along with dogs. They have to go somewhere else."

This was their home, not Pamela's. Still, Amanda remembered Seth's admonition. "They have to stay in here. I know another place we can go."

The dining hall was empty, and Amanda poured two coffees. She steeled herself for the reprimand as she handed Pamela her cup.

She didn't have to wait long. "That man works here?"

"Yes, he's the manager, and his grandparents own the ranch." Amanda braced herself for whatever Pamela meted out to her.

She deserved it.

Pamela stirred another dollop of cream into her mug, the steam dissipating in the air. Then she placed the coffee on a nearby table and folded her arms. "The man you were kissing last night is *our* client." Her tone was as cold as the coffee was hot. "That is conduct unbecoming to an employee of Parkhouse Promotions."

Amanda hung her head. "I agree. I'm sorry. It won't happen again."

Amanda kept holding her cup, wondering if she still worked for Pamela. The dude ranch had an exclusive contract with Parkhouse Promotions. If Pamela fired her, she couldn't work on Seth's account any longer.

Pamela pointed toward the beverage station. "Ice water." A slight tic pulsed near her forehead. "Please. I'm developing a migraine."

Amanda did as asked and handed the glass to Pamela. "Do you need any aspirin? Ibuprofen?"

"This should suffice." Pamela drained half the glass and sank into the closest chair, fanning herself. "This makes my decision to hire Paisley a sound one indeed."

Static rushed into Amanda's ears, and she waited for the buzzing noise to dissipate. Once it did, she sat across from her boss. "You hired Paisley?"

Pamela nodded. "She's bright and articulate. She'll be perfect by my side at presentations."

Amanda blew out a long breath and placed her coffee mug on the table. "Why won't she be working alongside me with the practical aspects of marketing, like branding, creating logos and updating websites? I've been begging for an assistant to aid with focus groups and data analysis."

Another sip, another minute of her fate still up in the air. Pamela downed the rest of the water and then set the glass on the table next to her cup of coffee. "We're fortunate to retain someone of Paisley's caliber. She graduated from my alma mater, and she has such a way with people."

Amanda reeled. "But I need an assistant, and I've been working for you for three years." This was a bad time, but she decided to forge ahead with the issue of her salary. "And I haven't had a pay raise in all that time. If you hired your niece, the business must be doing well enough for me to receive a cost-of-living increase."

Pamela arched her eyebrow and glared at Amanda. "You're fortunate I'm not firing you for kissing a client. For now, I'm willing to overlook that indiscretion. Your pay and position, however, will stay the same."

"What about my partnership?" Amanda figured she'd go for broke.

"My name is on the letterhead. I'm the person with the most to lose if rumors about my employees fraternizing with clients start flying around Arizona and beyond." Pamela raised her chin, the blunt edges of her haircut barely moving. "From now on, you can report to Paisley. Today you can turn over the information for the presentation. I'll supervise, and I know my niece will impress the dude ranch owners with her dynamic presence."

Amanda needed a minute to gather herself. Somehow, she'd have to tell Sami they were moving into a smaller space and explain to Seth that Pamela hadn't known his identity until today.

"I'll text you when you and Paisley can move into the cabin. Sami and I will collect our luggage and be out of there this afternoon."

Amanda fled the dining room, only to bump into Seth. How was she going to explain everything? She registered his comforting presence and ran for the library, shielding her eyes from his gaze.

AMANDA'S WORDS ECHOED in Seth's mind. *Collecting her luggage? Be out of here?* He'd known her time here was limited, but she was sprinting for Phoenix after their kiss.

Despite the rooms that needed cleaning, a stable that needed to be mucked out and his grandfather's request to set aside a minute for something important, Seth followed Amanda to the library. Why hadn't she told Pamela who he was earlier? Was she ashamed of him and this ranch?

His anger dissipated the second he entered the library. Her back was to him, her shoulders slumped. He fought the urge to take her in his arms; he wanted to make everything okay. For so long, he'd done just that for his siblings after their parents had died, but was that what she really needed?

While he'd have loved for their relationship to blossom into something more than friends, he wanted her to be happy. If she was still an employee of Parkhouse Promotions, he had to let her go.

Hap and Trixie revealed his presence, and Amanda turned, her face streaked with tears.

Putting her happiness first was the most important thing. That's what love was about. Being there for the other person even when your heart was breaking.

He wasn't sure if the deep ache inside him was at the thought of Amanda leaving or the fact she wasn't going to tell him first.

"Were you going to say goodbye to me?" The huskiness in his voice made it deeper and almost unrecognizable.

"I'm not leaving yet." Her eyes reflected hurt before comprehension flickered and caught fire. "You think I'm going home early."

It didn't escape his notice she called Phoenix home.

"Aren't you?"

Before she could answer, his grandfather appeared. "There you are, Seth." His grandfather tipped his Stetson at Amanda. "I knew I should have looked for you instead, fair lady. Wherever you are, there's my grandson."

"If you need Seth, I'll talk to him *later*." Amanda stressed the final word and started to leave the library.

"I'll be quick. Seth, there's a family conference tonight in my suite at nine. Jase is joining via video call from Denver. See you then." Grandpa Martin caught Amanda's eye. "Oh, and your boss introduced herself and asked if the presentation can be moved to Tuesday. I agreed to that."

Grandpa Martin ducked out before Seth had the opportunity to ask any questions.

He blinked and found Amanda, halfway to the door. "Going somewhere?"

Amanda halted and turned. "Hold Hap and Trixie, will you? I don't want them to escape."

"I can say the same about you." Seth joined her and guided her over to the overstuffed sofa. The dogs sat at their feet. "Do you still have a job?"

Her breaths came out in short spurts. "I thought Pamela knew who you were." She brushed her blond hair away from her eyes. "I didn't realize until a few minutes ago that she thought you were a guest. Now she knows I've become involved with a client."

Something gnawed at him until he finally hit upon the reason why. "Am I a client? You've been saying that since you arrived. Grandma Bridget hired you. She's your client."

"You're her grandson and work for her." She blew out a breath. "Same difference."

"Is it?" He lifted her chin with his rough hands. He wanted to see that smile again, her sad look sparking every protective cell to life. Keeping a light tone, he said, "As the attractive Virtue sibling, I'm just the pretty face who manages the place."

Her lips curled up in a tiny wink of a smile, and her body became less rigid. "I won't tell Daisy you think you're the prettiest of the group."

"She already knows." He liked that she was starting to relax.

"Then I'll just tell her you have a big head." She laughed as she reached up and lowered his Stetson over his eyes.

He stood and tossed his hat onto the table while the dogs returned to the hearth, curling up in balls on their beds. "My head is the perfect size." He whipped out his bandanna and wiped away her tears. "Will Pamela listen to Grandma Bridget if she puts in a good word for you? Or is that kiss the reason you're leaving in such a hurry?"

"What?" She rose and went over to him. "No, I'm just moving Sami's belongings and mine back to the Porcupine Suite since Pamela and Paisley need our cabin."

"Need or want? That cabin's plenty big enough for four. Pamela's taking advantage of you."

"I count myself fortunate she didn't fire me. That kiss…"

He tucked his bandanna back in his rear pocket

and faced her. Her gaze lifted to meet his. "Last night's kiss wasn't a mistake. It was everything and inevitable."

Despite the uncertainty in her eyes, she gave a slight chuckle. "That's a lot of pressure on a kiss."

"It was more than I ever expected." Amanda was more than he'd ever expected, too. "What's between us doesn't have to end."

She shifted her weight, a shadow descending over her face. "Yes, it does. You live here, and my life is in Phoenix."

"For now." This was moving fast, but there was no reason it had to stop because of distance. "We can get to know each other and then decide what we want in terms of us."

"Us?" She echoed his word but without a hint of shock or surprise in her voice, making it too obvious she had given that possibility some thought.

"Yep." He leaned closer to her and halted. "In case you have any doubts, we can see if last night's kiss was as good as I remember…?"

"Is a second kiss inevitable, too?" Her tone was light, and he liked that he made her smile.

"I promise it'll be *the* highlight of your trip."

At that, she raised herself on her tiptoes, and her lips found his. The sweetness of her flooded him, and he wrapped his arms around her until no distance separated them. This kiss somehow surpassed the one last night. A tiny sigh escaped, and he wasn't sure whether it came from him or her, but it didn't matter as the scent of jasmine tickled his nose.

It was like coming home in spring with the world in full color.

Seth was kissing Amanda here, but there were guests waiting for the welcome tour. With reluctance, he stopped but stayed close enough to see the slight freckles dusting her cheeks.

"You held your end of that promise." This time it was her voice that held a huskiness not usually there.

"I try my best." He moved toward the table and picked up his Stetson, placing it on his head. "Promise me you'll say goodbye before you leave."

She gave one hesitant but brief nod. Then tipping his Stetson her way, he departed from the library, the dogs safe and sound in their cozy spots. For a brief second, he stopped in the lobby, still tasting Amanda on his lips.

That kiss was *the* highlight of his life.

For sure.

CHAPTER FOURTEEN

WITH DINNER ON the horizon, Amanda wanted some fresh air and exercise. She waved hello to Buck, who was giving this week's guest tour, and shouted encouragement to the newcomers. "You're going to love it here!"

Not wanting to get in the way, she headed toward the pasture when she heard a raised voice coming from the direction of the goat pen.

"You impertinent animal." Pamela's distress was clear. "Get away from me this instant."

Amanda rushed to see what the commotion was about and stopped short. There, in the back of the pen, was Pamela with Winnie and three other goats surrounding her. Taking care so no goats would escape, Amanda entered the area.

"What's wrong?"

Pamela held up her designer leather purse, the one with the fringe covering the front. "These animals are impertinent and rude."

Amanda stopped her chuckle before it escaped. "They're wild animals, Pamela. Why are you inside the goat pen?"

"The wind knocked my sunglasses off me, and they fell in here." Pamela pointed at Winnie. "Then that one decided my purse was dinner."

Amanda hustled to the equipment station and scooped out a generous amount of goat feed pellets. "Here, Winnie!"

The goat hesitated as if contemplating whether Pamela's purse was the tastier haul before the other goats surrounded Amanda, who scattered the pellets on the ground. Winnie gave a regretful glance to the purse, if such a thing were possible from a goat, and moseyed toward Amanda.

Pamela, however, made a beeline for the exit. A few minutes later, Amanda joined her boss, who was fanning herself with her hand, her black oversize sunglasses hiding her full expression. Pamela harrumphed. "Some animals have no respect."

"No harm done." Amanda noticed a slight nick on the black frames but decided not to mention it.

Pamela tapped her chin with a manicured finger. "Perhaps we ought to move the presentation to tonight." Then she shook her head. "Paisley needs to practice her delivery, so tomorrow it is. The poor dear has been working so hard. After graduating college, she deserves a few days to soak up the sunshine and be pampered by having someone else do the cooking. We'll keep to the schedule and impress our clients on Tuesday morning."

At dinner, Amanda took the opportunity to introduce herself to a bunch of new guests to get their first impressions of the ranch. Afterward, she entered the Porcupine Suite, where she and Sami were staying.

Unsure of whether this was a bad time, she paused at the doorway. Sami held a blow dryer and was brushing out Daisy's hair with Bridget sitting on the comfy chair in the corner. Bridget motioned for Amanda to come sit near her.

"Your sister is excellent at her job." Bridget's raised voice made it possible to hear her over the hair dryer. "You must be very proud of her."

Amanda waited for a jealous feeling to rise up after a lifetime of hearing how wonderful Sami was. *Nothing.* Instead, she readily agreed with Bridget. "I am."

Her parents might have placed a wedge between them, but that ended here and now. There was so much they could do in Phoenix together. Go horseback riding. Share shoes. Stay up late with hot fudge sundaes or appletinis, talking and telling each other everything they'd missed over the past few years.

Except she didn't know if she'd be able to talk about Seth. Just the thought of leaving him and not hearing his corny jokes or seeing his broad smile brought a deep ache to her chest.

After a few minutes, Sami flicked off the hair dryer and finished styling Daisy's hair. "There. How do you like it?"

Sami handed Daisy a mirror. "I love it!" Daisy exclaimed and examined her new hairdo from all angles while Sami smiled at the praise.

Daisy grinned and said, "I can see why Grandma and Grandpa have offered you a job. They're serious about their offer, you know. I hope you'll take it under consideration."

Martin's offer to Sami at the dance was genuine? Amanda looked at Sami, who nodded. "I'll need more information, but I'll think about it."

The glow on Sami's face stunned Amanda. What happened to them taking Phoenix by storm together?

Bridget reached for her cane and rose from the chair. "Come on, Daisy. We don't want to keep Seth and Martin waiting." She hobbled over and patted Sami's arm. "Arrive around nine thirty, dear, for our discussion about the fine print about the job. That way you can meet Jase even if it's on a computer screen. These days, I only see my grandson online, but I'll take it."

Daisy and Bridget departed, and Amanda watched Sami replacing the hairstyling equipment in its case.

Her sister faced her, practically glowing. "Isn't this the most wonderful day?"

Earlier when she kissed Seth in the library, Amanda would have agreed with Sami in an instant. Now? Everything she wanted was slipping through her fingers, and fast.

"Are you really thinking of taking the job offer?" Amanda asked.

Sami snapped the equipment case closed and beamed at Amanda. "They're finalizing the details, but if I like their terms, they'll vote in favor of my six-month job contract."

It was already a done deal. Amanda fell into the chair, dinner churning in her stomach. "If you live here, you won't be in Phoenix."

Sami glanced at Amanda, and her mouth dropped open. "I didn't think you'd be upset. After all, we haven't lived in the same town for years."

Would she and Sami end up like Jase and his siblings, only communicating on the phone or online? Then Amanda mulled over the job offer and perked up. "You're only signing for six months?"

"Just until the holidays." Sami confirmed. "Then I'm off on my next adventure."

"In Phoenix?"

Sami gave a winsome smile that held no sense of forever, unlike Seth's expression after they kissed. The promise of forever had been written all over on his expressive face. Sami shrugged. "I don't know where the wind will take me." Then that gleam in her eye returned. "Why don't you move to Violet Ridge with me?"

"I have friends in Phoenix, and my savings are tied up in my new house."

"Why Phoenix?" Sami gripped Amanda's hands in her own. "Why not flip your house and move here? It'll be a fresh start for both of us. Just like when we were growing up and moving around."

Amanda couldn't believe what she was hearing. While she'd grown more weary after each move, wanting to settle in one place, apparently Sami must have viewed the constant relocation as a grand adventure, enjoying the experience.

"Mom and Dad went through jobs more often than some people shampoo their hair. I promised myself I wouldn't be like them."

Sami startled and shook her head. "You're not. You're conscientious, and you took me in when they threw me out." Sami squeezed Amanda's hands. "Besides, there's something in Violet Ridge that's not in Phoenix."

Sami didn't have to spell out what that something was.

"Seth." Amanda said his name anyway.

"Exactly. The way he looks at you." Sami delivered a low whistle. "Like you lassoed the moon. Like the way Martin looks at Bridget."

Amanda brushed away her sister's concern. "While you're talking with the Virtue family, I have to update social media posts for other clients. Pamela outlined what she wants to see by dinnertime tomorrow. I'll review the presentation one more time before I hand it over to Pamela and Paisley. I need to work. There are still parts of the presentation I should fine-tune."

She started for the table and her laptop, but

Sami blocked her way. "You know that presentation inside and out. You even mumble it in your sleep." Her sister flipped her hair over her shoulder. "How about some girl talk? I'll do your hair, and you can tell me everything about Seth."

If she stayed in this suite, Sami would force Amanda to confront her feelings about the cowboy. "I'm not sure I'm ready to discuss Seth. But it's a definite yes to the hair." That second kiss was still seared on her lips.

Sami chuckled and reached for her equipment case. "Many of my new clients don't intend to spill any personal details when I'm styling their hair, but then I ask a few questions and they start talking. It must be my magic fingers." She wiggled them in front of Amanda for good measure.

With only a few days before she would leave, Amanda wondered if there was a way forward for her and Seth. If not, she'd much rather end things now before her heart became irrevocably involved.

Though she had a feeling it was already too late for that.

Seth arrived at his grandparents' suite thirty minutes early. After he knocked, the door swung open, and Grandpa Martin waved him inside.

"Honestly, I expected you some time ago." Grandpa Martin went directly to the beverage cart. "What can I get you? Water? Soda? A beer?"

"My usual." Seth accepted a root beer and settled on the sofa.

Grandpa Martin uncapped a homemade local microbrew from Brewer Brothers and sat opposite Seth on the matching sofa. "Trouble with Amanda?"

Seth placed his glass on a coaster and leaned forward. "What makes you think that?"

Grandpa Martin produced his bandanna from a back pocket and tossed it to Seth. "Amanda wears the shade of lipstick that's on your lips, and she's not with you."

Seth gratefully accepted the bandanna and the hint. "What of it? Amanda's made it clear she lives in Phoenix." If he said it loud enough, that might cover the thunderous beating of his heart.

"How do you feel about her?" Grandpa Martin stared at Seth, his gaze full of that same wisdom and love that had always been reflected there.

Seth would draw on that soon enough, but for now he wiped his lips. "I've only known her a week."

"When you know you've met the right one, you know." Grandpa Martin nodded and took a long swig of beer. "I remember your grandmother coming out to the ranch for a community square dance. She was eighteen, and I hadn't seen her for a couple of years. The second I laid eyes on her I knew she was the one. Something deep down told me I'd never be the same if she got away."

Seth sipped at his root beer, knowing that exact

feeling all too well. "That's different. Grandma Bridget lived in Violet Ridge."

Grandma Bridget walked in and set her cane beside the sofa while Daisy pushed a cart of food inside the suite. "I heard my name, young man. What's going on?"

Once his grandmother was seated, Grandpa Martin reached for his wife's hand, kissing the back of it, his eyes twinkling with a love that time had not diminished. "I was telling Seth about seeing you at the square dance. You were as lovely then as you are now. Your new hairstyle suits you, my darling Bridge."

Was that a blush on his grandmother's cheeks?

"A good reason to vote to hire her," she said.

A look at the books had ended any hopes Seth had of expanding the services. "We can't afford to hire a full-time hairdresser."

Grandma Bridget accepted the decaf coffee her husband brought over for her. "I already crunched the numbers. Sami will live on-site rent free for one month, a trial period—she insisted it be a temporary setup to start with. In lieu of the room fees, we'll split the profits with her. We've had so many guests that have asked for Sami's talents, I'm sure she'll end up staying. We're converting the Snowshoe Hare Suite into her salon. It'll be a snap."

Seth's breath caught. He'd been suggesting a more upscale version of this all along. "It might be too little too late, but I'm glad you're finally listening to my suggestions."

"We've always listened." Grandpa Martin frowned and placed his arm around Grandma Bridget. "But now we're moving ahead as a family."

Frustration bubbled under the surface. Was this ranch really a *family* enterprise? He loved his siblings but… "Jase isn't coming back, and Crosby has no interest in ranch management."

Daisy glared at him while Grandpa Martin unwound his arm from his wife and mimicked Seth's stance, his elbows on his knees. "There's more to family than blood. Every employee, every guest becomes our family while they're here."

Before Seth could answer, a knock preceded Crosby's entrance. Grandma Bridget hugged him and then connected Jase to the meeting. "How are you, Jase, sweetie? Have you met anyone nice lately?"

"Hello, Grandma Bridget. The weather is lovely in Denver, and my partner and I cracked the tough case we've been working on for six months. It's kept me too busy to meet anyone. Thanks for asking." Jase's droll voice matched his no-nonsense image projected on the big screen over the fireplace.

Jase exhaled a deep breath, his eyes moving over each of them as though he was obviously zeroing in on the best person to draw attention away from himself. "Daisy, how are my favorite nieces and nephew?"

"They're your *only* nieces and nephew." Daisy pointed out the obvious. "Rosie was just cast in the summer play, and Lily is looking forward to Grandma Bridget's knitting lessons. Aspen is learning how to ride a sheep for the children's rodeo thanks to his uncle Lucky, and they all love their toddler cousin, Cale."

Sometimes it was hard for Seth to remember the triplets now counted Daisy's new husband's family as their own. Ben's sister, Lizzie, married a former rodeo star, Lucky Harper, and they had welcomed their first child shortly after the play wrapped up seventeen months ago.

"They're also attending my history camp this summer." Crosby reminded Daisy, and they began discussing details while Grandma Bridget interrogated Jase more about his dating life.

Seth finally had enough of the small talk. "We have serious issues at the ranch." Everyone stared at him. "We need to vote on hiring Sami Fleming, and I have a meeting at the bank tomorrow to discuss refinancing the mortgage."

"What mortgage?" Jase interrupted.

So Grandma Bridget wasn't the last to know, after all. Seth summarized for Jase and continued, "I'm asking Mateo to reconsider the terms given it was the bank that leaked our financial information to Killian Wilshire."

"Back up a second." Jase never missed anything. "The bank wants to work with you rather than Grandpa Martin?"

That would be what Jase focused on. "Mateo Rodriguez knows me. It's nothing personal against Grandma Bridget or Grandpa Martin."

Grandpa Martin cleared his throat. "The Lazy River Dude Ranch is still all of us. I say we hire Sami Fleming and adapt the Snowshoe Hare Suite into a salon."

Everyone in the room voted in favor of offering Amanda's sister a contract. Seth's gaze went to Jase, whose image loomed as large as the lack of his presence. "I shouldn't have a vote. I have no intention of living in Violet Ridge again," Jase said. "I'm not coming back to the ranch."

Passing sadness flitted over Grandma Bridget's features before she nodded. "Your mother and father would have wanted you to follow your heart and your dreams. If those are in Denver, so be it."

Following his heart. Was the ranch Seth's heart?

Or was it Amanda?

This week, she rode alongside him, bringing a lightness to him he hadn't felt in years. She made all of this enjoyable again and now he couldn't wait to find out what shenanigans this week's guests would get up to.

He'd do whatever he had to, to ensure Wilshire didn't purchase this land.

But could he work up the nerve to ask Amanda to stay?

CHAPTER FIFTEEN

IN THE MIDDLE of the night, Seth caved and got out of bed since he couldn't sleep. The family conference confirmed what he'd already known in his heart. This dude ranch depended on him for its survival. There'd be no buying another ranch in Arizona, not that Seth had really entertained that thought for more than two seconds. Colorado was part of him, and there was no way he'd give anything less than his all for the survival of his parents' legacy.

He crept to the library, eager to find a book that would enthrall him for a few hours or put him to sleep.

He cracked the door enough so as not to alarm Hap or Trixie. To his surprise, the dogs weren't the only ones there. His gaze flitted to Amanda, knitting by the hearth. His heart leaped at the sight, but he wanted a romantic setting for his speech. The pond with the ducks nearby or the stable with Rosa and her new foal. He tried to sneak away, but she noticed him.

"Come on in." Her face puckered with concentration, the clacking needles a soft whisper.

Seth entered, and the dogs lifted their heads before resuming their slumber. "I thought a book might help me sleep."

She lifted her eyebrows. "That's funny. I usually read so I stay awake."

"Is that why you're knitting instead of cuddling up with the dogs, a fire and a book?"

Amanda focused on her stitches. "Don't tell your grandmother but knitting lulls me to sleep faster than anything else."

Seth laughed but kept a respectful distance. "Is that a scarf or a blanket?"

"Don't you know?" Amanda held up her massive undertaking, and he stared at it. It was too narrow to be a blanket and too long to be a scarf. She sighed and set it aside. "I don't know, either."

Her gaze met his. In that moment, the lines blurred, and he knew she was talking about more than knitting. Whatever was between them was too special, reaching deep into the depths of his soul, to cast aside, yet there wasn't an easy solution. Seth had lost people he'd loved before, and he'd been devastated. He couldn't lose Amanda, too. The place where he told her wasn't as important as just confiding his feelings to her.

He sank into a chair, the emotions catching up to him. "This week was only the tip of the iceberg as far as I'm concerned. I want to know your middle name, your favorite flavor of ice cream and your suggestions for what to call Rosa's colt."

"Jayne, strawberry and Leo."

The calm manner in which she delivered relatively mundane information sent a surge of energy through him. There was something about her that spurred hope in him. How? He didn't know, but it had been like this all week.

He couldn't control what had happened to his parents. He hadn't gone after Felicity. Yet he knew if he didn't try with Amanda, he'd regret it his entire life.

"There's a place in town. Miss Tilly's." The steakhouse was a special-occasion restaurant, and he wanted his first date with Amanda to be as unforgettable as possible. "Before you go home to Phoenix, will you have dinner with me?"

"Like a date? Nothing can come of it. I'm not moving to Violet Ridge." Conflict clouded those beautiful blue eyes.

He rose out of the chair and pulled her to her feet. "Something has already come out of this week. *Us.* That is, if you want there to be an us."

Her gaze traveled along his face, seeking reassurance, which he had enough for both of them. "To think, if the kitchen had been open, I'd have missed all this."

"Remind me to give Ingrid a raise." He chuckled and then grew serious. "I would have asked you earlier today if we'd had the right moment."

Amanda reached for him, her hands surprisingly cold. He pressed them against his chest in an effort to warm them before bringing them up to his lips and kissing her fingers.

She freed one hand and began caressing his ear. "I didn't take you for a romantic."

"I do teach a class under the stars." She hadn't accepted his offer, and he was desperate to know either way. "One date. Tuesday night. Then you can decide if you want to say goodbye or do me the honor of continuing our dates online."

Her throat bobbed, and he stilled, his heart racing.

"Whenever my dad lost yet another job, I always had to say goodbye to my friends and the neighborhood. It never gets any easier. That's why, when I say goodbye, I make a clean break."

Seth threaded his fingers through her silky hair. "This is different?"

Amanda leaned into his touch. Something inside him softened, something he believed was hard and impenetrable and gone forever.

Then she stepped away from him. "If I quit my job and leave Phoenix, I'll be just like my father."

"What if this is your home?" He hoped that might be the case someday. "What if Violet Ridge is the place you were meant to be?"

She let out a small sigh that sounded like contentment. "One date."

"Just me and my silver dollar. And if you say

goodbye to me, I'll…" He stopped, for he didn't know what he'd do as there was no doubt this ranch was his home.

"Let's hope I never say *goodbye* goodbye." She moved forward on her toes and kissed him.

How did each kiss keep getting better? He savored the moment. He had one chance to make a case for long-distance dating and he'd make the best of it so hopefully he'd never hear the word goodbye uttered from her lips.

Monday

AMANDA PLUMPED HER pillow and placed it over her head, ignoring Sami's plea to attend morning paddleboard yoga with her. Sami sighed and left. As tempting as it was to linger in bed, Amanda showered and headed to the breakfast buffet, eager for a Seth sighting.

Yet only the new guests occupied the dining room tables. Seth must have already departed for his early-morning meeting with Mateo.

Ingrid had outdone herself, and Amanda piled her plate with waffles. She looked around, almost expecting Mabel to pop out from behind a table, but she was back in Birmingham. How did Seth adapt to a new group of guests each week?

That was just part of what he did, and he loved the constant hustle and bustle of the dude ranch. She knew something about adapting. Every time she and her family moved, she found new friends and adjusted to a new apartment layout.

One benefit of moving around, though, was learning how to stay in touch. Before they departed, Amanda had exchanged phone numbers with Colleen Carr and Whitney Berggren, both of whom promised to come back next summer.

She introduced herself to a family and accepted their offer to join them. Bolstered by new friends and an infusion of caffeine, Amanda snagged a rare second cup of coffee and returned to her suite, where she found a note from Sami. She'd returned from yoga long enough to change and head off for the mountain bike excursion.

Amanda logged onto social media and laughed at Colleen's post about Mabel's new calendar, marking off the days until they returned to the dude ranch. Moving past her procrastination, she opened her inbox and gasped at the flood of emails on this Monday morning. Client after client complained that no one at Parkhouse Promotions had returned their calls or scheduled their social media posts. What would the company do without her?

Amanda considered texting Paisley and asking for help, but she'd get it done faster by herself. She'd learned that the hard way over the past three years.

One by one, Amanda fixed each problem. The morning passed in a blur until she received a text from Seth, inviting her on an afternoon trail ride. She replied in the affirmative before she realized it was time to meet with Paisley and Pamela at the Bluebell Cabin. After hitting Send on the last email, Amanda crammed everything into her messenger bag and left the Porcupine Suite.

Being outside, even if only for a few minutes, was just what she needed. She traversed a shortcut to the pretty guest cabin and stared with awe at the majestic sight surrounding her. The duck pond glistened with the spring breeze, sending beautiful silver ripples along the surface. That same breeze carried the nickers of the horses in the paddock toward her. Anticipation welled within her for a late-afternoon horseback ride on Cybill. That it was with Seth made it that much more special.

With that in mind, Amanda hastened her steps until she passed by the circular pool. She blinked, unable to believe her eyes. There was Paisley, sunning herself on a chaise lounge rather than working in the cabin.

Amanda followed the trail of cedars, opened the latch and entered the pool area. "Paisley, what are you doing here?"

Paisley lowered her designer sunglasses. "Aunt Pamela and I had the most hectic morning." She motioned for Amanda to approach. "We worked our fingers to the bone polishing the proposal for the architect firm that's taking place next week. She said I should relax for an hour before lunch."

Amanda blew out her frustration. It seemed to her they needed to start taking care of their current client list before signing new ones. "I was headed to the Bluebell to review my research about the dude ranch with you. It's one of the best campaigns I've done."

Paisley stood and grabbed her cover-up. "I'll be the judge of that. Aunt Pamela has some ideas, and I took classes in hospitality management."

Amanda clenched her jaw. "I've been at the ranch for a week, and I've seen what the Virtue family expect from us. My presentation reflects that."

There'd been more than a few times they lost out on clients when Pamela tweaked Amanda's campaign beyond all recognition and the company didn't sign the final contract.

However, this wouldn't be one of those times. Amanda was sure this campaign was truly great work.

"Aunt Pamela says I'm a natural." Paisley adjusted her sunglasses on her nose. "Since I'll be presenting, I'll put my own touches on it."

She prided herself on staying calm, an important trait in maintaining steady employment. After getting fired from her first position, she made a pledge to herself to be as steadfast as possible. Paisley and, by extension, Pamela, were starting to make her resolution impossible.

While she didn't want to become her father, there was also a point where she wouldn't be a doormat. She was good at her job, more than good really. Working under Paisley and committing to an approach she didn't believe in might be the dealbreaker that resulted in her putting her foot down.

Then Amanda noticed something on Paisley's legs. At first, she thought they were lines from the chaise lounge, but now she gasped. "Paisley, did you go off the trail when you walked from the cabin to the pool? Specifically, where there's a sign to keep off the grass."

Paisley sniffed and held her head high. "Of course. What harm can come from walking through grass?"

"I'll show you the problem." Amanda led Paisley to the path to the cabin. She pointed at the plants near the tree. "That's poison ivy."

Paisley looked down at the rash spreading over her legs and screamed.

CHAPTER SIXTEEN

LATER, AT THE STABLE, Amanda adjusted her Stetson and fed Cybill an apple slice. "You don't know how much I need this ride."

Especially after soothing Paisley, who'd been beside herself when she wasn't itching at the rash. Amanda had contacted Bridget, who sent over some soothing ointment. It had taken quite some time to reassure Pamela that she wouldn't break out in a similar rash.

"Why does it not surprise me that you beat me to the stable?"

Amanda's heart soared at the strength and steadiness in the timbre of Seth's already familiar voice.

She faced him, and he plucked the hat off her head. Confusion trilled through her until his lips met hers. The simple peck deepened into a real kiss, and every fiber of her being awakened. His beard tickled, but she liked it. It was solid and real, the same as the rest of Seth.

That scared her, and she moved away from him.

"You're making it hard to go back to Phoenix."

She reached for her Stetson, planting it on her head once more. "Let's just enjoy the afternoon. Come on."

"Give me two shakes of a horse's tail, and I'll be ready to go. Buck's taking over the lasso lessons for the guests. I need to get some ranch maintenance done and thought I'd ride. You're the best company I could ask for."

While he was otherwise occupied, Amanda checked Cybill's saddle pad. *Good.* There was nothing slick and no burrs. She adjusted the cinch and mounted Cybill at the same time Seth appeared on Mocha. He nodded, and they set off on a new trail with the express intent of checking acres of fencing for holes and other issues. Slopes of wildflowers and grass gave rise to hillier terrain with green scrub trees and red rocks greeting her. Only the screech of an overhead hawk and the horse's nickers broke the steady, comfortable silence.

The horses continued to climb, and she kept a steady gaze along the miles of fence and open sky. No signs of damage from predators or wear and tear from the weather. After a while, Amanda called to Seth for a break. He obliged, and they saw to their horses before themselves. Only after Cybill and Mocha were settled did Seth offer her water and a protein bar, which she gratefully accepted.

The peace Pamela and Paisley sorely tested this afternoon seemed restored. She munched happily on her protein bar and sneaked a peek at Seth. If only she'd met him in Phoenix. Then she gave a soft chuckle. In that case, he wouldn't be Seth Virtue. The Lazy River Dude Ranch was as much a part of him as he was part of this experience for the guests.

And being Seth, the future of the ranch was paramount to him. Much of that hinged on this morning's appointment with Mateo.

"How did the bank visit go?" she asked.

"Mateo wasn't the leak. He promised to investigate how Killian Wilshire had access to what should have been privileged information. He also said any future negotiations depend on a new business plan." Seth downed the rest of the protein bar, followed by a second swig of water. "But right now, I just want to concentrate on this. And you."

"Well, the presentation is tomorrow. That's something else to consider." She had poured her heart into the campaign with its vibrant colors, new branding and a focus on the family while emphasizing the adaptability of the ranch.

"You sound sure of yourself." He came over and placed his arms around her waist.

"You're going to love the presentation." Pride trickled through her. Then Amanda batted him away and scrunched her face. "I can't concentrate when you're so close."

"Then we're even." He kept his arms where they were. "Because I can't concentrate when you're not close by."

His beard may have shielded his expression,

but Seth's eyes gave everything away. They were heading into dangerous territory, but it wouldn't last. Once she left, they'd realize it was the vacation talking and go their separate ways.

"We'll see where we are a month from now," she said.

Mocha whinnied, and Seth checked on his horse. Although she'd have liked reassurance this was more than a whirlwind vacation romance with no hope for tomorrow, she knew he couldn't give that promise any more than she could.

Seth mounted Mocha, and Amanda hooked her boot through the stirrup before swinging her leg and body over Cybill. She grasped the reins and met Seth's gaze.

"This isn't a shooting star. This is the real thing." He clicked his tongue against the roof of his mouth and dug his heels into Mocha's flanks.

Mocha began galloping, and Amanda gave Cybill her lead until the Tennessee walking horse was going all out. The breeze caressed Amanda's cheeks, and she knew the invigorating ride was only part of the reason her heart was pounding. The other revolved around the handsome man astride Mocha.

THAT NIGHT, Seth concluded the astronomy lesson by asking if anyone had questions. This program would have been perfect if Amanda had joined the group, but a client paged her earlier seeking her attention.

The crowd thanked him, and he launched into the next day's itinerary along with a reminder about the library and rec room. Most guests set forth for their cabins, no doubt eager for tomorrow's long trail ride. Buck would be taking Seth's place since he'd be beside his grandparents at the marketing presentation.

Returning to the lodge, he headed toward his grandparents' suite and the second family conference in as many nights. No matter what was said, though, he wouldn't be attending another family conference tomorrow. He had set aside that time for his first date with Amanda.

Seth couldn't shake the feeling Amanda thought this was a diversion, that absence would make the heart forget. How could he convince her how much he'd miss her? And how much Violet Ridge needed her here. How much he needed her.

Seth hesitated at the closed door to his grandparents' suite. Was that Crosby's voice? Seth checked his phone for the time. It couldn't be. As it was, Seth was early, and Crosby?

Well, his younger brother was born two weeks late and had continued his streak of tardiness ever since.

Seth gave a perfunctory knock and entered, halting in his tracks. Jase's face loomed large on the screen over the stone fireplace. Grandma Bridget and Grandpa Martin sat on one sofa while Crosby and Daisy occupied the matching one. Everyone stopped talking and stared at him. What was going on?

Jase broke the silence with deep rumbles of laughter. "You owe me a microbrew the next time you visit Denver, Crosby. He's ten minutes early on the dot."

Shrugging, Crosby pushed his glasses up the bridge of his nose and faced Seth. "I thought that new colt would keep you busy."

Daisy flipped over her phone on the coffee table between the two sofas while shaking her head. "And I thought you'd be sidetracked with Amanda."

Seth poured himself a tall glass of root beer before settling between Crosby and Daisy. "What's this intervention about?"

"It's nothing of the sort." Grandpa Martin handed a stack of papers to Seth. "Bridge and I wanted to explain ourselves to your siblings first."

"I'm still willing to sign away my share. You don't have to prove to me that you love me," Jase chimed in before Seth had a chance to read anything. "I know you do."

Unease traveled through Seth as he caught the words *transfer* and *trust* in the first paragraph. He laid the paper back on the coffee table. He'd been positive his grandparents wouldn't sell. Had he misjudged the situation that badly?

Once again, Amanda's admonition to not assume calmed his inner turmoil and need to act on impulse, and he relaxed his shoulders.

"Why don't you fill me in on what's going on?" Seth took a step forward.

Grandpa Martin tapped the paper. "I'm doing what I should have done years ago. It's time your grandmother and me think about what's best for everyone."

Seth's jaw tightened. "That's it? Without consulting me?" Never before had he been so disappointed in his grandparents. He could understand the mortgage. He'd have done the same, anything for Grandma Bridget. Yet this? Bile rose as he thought of what had been in their family for four generations being handed over to Wilshire.

Daisy leaned forward and placed her hand in his. "This is for the best. We're all in agreement. You've done so much to hold everyone together all these years, but this was inevitable."

Crosby nudged Seth's side. "This makes perfect sense. Grandma and Grandpa are being more than generous in the way they designed this."

Seth jumped up and ran his hand through his hair. "This ranch is part of our family, and we're in this together." He couldn't even spare a glance at his grandparents. How could they? "I thought it would be this way forever."

It was the end of an era. Everything his grandparents had taught him about family crashed down on him. He finally understood what they meant all these years, and it was too late.

Grandma Bridget grasped her cane and rose, making her way over to him. "Why don't you read the details?" She laid her gnarled hand on his cheek. "We didn't sell to Wilshire."

Seth paced the room as he studied the document. The blood drained from his face as the repercussions of what he was reading sank into his system. "This can't be right." It was saying he would own thirty percent of the ranch with each grandparent keeping a twenty percent stake, which would be run through a trust and go to him after each passed. He glanced at his siblings and then up at Jase on the screen. "This ranch is your legacy, too."

Daisy joined him and grasped his hands. "Not in the same way as it's yours. You've put your blood and sweat into this place."

Emotion lodged in his throat. He'd have done it again in an instant, but without all of them sharing this together?

He wasn't enough to keep this ranch afloat. "This is a family enterprise."

"Family endures, and you've done a good job with your siblings. They're happy and leading their own lives. And, for the record, Bridge and I aren't leaving." Grandpa Martin joined Seth, patting him on the back.

"Far from it. Martin and I had a long talk." She settled back on the couch, her cane resting next to her. "He and my doctors will take care of me so we can be around a long time for the triplets and all of you."

Grandpa Martin reached for his wife's hand. "Change happens. This trust ensures positive growth."

His grandparents had obviously given this a lot of thought and sought out legal representation to make sure it was aboveboard.

"I have to go, but Seth?" Jase spoke up. "The ranch is in good hands."

The screen went dark. Crosby and Daisy echoed their brother's sentiments before taking their leave.

The suite seemed empty without his siblings.

"This is a celebration, you know." Grandma Bridget broke the silence. "You've been in charge, and now you're officially a co-owner."

"But Daisy, Crosby and Jase…" No other words escaped from his dry mouth.

After his parents passed away, everything Seth did, he'd done for his siblings, anticipating they'd one day run the ranch as a team. The past two nights showed the futility of that hope.

"We'll always be there for you. Daisy will still be in charge of the silversmithing classes and gift shop, but you've proven yourself." Grandpa Martin came over to Seth and smiled. "You're the one who'll keep this ranch going. This past week you've shown how you can adapt and do what's best for the ranch even when you have to come around to another way of thinking. We're proud of you."

His grandfather's wise words calmed Seth's worry. "Thanks." A simple word, a powerful word, and yet maybe not enough for this occasion.

"We love you, Seth." Once again, Grandma Bridget put everything into perfect perspective.

His family loved him, and he'd been there for them when it counted. It was time to let them be them. He was strong enough to keep this ranch afloat with the help of his wider dude ranch family, which included Ingrid and Buck and countless others who would be beside him every step of the way.

Would Amanda join his family someday? That possibility made his heart soar. As much as he wanted to spend the rest of his life with her, they needed time to prove this was no temporary fling. His breath caught. He was now part owner of the ranch, and Amanda's boss had a strict no-client-relationship rule. Just when he'd felt things had gotten easier...

And if she never chose him and the Lazy River Dude Ranch to become a part of her life?

He'd cross that bridge then. For now, though, he had to keep a wrap on this news.

"Can we wait until Wednesday to make the announcement to the staff?" Seth asked.

Grandpa Martin poured himself a cup of decaf coffee. "Why? Seems to me it would be easier to announce it as soon as possible." He drank and then met Seth's gaze. "Unless this has to do with whatever's going on with you and Amanda. You're in love with her, aren't you?"

Even Grandpa Martin saw the sparks between them. "Her boss interrupted our first kiss, and Amanda's been in the hot seat ever since. Moving here has to be her decision."

"I see what you mean." Grandpa Martin glanced at Grandma Bridget and nodded. "I won't call the staff together for the announcement until everything is signed and notarized at the attorney's office."

Grandma Bridget grinned. "The two of you are so right for each other. Amanda is lovely, but I'm concerned history will repeat itself. I remember what happened when Felicity left."

"Thanks for the concern, Grandma." Seth grinned back. He loved his grandmother dearly and for everything she did for each of his siblings, especially helping them all face their grief after their parents' death. "Amanda and I will work this out for ourselves."

"I see so much of your grandfather in you." Her eyes twinkled, that aspect of her unchanged. "And since I'm in love with him even after he kept the mortgage a secret from me, I can see why Amanda is falling in love with you. I think she already has."

Seth wanted the type of love his grandparents shared. For the first time, he believed he was enough to claim that future for himself.

CHAPTER SEVENTEEN

Tuesday

SETH STARED AT Rosa and Leo in their stable stall. The mare and her foal had bonded over the past few days, a strong connection linking the pair. It wasn't the amount of time that mattered; it was the intensity of the relationship. He and Amanda hadn't known each other a long time, but he was convinced they had something as rare and special as this.

He consulted with the groom about Rosa's feed before heading toward the lodge for the presentation. He came upon Amanda, chatting with one of the new guests.

Her different outfit stopped him short.

She caught sight of him, said a quick goodbye to the new guest before catching up with him. "This is it. The big morning. Are you ready?"

He tried to respond but wasn't able to, so he nodded. He'd never seen her in a power suit before. He was used to her Western gear and pretty floral dresses. Would she change before they went to Miss Tilly's tonight? Maybe she'd at least wear her Stetson. The anticipation for their date made the wait that much sweeter. "I am now. I needed a minute to collect myself."

"And you went to the stable, didn't you?" She smiled. "I'm a little nervous myself. Can I see Leo before we get down to business?"

His apprehension about whether she fit in at the ranch faded with that simple statement. "Come with me," he said.

He led her to the foal and watched as joy lit Amanda's face when she spotted Leo.

Seconds passed and she squeezed his hand. "I'm glad I had this moment with you. And Leo." She took a deep breath. "While it's just us, I want to give you a preview of the presentation. I took what makes this ranch great and poured my heart into the campaign. My suggestion for your new slogan is 'Let our family be your family for a week.' The social media and ad blitz will communicate your new brand, which shows how families come in all shapes and sizes and weather any situation together. There will also be video blogs on different platforms."

He knew how well she'd handled the Ducks for Dogs Derby, but this level of passion and commitment for the Lazy River Dude Ranch blew him away. No wonder Parkhouse Promotions was in such high demand. "The cabins will be booked months in advance."

For the first time in a long time, hope turned

into certainty. She'd taken the diamond and polished it until it shone again. Everything was falling into place businesswise. He hoped for the same with their relationship.

A grin spread across her face, bringing a ray of sunlight into the stable. "I can't wait for you to see the presentation. I included the first video, too. Your grandparents are sure to sign the extended contract on the spot."

How did he tell her he'd be signing the contract as well? Look what happened the last time he kept something a secret. Guilt wrecked the moment. "Amanda…"

His grandfather entered the stable and stopped in front of Rosa's stall. "That's a pretty sight." Then he tipped his Stetson toward Amanda. "You and my grandson look mighty good together, too."

Seth let out a nervous chuckle. It might be for the best to steer everyone toward the library before his grandfather revealed the terms of the trust to Amanda. "Time to head to the lodge, isn't it?"

Seth stole another glance at Rosa and Leo, the mare and colt content with each other. Everything was coming together, yet he was aware it could unravel at any minute.

AMANDA ENTERED THE library and missed Hap and Trixie's usual welcome. The dogs were presumably content in Seth's quarters since Pamela was allergic to them and this was a business meeting.

Her stomach clenched. She was going to miss everything about the ranch from Bridget's knitting lessons to rides with Cybill.

Who was she kidding? Seth topped the list. If she went with him to Miss Tilly's tonight, she feared she'd leave her heart behind when she returned to Phoenix and he stayed here. Then they'd come to their senses and see this was all vacation magic.

Except what if it wasn't? What if their attraction was the beginning of something special that didn't come along every day?

What if she was special enough for someone to love?

That thought jolted her almost as much as the person who collided with her. With no apology, Pamela and Paisley sailed past her and began setting up their laptop. They connected it to a projector linked to a portable screen set up for today, opposite the stone fireplace and bookshelves.

Paisley stopped and scratched her arms, the poison ivy rash having spread there. Amanda thought she even saw a few spots on Paisley's face.

Amanda concentrated on work. This presentation had to go well so she and Seth would continue to have a reason to connect. "How can I help?"

Pamela crooked her finger at Amanda. "I have the most marvelous news. Let's go to the lobby, shall we?"

Amanda's nerves were already on edge with the

presentation so near, but she followed her boss out of the library, catching Seth's confused glance as she passed. She shrugged and kept moving forward.

Her palms became more clammy with every step. What if Pamela decided her kiss with Seth violated company rules and dismissed her? Amanda held her head high. She wouldn't apologize for her growing feelings for Seth, and neither would she believe she was like her father. Her work ethic was impeccable, and she'd logged more hours last week than she spent riding Cybill or enjoying the ranch's amenities.

In the lobby, Pamela found an alcove where she and Amanda were alone. Amanda stiffened, determined not to show emotion at whatever Pamela had in store for her.

"Relax, Amanda." Pamela smiled, a rare sight indeed. "Last night Paisley and I were quite busy with reorganizing the company structure when Paisley wasn't itching from that nasty rash. It's so unfair. She's such a trooper. She insisted on following through with the presentation and says she's feeling better."

Amanda's jaw clenched. She should have been invited to that meeting. Then she put everything into perspective. Getting fired wouldn't be the end of the world. Not with the family she'd found this week at the ranch. Losing her escrow deposit, though, would be a hardship, but maybe she could rent the house until she recouped her savings. Sami already intended on moving here. Life was always easier with a friend, especially if that friend was your sister.

Then she caught sight of her boss's face. Pamela always had a motive for everything she did. "I'm glad Paisley feels better, but why did you wait until the clients were ready for the presentation to tell me this?"

"Because it's such good news, darling." Pamela reached out and patted her arm. "You know that raise you asked for?"

"For the past three years?" Amanda folded her arms.

"It's yours along with your new job title— Client Liaison and Social Media Coordinator." Pamela beamed as if extending Amanda the ownership papers to a thoroughbred.

Shocked, Amanda stood still and said nothing. That was what she did now and the title sounded less impressive than her current title of Account Manager. She heeded her own advice to Seth to listen and not make assumptions. "How does that connect to your corporate reorganization?"

"I'll continue to be the public face and persona of the company, and Paisley will be the Vice President of Branding. You'll report to her and she'll monitor your work with our clients." Pamela's frown turned into a smile. "Paisley is already showing her remarkable ability. She made a few tweaks to your presentation so we'd stay on brand with the original concept."

A few changes were the norm and would be okay as long as she stayed true to Amanda's vision. She kept calm and nodded. "You do the same with each client. Shall we get back to the library?"

Amanda didn't wait for Pamela's response. She entered the room, where Paisley was rising to her feet. Amanda slid into a chair as did Pamela, who gave the go-ahead to her niece for the presentation before turning off the lights.

Paisley launched the slideshow, and Amanda's jaw dropped. A few tweaks? Instead of a traditional font with a faded color scheme emphasizing family values, this was a brand-new approach with bold lettering and bright hues. Paisley's approach centered on the Lazy River becoming a competitor of Wilshire's. She dared a glance at Seth, his original outlook encapsulated in these graphics. His face gave nothing away although the tense set of his shoulders told her everything.

"New teak loungers, a sauna room and massage table will add value to the pool area, which right now needs a facelift with its faded tiles and outdated furniture. Your maintenance staff also needs to prune away the poison ivy." Paisley emphasized everything the ranch lacked, reviewing its faults rather than drawing on its strengths. She stopped for a second to scratch her arm and then continued, "The slogan will be 'Where the mountains rise to reward you.'"

Soon, Pamela switched the lights back on, and a stunned silence fell over the room. Paisley beamed, obviously mistaking the tension for platitudes on a job well done.

Seth faced Amanda. "Is this your recommendation? Do you agree with this approach?"

His stone-cold voice held none of the warmth she had experienced since their awful first meeting.

Pamela placed herself between Amanda and Seth. "My employees are always in accord for the final presentation."

Martin cleared his throat, and Amanda switched her gaze to him and Bridget. The disappointment in their eyes was clear, and Amanda fingered the flash drive in her pocket, the one with the presentation she'd designed.

If she went against Pamela, she'd be fired on the spot.

If she didn't speak up, she'd lose Seth's respect.

"Thank you for your time, Ms. Parkhouse." Seth rose, his mouth set in a grim smile.

"It's our pleasure." Pamela reached for the attaché case under the table and pulled out a sheaf of papers. "Once you sign the contract, we'll be on our way back to Arizona, where we'll start the promos."

Seth glanced at his grandfather, who nodded.

Then he faced Pamela once more. "We won't be signing with Parkhouse Promotions at this time, or any other."

Pamela startled and blinked. "Excuse me, but this campaign is flawless."

"It doesn't fit the family vibe that makes us stand out from our competition." Seth said. Then he pursed his lips in a straight line.

Pamela huffed out her displeasure. "It's obvious you don't appreciate the vitality and vibrancy of this presentation. You're also acting like you don't want Parkhouse Promotions here any longer."

"Can't say as I do," Seth said.

Amanda's heart spiraled. She was part of Parkhouse Promotions. She waited for some sign from him that he wanted her to stay at the ranch.

Pamela faced Martin and Bridget. "You are the owners of the ranch, and therefore, you have the final say. This campaign is a positive step forward, one that will ensure new clients and provide a glossy image."

Martin scrubbed his chin and then motioned at Seth. "As of last night, Seth is now the primary owner of the ranch. He's made his decision."

It was as if someone yanked a rug out from under her. Seth could have told her about the change. He would have told her if she meant anything to him. They'd been alone in the stable, and he hadn't shared this momentous detail with her. After this week, she knew how he felt about keeping secrets from people he cared about, and he hadn't told her. A chill ran through her despite the ambient heat. She felt hollow and weak.

Pamela tapped Amanda's shoulder. "Paisley is quite distraught. You'll drive us back to Phoenix at once."

A week ago, she couldn't wait to return to Phoenix. Now? This ranch had taken her in and made her feel like she was part of the Virtue family for a week.

It was too easy to envision what that would have looked like for keeps, living in Violet Ridge, starting her own business with the ranch as one of her main clients. Riding Cybill on a regular basis. Coming home to Seth every day would be the cinnamon ice cream on Ingrid's apple crumble pie. Yet her upbringing had taught her one important lesson. All good things come to an end.

She swallowed the lump in her throat and nodded. "Goodbye, Seth."

CHAPTER EIGHTEEN

One week later

IN HER PARKHOUSE PROMOTIONS OFFICE, Amanda outlined the social media updates to her client over the phone. Then she rejected Neil's second appeal for her to strike out on her own and sign his landscape architect firm as her first client. "Thanks for the encouragement, but I like the predictability I have here."

Amanda placed her cell phone on her desk, then found herself gazing out the window, the parking lot its usual bevy of people rushing home on a typical evening. She'd love to head home, but she still had a mountain of work to do. It seemed to get larger every time she thought about how much she missed the ranch and one cowboy, in particular.

She rubbed her neck, tried a stretch or two.

The door opened, and Pamela and Paisley entered the office, laughing. "You're brilliant, Aunt Pamela." Paisley collapsed into her desk chair, rubbing her stomach. "That dinner was scrumptious."

As Pamela strode over to Amanda's desk, her fingers were flying across her phone's screen. "I'm forwarding the information about our newest client. I'll need their updated website done by tomorrow, Thursday at the very latest. They're paying premium prices for expediency."

Amanda's muscles ached, and she rubbed her neck while her laptop chimed receipt of the documents. "Paisley can do it."

The younger woman scoffed. "I'm the brand marketer. You're in charge of websites."

Pamela frowned. "Amanda, this is your job. Paisley has other obligations."

Something inside Amanda finally snapped. She wasn't her father; she never would be. But being miserable at her job in a career she loved and was good at doing was no type of life. She deserved better for herself. Last week, she'd been riding horses, knitting some concoction that was a cross between a blanket and a scarf and kissing Seth. This week, she'd been working her fingers to the bone, trying to prove something to herself, trying to forget the expression on Seth's face when he said he didn't want Parkhouse Promotions there.

She no longer wanted to be part of Parkhouse Promotions. This company didn't define her, or her abilities.

It boiled down to this. What she and Seth had was unique, and she'd left Colorado without a second glance. Even now, she could see him in her mind, a piece of hay in his beard, his shirt untucked and his jeans stained with mud from a hard day's work that he loved.

She missed him with every fiber of her body, and she'd turned him away.

Her heart ached at the thought of never seeing him again, but goodbyes didn't have to be final.

However, her next one would be.

Amanda glanced around the room. Nothing here belonged to her. Pamela was a stickler for a clean workspace with no personal traces. Well, that was fine, as far as Amanda was concerned. She glanced at Paisley's desk covered with digital photo frames and college memorabilia. Amanda opened the bottom drawer of her desk and pulled out her purse, slipping her phone inside. "Thank you for hiring me when no one else would, but I quit. Effective immediately."

Pamela sputtered and then laughed. "Okay, you can have until Friday for the website." She waggled her finger at Amanda. "Just this once. Don't pull this stunt again, though."

Amanda closed her company laptop and wouldn't regret leaving it here. Anything she needed was on her personal laptop. "It's not a stunt. I quit. You and Paisley can hire someone to take my place or do everything I do by yourselves. Goodbye, Pamela."

Her former boss turned ashen white as if she understood Amanda was serious. "You drive a hard bargain, but okay. I'll give you a three percent raise."

Amanda rose and pushed her purse strap into position at her shoulder. "No, thanks."

Without looking back, she hotfooted it out of the office, ignoring Pamela's concession for a four percent increase and not a penny more. Amanda made it to her car, sliding into the driver's seat, before nervous laughter bubbled to the surface. If she had quit the day of the presentation, she and Seth might be riding Mocha and Cybill this very minute, riding off into the sunset together.

And yet she'd have always wondered if she was like her parents, going where the grass was greener, in search of something elusive. If anything, that elusive part of embracing love and family had finally been in her grasp, and her stubbornness had kept her from clenching it tight.

She finally acknowledged what had been in front of her all along. She was more than good enough to have a home. To have love in her life.

How could she have thought that what she and Seth shared was just a vacation romance? Amanda was in love with Seth.

The thought she'd never see him again shattered her heart into a million pieces.

THE GRAY SKIES opened in a spring deluge, a gully whopper of a storm. Rain pounded Seth's office window, water streaming down the glass. It had been nine days, fourteen hours and ten minutes since Amanda had left the ranch, taking his heart with her.

Nothing was the same without her. Ingrid's waffles tasted like rubber. The stars didn't twinkle half as bright. Even the stable was lackluster although Rosa and Leo were as beautiful as ever. Seth rubbed his eyes and groaned at the computer, the numbers on the screen running together, becoming one big blur.

Someone knocked, and Seth welcomed the interruption. Come to think of it, though, no one had crossed that threshold all morning. Everyone around him was giving him a wide berth since he'd been rather temperamental, and that was putting his bad mood in the best possible light.

Crosby entered and fell into the closest chair. "Sami found something important. You need to see it."

"What are you doing here this early?" Seth checked his phone and found it was, indeed, still morning. "Are you visiting our newest employee?"

"I am. I took the day off. Blame Sami. First activity is foosball. I can't wait for her to teach me all about it, whatever it is."

"Sounds great, but some of us have a ranch to run." Seth exhaled a long breath.

"Well, Sami will be right here." Crosby leaned his elbows on his thighs. "She found something that Amanda must have left behind. It's important."

"Did someone say my name?" Sami entered the small office and settled in the chair next to Crosby.

The two were spending a lot of time together. Seth's breath caught. Would Amanda come back to the ranch if the pair fell in love and got married?

Sami met his gaze and started laughing. "Seth, I don't know you that well, but I recognize that look in your eye. Crosby and I are just friends." She reached over and ruffled Crosby's hair. "He's the best buddy I never had."

A disgruntled expression came over Crosby's face, and Seth sympathized for his little brother who'd be in for the same problem as Seth if he didn't protect his heart. He resolved to have a talk with him so Crosby might be spared this level of heartbreak.

"So, what's going on?" Seth set aside the papers on his desk and Sami dropped a flash drive on his desk.

"Amanda left this in the Porcupine Suite. It's her vision for what the ranch's campaign should be."

Seth opened the file on his laptop. His chest caught in a tight vise. The mission statement and brand information had her fingerprints all over it.

"Seth?" Crosby's voice became more insistent and until something rapped his hand.

Everything came into focus once more. Seth

moved his hand away, the stinging sensation continuing for seconds. "That hurt, Crosby."

"You've been in a fog all week. Business plans aren't that moving. What gives?" Crosby reclaimed his seat, his voice holding concern that wasn't right. Seth was the big brother. He should be looking out for Crosby, not the other way around.

"This is so like Amanda, and I miss her." The admission had been on his heart all week.

"She left because you rejected her, Seth," Sami said. "That's what she told me. It took a lot for me to stay here and not go to Phoenix to be with her. I still feel bad about that."

Seth's body stiffened, and he kept from jumping out of his chair. "I did no such thing. I rejected Parkhouse Promotions." Then his shoulders slumped, and he fell back into place. "I see it now. To Amanda, it must have seemed like I was rejecting her."

Seth returned his attention to Amanda's campaign. He found the silver dollar and held it tight while taking in her meticulous details. Amanda's approach was subtle yet brilliant, so much like her. The vision statement, the slogan, the videos. Everything was perfect. There was only one person he trusted for the job of marketer for the ranch, and that was the one person he drove away after the presentation.

That empty ache he'd felt for the past nine days gripped him once more.

He brought the silver dollar out of his pocket until it rested on his desk, the ridged edges as familiar as Mocha's reins.

The silver dollar. Chills ran through his body. Parting with this gift was the last thing he ever wanted to do, but it might be the only way to win Amanda back or at least see her in person to apologize.

He had to try.

AMANDA PARKED THE rental van with her personal belongings in her new driveway. The professional movers had delivered her large furniture items yesterday. Thank goodness she'd closed on the house before she quit her job on Tuesday. The rest of the week was still a blur as several Parkhouse Promotions clients had called and insisted she take over their accounts. Even without Pamela's reference, she already had two full-time job offers at almost double her old salary and with benefits.

None of that, though, eased the ache in her heart from leaving Violet Ridge and the Lazy River Dude Ranch. By now, Leo was probably eating solid food and hay. The farrier might even have examined him by now. Grandma Bridget might have completed those beanies for the triplets. And Seth?

Had he made progress on finding replacements for Rich and Vickie although, in his words, they were irreplaceable? Was he sparing time to ride

Mocha? Was he going through the motions, feeling a giant ache inside the same way she was? She blinked away her concern about Seth and opened the sliding door of the van. Boxes stared back at her the way they'd done so often over the course of her life.

This time, like so many others, she couldn't shake the feeling this wasn't where she was supposed to be, that Phoenix wasn't her ultimate destination. No longer did the small stucco ranch give off vibes of her forever home, not when the Lazy River Dude Ranch filled that part of her heart.

The hurt was still fresh. A year from now, she'd look back at the experience and what? Laugh it off? Smile? Have regrets that she didn't go back and tell Seth she loved him?

Amanda unloaded a box and set it on the granite countertop in her new kitchen. A knock at the front door surprised her, and she glanced through the peephole. To her delight, she found Sami waving hello with a big basket in her other arm, pretending to collapse under the weight.

Amanda threw open the door, a flicker of happiness running through her.

"Surprise!" Sami announced. "We couldn't let you move all by yourself."

"We?" Amanda's heart leaped at the thought of Seth traveling with her sister until her gaze landed on Crosby coming up the path, his nose stuck in a book.

"Crosby doesn't get carsick reading so I drove. Beautiful scenery, a once-in-a-lifetime road trip with yours truly, and he doesn't stop reading." Sami sighed and then lifted a basket filled with goodies. "This is for you. Loofahs, lotion, bath bombs, guest towels and a scented candle."

Amanda swiped the tear at the corner of her eye. "Come in, both of you." Despite everything, Amanda couldn't regret her time at the Lazy River. It had brought her and Sami together. "I don't suppose anyone else made the drive."

"Hap and Trixie jumped in the car." Crosby closed his book and tucked it under his arm. "They miss you."

Amanda noticed someone was missing on that list, but she didn't mention Seth. It hurt too much to even think about him. His name would inevitably come up, but she didn't want the first five minutes in her new house to become a cryfest. Instead, she set the basket on the floor and extended her arms for a Sami hug. She missed her sister and Crosby. Bridget and Martin. Cybill and Mocha.

She missed Seth more.

"You'll help me unload the van?" Her muscles breathed a sigh of relief when Sami and Crosby nodded.

Amanda headed outside when Crosby tapped her arm. "First, though, I have a business proposition for you."

Sami elbowed him in the ribs. "We agreed we

wouldn't mention Seth until everything was unloaded."

"But it only makes sense to do the offer first.
Why move everything twice if we don't have to?"
Crosby shrugged at Sami.

Sami simply laughed at the tall cowboy historian. "You know the worst part about being your
new best friend?"

"There's a bad part?" Crosby nudged his glasses
until they were back to the top of his nose.

"It's that you're always right." Sami grinned and
kept her attention on her driving partner.

Crosby chuckled and then pointed toward the
living room. "Can we talk in there?"

"With some water?" Sami fanned herself, not
a trace of sweat on her pretty forehead.

Her first guests in her house and Amanda was
failing in her manners. Heartache or not, she resolved to do better. Since she hadn't unpacked
her glasses, she brought three water bottles to the
living room.

Crosby accepted the bottle of water. "Seth meant
he didn't want Parkhouse Promotions at the ranch
anymore. To him, Pamela and Paisley represent
the company, not you," he said.

"You left your flash drive behind, and I showed
him your presentation," Sami continued as Crosby
sipped his cold drink. "I felt so guilty about not
coming back with you, I couldn't wait any longer.

I had to check on you. I'm here for you. Seth is on his way. I had to get here first and warn you."

"And I came because he's my big brother. I don't want to see him get hurt. Or you." He smiled at her. Amanda was stunned. What was happening?

Crosby pressed on. "Seth wants to hire you as the ranch's marketing manager and Mayor Ben reserved nine on Monday for a job interview with you. The town wants to hire you, too, if you're available…?"

Sami leaned forward and met Amanda's gaze. "That's not the important part. This is. Are you in love with Seth?"

Crosby and Sami neared each other on Amanda's sofa, presenting a solid wall and waiting for her to say something.

But what was there to say? Seth should have told her he'd signed the trust papers.

Then it hit her. He hadn't wanted to force Pamela's hand into firing her before Amanda had quit of her own volition. Ultimately, it had to be her decision to relocate to Violet Ridge.

Amanda looked around her new living room. This house represented everything she'd worked so hard to attain, everything she wanted to prove she wasn't like her parents, searching for that elusive pot of gold at the end of the rainbow. In this case, it wasn't gold but love waiting for her.

That was, if she was brave enough to grasp it with both hands.

"Crosby, change of plans. And Sami, yes, I'm in love with Seth." That came first. Always.

Seth's brother had been right when he suggested hearing him out before unpacking the van. "By the way, Crosby, you're a genius."

"Like he didn't know that before." Sami guffawed and rolled her eyes before a grin overtook her. "But what you don't know, Crosby, is you're driving home so you actually see the scenery this time."

Home. The mountains, the air, the goats, horses and even the ducks. Amanda couldn't wait to see Rosa and Leo, Bridget and Martin, Cybill and Mocha.

Seth.

CHAPTER NINETEEN

Saturday

SETH FINISHED MUCKING out the stable and headed toward the lodge. This weekend, the first without Rich or Vickie, who had served out their two-week notices, was even more hectic than normal and kept him from driving to Arizona.

He had to apologize to Amanda in person. Only then might she see his sincerity.

He sniffed himself and winced; even a shower would have to wait. Besides, he was set to start weeding the gardens in front of each cabin, a messy task that would only add to his pungent odor.

Seth unlocked the maintenance shed and started loading a cart with gardening implements.

"Hello?" A voice from the entrance startled Seth, and the spade fell to the ground.

Seth whirled around and found Rich and Vickie standing at the doorway. He blinked and rubbed his eyes, only they were still there. "What are you doing here? Shouldn't you be at Wilshire's?"

Rich shuffled his feet and glanced at Vickie. "About that." He hesitated, his voice full of something Seth could have sworn sounded like regret. "Turns out the grass isn't always greener."

Vickie looked just as sheepish as Rich. "My daughter's upset with me. She loves the two weeks a year you open up the ranch for the employees to be guests, and she was counting on starting riding lessons at the stable."

Thirty years ago, Grandpa Martin had hit upon employee week at the beginning and end of each season as a way of thanking everyone for their hard work. Chuckwagon dinners, glamping and a week of horseback riding over the open range. Those were two of the weeks Seth loved the most, as well.

"What are you saying?" Seth didn't have time for nice speeches. After gardening, he also had to help clean two of the cabins.

Vickie tilted her head at Rich, who stepped toward Seth, his gaze roving over the gardening equipment in the shed.

"Are our jobs still available?" Rich removed his cap and scratched his bald head. "Even if we have to start at the bottom of the pay scale. I talked to a couple of other former employees as well. Wanda and Chuck want to come back, too."

"Courtney and Lisa are wondering about their positions, as well," Vickie added.

Along with the three other new hires thanks

to the derby applications, this would practically bring the dude ranch back to full staff.

If only Amanda were here to see what she'd set in motion. That empty space in his heart ached until it hit him. Tomorrow when he traveled to see her, he hoped she'd accept his apology. It didn't matter where they had their first date, as long as they did. And a second. And a third.

"We'll go to the lodge and get the paperwork in motion, but as far as I'm concerned, you never left." He nodded at the pair. "Spread the word. The others can come back at full salary with the employee weeks intact."

Rich leaned backward and motioned at something with his fingers. There were Wanda and Chuck, Courtney and Lisa, all familiar and welcome faces. Seth's throat constricted, and he couldn't talk for fear of letting loose the emotion building inside him. Still, he accompanied the group to the lodge and added their names to the schedule, getting everyone back on the payroll.

Rich lingered after the others left and fingered his baseball cap. "There's no place like the Lazy River."

Seth couldn't agree more and only wished a certain marketing expert were here to celebrate with him. Rich departed, and Seth would have felt giddy with the newfound extra time on his hands. Instead, he walked toward the lodge exit, bound for the stable to check on Rosa and Leo, when he bumped into Crosby.

"What are you doing here, Crosby?" Seth asked. "I thought you'd be at home in town, preparing for your doctorate."

"I wanted to check on my big brother, especially since you're taking Amanda's departure really hard." Crosby looked as though he was hiding something rather than lending his support.

Seth dismissed the thought. The important thing was Crosby was here, looking out for him. "Just counting down the hours until I leave for Phoenix."

"About that—" Crosby started before Seth interrupted him.

"I have more good news. Six employees came back." A weight had lifted off his shoulders. "I can't wait to tell Amanda all about it. I hope she'll give me a chance to explain everything." That was what he should have done in the first place.

Crosby ran his hand through his disheveled hair. "Seth, don't get mad, but Sami and I went to Phoenix."

Seth reeled at the revelation. "Why?"

"If Amanda didn't want to hear you out, I wanted to break it to you gently." Crosby sniffed and fanned the air around his nose. "Ew, you stink. Why don't you take a shower before we have a heart-to-heart?"

A pair of empty nesters from California approached Seth. Mrs. Barrett spoke first, "How fancy do we need to dress for tonight's dance?"

Seth smiled. "Some guests do get very fancy, while others wear jeans and their cowboy hats. Feel free to do what's comfortable for you."

The guests thanked him and strolled toward the duck pond. Crosby tsked. "It's so busy around here, and I want your complete attention. Meet me at our old house, okay?"

He left before Seth had a chance to suggest meeting in Seth's quarters on the third floor. Then again, his suite was a mess with unfinished packing and suitcases everywhere.

Seth sniffed around him. Okay, the smell was that bad, but what was so important that Crosby couldn't just blurt it out? And wanting to meet at his parents' house of all places?

What was that all about?

AMANDA PLUMPED A pillow on the couch. She was finally home. The word didn't even begin to capture the essence of the moment. For so long, she'd wanted roots and a place to belong. She'd worked long hours to afford the perfect house in Phoenix, only to travel to Colorado and spend a week at a dude ranch to find her heart.

Staying in one area for the wrong reasons was more detrimental than moving for the right ones.

Unlike her parents, though, she uprooted herself and planted herself in this environment so she could grow and thrive.

A sound broke the silence. Amanda froze. Goose bumps pebbled on her arm. She heard someone on the front porch, but Sami and Crosby weren't due for another hour. Besides, Crosby would be invariably late anyway. Her eyes widened when she heard scratching near the door. Her heart almost leaped out of her chest. City habits were hard to break, and, for some unknown reason for which she was very thankful, she'd locked the door. A second later, she saw the knob turn. Pulse racing, she glanced around the room, searching for something, until her gaze landed on the umbrella stand. She ran over and grabbed a large black umbrella.

Her body tense, she stood behind the door as it opened. Poised to strike, she stopped with the makeshift weapon in midair, recognizing the person who entered. "Seth?"

He had raised his arms in an effort to protect his head. Lowering them, he met her gaze, his mouth dropping. "Amanda." The umbrella clattered to the ground, and he ran to her, embracing her in his arms. "What are you doing here? I'm driving to Phoenix tomorrow to see you."

"Crosby and Sami told me." Her voice was muffled, her cheek nestled against his chest.

Seth stepped away, and it became clear. A house was a house. People made it a home. Wherever he was, there was her heart, for she loved Seth Virtue.

"I should have come straight away. The past week without you has been the worst." Seth picked up the umbrella and placed it back in the stand before a frown came over him. "That's new."

He glanced around the living room and scowled. "What's going on?" Seth went over to her couch and picked up a pillow. "This shouldn't be here. Everything's changed."

Amanda bit her lip. "I've got something important to tell you."

"Tell me what?" Seth faced her, uncertainty written all over him.

"I've quit my job." She gathered her strength to tell him the rest when a smile lit up his face.

"I'll hire you." He reached in his pocket and pulled out his wallet. "Except I don't have any money for a retainer."

"Seth—"

"Actually I do have a dollar." He patted his pocket and the uncertainty left his gaze. In its place was love and acceptance. "Amanda, will you accept this and come work at the Lazy River?"

He held out his special silver dollar to her. For him to be willing to part with his most cherished possession and give it to her? Any last twinges of concern about the move or Seth's feelings for her disappeared. This was where she belonged.

Amanda smiled and curled his fingers around the coin. "No. The coin is yours. Your grandparents already hired me, contingent on your being okay with it, and I'll lease this house as part of the deal. I also have an interview with Ben about working for the city of Violet Ridge as their marketing manager, as well, as long as he knows the ranch is where my heart is." She waited until Seth tucked the coin in his pocket and then closed the distance between them. He placed his arms around her waist. She savored the feel of his touch. "You see, there's a horse named Cybill who needs a rider, and a colt named Leo, who I want to see grow up. And Bridget promised to teach me how to knit socks."

More lessons with Bridget were a necessity, especially on snowy winter evenings come later this year.

"I can't believe you're really here." He unclasped his hands from behind her waist and began rubbing her cheek with his rough fingers. "This isn't just a vacation fling. You and me, I mean."

"I know that now." Amanda leaned into his touch. "I'm falling for you."

His eyes shone bright, his emotions reflected there for her to see. "Then would you do me the honor of going to Miss Tilly's for our first date tonight? We can celebrate your move and new job."

"I love your efficiency." She glanced over his shoulder and found Sami and Crosby holding up their thumbs with Sami puckering her lips and making kissing motions. "By the way, we have an audience."

Seth glanced behind him and left Amanda's side. "We'll be with you both in a minute. I have some unfinished business with Amanda first."

"Aren't you glad I told you to take a shower—" The rest of Crosby's sentence was lost as Seth ushered the pair outside and closed the door.

"Amanda, I meant what I said earlier. I had every intention of going to Phoenix tomorrow. I'll give you as much time as you need. For now, though, let's follow our feelings and see where they lead. Starting with this kiss." He waited until she nodded.

Then his lips met hers.

She knew she was home to stay.

EPILOGUE

TONIGHT MARKED THE end of summer. This fall, he'd begin work on the long list of improvements, which would be easy to cover the cost of thanks to all the bookings. The full staff would keep plenty busy right up until December for the holiday season.

"You're doing it again." Amanda murmured while nestled against his shoulder. "You're thinking about the imperfections of the ranch rather than seeing its beauty."

"Old habits are hard to break."

But he'd been working at it over the past few months. In the morning, he spent time with the guests while she traveled to city hall and worked with Ben and the business owners of Violet Ridge. Afternoons were their time together leading trail rides on Cybill and Mocha, where she matched him stride for stride. He loved how she met each challenge with her calm, implacable style almost as much as he loved her. At night they spent quiet evenings with Hap and Trixie in the lodge library or her living room. She had settled into his parents' house, bringing her own unique style to the place, turning it once again into a charming home.

In the barn, for this week's cowboy dinner and dance evening, he savored the feel of her in his arms while they danced to the Elvis standard the band was performing. She smiled at him, that unforgettably sweet smile that reassured him everything was fine.

"You just need a positive spin. Think of fall as a new opportunity to enhance what's already special."

Her innate optimism and her positive spirit were only two of the reasons he'd fallen deeply in love with her since she arrived in Violet Ridge. The past few months had only cemented their relationship, taking the strong beginning to even greater heights. "Have I told you today how special you are?"

"Once or twice."

"And that dress? You take my breath away." He gazed at her, a vision in copper.

"Thank you, but the music's stopped, and we're the last ones on the dance floor." Amanda led him toward the gallery of pictures that now dotted one barn wall.

Vickie and her family slowed their progress, and they chatted with them. Everyone thanked Seth for a wonderful employees-only week at the ranch. He agreed it was a great success but brushed off their praise of him. "Glad everyone enjoyed themselves."

Amanda made their excuses, but rather than escaping out of the barn, she brought him to the new retrospective gallery that highlighted the ranch's history. Crosby had organized the display but, as usual, he was running late. No longer did seeing the pictures of his parents at their wedding, so young and in love, bring a lump to Seth's throat. Instead, he relished the time he'd had with them. If only Jase could accept that and come back…

Seth patted his pocket and the black velvet box resting there, hoping a wedding in the near future might draw Jase's return to Violet Ridge. That was, if she said yes. "Amanda…"

"I still can't get over how much you look like your grandma Lou," Grandma Bridget cut in to finish the sentence as she and Grandpa Martin joined Seth and Amanda at the photos.

"I feel like I know her so much more now." Amanda reached out and grasped his grandmother's hands. "Thank you for sharing her with me."

"I'm so glad Lou brought us together." Grandma Bridget hugged Amanda. "I know it's been a difficult time with your parents."

"I told them flat-out there'd be no more money from me. They're in New York and know where to find me if they want a real relationship." Amanda broke the contact and moved closer to Seth.

"You have Lou's optimism, and Sami has her wanderlust." Grandma Bridget smiled, her eyes misting; no doubt she was thinking of long-ago memories.

Speaking of Sami, her best buddy Crosby rushed into the barn and headed their way. "Sorry I'm late. Did she say yes?" Crosby's gaze went to Amanda's hand.

"Sami said yes, she'll enjoy her vacation in Galveston and bring you something special for a souvenir." Seth interrupted his brother before Crosby could ruin the moment Seth had planned for weeks.

Thankfully, his brother understood what Seth was trying to convey. Crosby turned to his display. "I'm quite proud of how well this turned out. There's something solid about the past, how it grounds us in who we are today."

Seth's heart went out to his brother, who obviously was in love with Amanda's sister, yet the two of them had too many differences, mainly that Sami was determined not to settle in one place whereas Crosby seemed too settled in his ways and very content to stay in Violet Ridge.

However, it wasn't Seth's place to interfere with their lives.

On the other hand, he'd like nothing more than to interfere with his brother Jase's life. Only by confronting his past would he have a future, but that was for Jase to figure out.

Seth tried once more to get Amanda outside, yet everyone wanted to talk to them, either thanking him for a wonderful employee week or asking if he had room for a cousin or family friend on the employee roster. Seth accepted their thanks while replying he was always on the lookout for good workers and they should check the website Amanda updated on a regular basis.

Same as he was on the lookout for some way to get Amanda to himself. Some things were just too private for many sets of eyes watching him.

Finally, he crooked his arm, and Amanda linked hers in his. With her by his side and his silver dollar in his pocket next to a black velvet box, anything was possible. The sky was the limit, and the night stars twinkled their brightest, putting on its finest show for him and Amanda.

A few minutes later, they strolled alongside the duck pond until they came upon the boat shelter. He led her to the bench, and she nestled her head on the crook of his shoulder.

He pointed to the dazzling sky. "Do you know the story of the fall constellations?"

"I'm looking forward to hearing them." She snuggled against him, and he reveled having her in his arms.

Seth took off his jacket and placed it over her shoulders.

She startled and reached into the pocket, pulling out the black velvet box. "What's this?"

His breath caught, and he composed himself. Kneeling before her, he reached for the box. "I had a fancy speech about how Perseus rescued Andromeda and they fell in love, but how we're the reverse. You rescued this ranch, and I fell in love with you." He opened the box to reveal a diamond solitaire. "This is to remind you of the stars that shine so brightly on the ranch, Amanda Jayne Fleming, will you marry me?"

"Yes!"

The full moon shone on her face, and he etched the image in his mind forever. "I love you."

"I love you, too, Seth." She nodded and held out her hand. He slipped the ring on her trembling finger. "Let's tell your grandparents and Crosby and everyone. The whole family. Then you can call Jase while I call Sami."

He rose and stared deeply into her eyes, that love shining bright. Their lips met, and the kiss sealed the deal. Her jasmine scent filled him, and she tasted of hope.

Forever started now.

Together, they strolled to the bustling barn, the dancing in full swing, hands locked, hearts entwined, the rest of their lives waiting for them. There would be challenges around every bend, same as there had been heartbreak and triumph in his grandparents' marriage, but Amanda would be by his side every step of the way, her steady positivity bolstering him and giving him confidence to meet whatever life threw at them.

Wherever they went, the stars would guide them home, their love for this land, the horses, each other, keeping them together for a lifetime.

* * * * *